Rain Shadow slammed into a hard chest. Her breath escaped with an unladylike ''oof.''

Anton grasped her shoulders and steadied her. ''Sorry. I seem to be knocking women left and right tonight.''

The scent of his heated skin assailed her senses. He slid his hands to her upper arms. Through her soft dress, his touch was warm, the effect on her pulse swift.

He knew he should release her, but his fingers refused to obey. Instead they wanted to glide down her arms, caress the supple skin beneath her dress, linger at her narrow waist and explore the gentle curve of her hips. He knew he was lighting a match next to a keg of gunpowder, but he couldn't release her just yet....

Dear Reader,

It's March Madness time again! Each year we pick the best and brightest new stars in historical romance and bring them to you in one action-packed month!

When the hunt for a spy throws the cynical Duke of Avon and Emily Fairfax together in *The Heart's Desire* by Gayle Wilson, one night of passion is all they are allowed. Yet their dangerous attraction is too hard to resist.

Anton Neubauer's first glimpse of *Rain Shadow* was in a wild West show. Although Anton knew she could never be the wife he needed, why was the Indian-raised white woman the only one he desired? A wonderful tale by Cheryl St.John.

My Lord Beaumont by Madris Dupree brings us a wonderful love story for readers with a penchant for adventure. Rakish Lord Adrian Beaumont rescues stowaway Danny Cooper from certain death, but finds that beneath her rough exterior is an extraordinary young woman willing to go to any lengths for her true love.

And rounding out March is Emily French's *Capture,* the story of Jeanne de la Rocque, who is captured by Algonquin Indians, and Black Eagle, the warrior whose dreams foretell Jeanne's part in an ancient prophecy.

We hope you enjoy all of our 1994 March Madness titles and look for next month's wherever Harlequin Historical books are sold!

Sincerely,

Tracy Farrell
Senior Editor

Please address questions and book requests to:
Reader Service
U.S.: P.O. Box 1325, Buffalo, NY 14269
Canadian: P.O. Box 1050, Niagara Falls, Ont. L2E 7G7

RAIN SHADOW

CHERYL ST.JOHN

Harlequin Books

TORONTO • NEW YORK • LONDON
AMSTERDAM • PARIS • SYDNEY • HAMBURG
STOCKHOLM • ATHENS • TOKYO • MILAN
MADRID • WARSAW • BUDAPEST • AUCKLAND

ISBN 0-373-28812-3

RAIN SHADOW

CHERYL ST.JOHN

remembers writing and illustrating her own books as a child. She received her first rejection at age fourteen, and at fifteen wrote her first romance.

She has been program chairman and vice-president of her Heartland RWA chapter, and is currently proud to serve as president.

A married mother of four and grandmother of three, Cheryl enjoys her family. In her ''spare'' time, she corresponds with dozens of writer friends, from Canada to Texas, and treasures their letters. She would love to hear from you.

To the romance authors of the Heartland,
who critique to sell;
Mom, who taught me I could be
anything I wanted;
Jen, who prayed;
Sis, who cooked and cleaned for holidays;
Jared & Kris, who think pizza is a nutritious meal;
and Jay, who gave me time to make my dream
come true.

This one's for you.

Prologue

1875

An unfriendly wind carried the pervading stench of scorched wood and canvas. Two Feathers, crouched in an outcropping of boulders, ignored the odor as well as the rocks biting through his moccasins, his attention focused on the ruinous scene below him.

The charred skeletons of two dozen covered wagons lay on their sides like so many smoldering carcasses on the Nebraska prairie. Thin gray trails of acrid smoke curled into the darkening sky. Growing bolder as night drew near, black scavengers circled overhead, occasionally swooping toward the scattered bodies of the slain whites.

He examined a few overturned rocks. A small war party had lain in wait earlier. The arrows in the bodies were Crow. Two Feathers wasn't worried that they would return. They had scalped and looted and were long gone.

Ominous thunder clouds had obliterated the setting sun the better part of an hour ago, and the purple sky boasted the unmistakable aura of rain.

Through the stillness a pitiful wail carried, wafting with the dry, acrid stench of gunpowder. The sound had grown weak—at times almost a mewling—but its effect was no less profound than the first time Two Feathers had heard it.

Several yards from the violent scene, Two Feathers saw a small figure take a few reeling steps and crumple on the short-cropped buffalo grass. It was a girl child, tiny and dark-haired. The sun, her foremost enemy earlier, had disappeared, and now her true peril began.

The Indian gestured to the spotted pony behind him, covered the velvet nose and whispered a command. The animal stood unmoving, its eyes watchful. Two Feathers crept stealthily from his hiding place, silently closing the distance between his horse and the child.

Catching sight of the lithely muscled Indian dressed only in deerskin leggings, a knife at his hip, her dark eyes registered surprise. Her head rolled tiredly, but the soft keening lessened.

She was no more than three or four summers, dressed in the muslin and aproned fashion of the whites. Her exquisite hair, near black and flowing, held bits of dry grass and twigs. A heart-shaped gold locket with a stone Two Feathers didn't recognize dangled from a chain around her neck. Was the ornament a bauble to pacify her during the day's journey, or perhaps a mother's last frantic attempt to leave the child a shred of her identity?

Two Feathers crouched over her.

She stared back fearlessly, her stormy violet eyes taking in his angular features, his beaded headband and the two red feathers dangling over his left ear.

What had she seen here this day? How much had she been spared? Her lack of fear showed a brave and strong spirit. Wandering away from the others as she was, he imagined a parent thrusting her from the wagon when the attack came. He would have done the same. He would have taken any measure to save his own child—had she lived.

"Mama," the girl child managed in a raw-throated voice, and touched the feathers. Was she asking for a parent or was his long, black hair familiar? She placed a dirty palm on his mahogany cheek, and his warrior's stoic heart admitted her.

To the west, an enormous dark cloud covered what little remained of the sun, and rumbling thunder shook the ground. He couldn't leave her to die. Not this child with a strong spirit and will to live. Wakon Tanka had spared her for a reason.

Lightning forked from the dark sky, punctuating Two Feathers' decision.

There'd been no movement near the scattered wagons since he'd come upon them. If anyone lived through the massacre, he would soon be dead. Once darkness settled on the plain, the night predators would close in. The child would be prey to scavengers and the ominous storm.

He didn't know which wagon the child belonged to, and if he ventured any nearer, a dying white man might mistake him for one of the Crow attackers and shoot. With deft movements, he plucked her from the ground and ran silently to his waiting pony. She didn't weigh as much as most game he brought down and gave less resistance.

Astride, the girl in one arm, he kicked the pony with a moccasined heel and skirted the carnage of the wagon train. A jagged streak of lightning pierced the sky, momentarily illuminating his granite-cut features. Before the rain fell, Two Feathers pulled a deerskin from his bundle and covered the sleeping child. His child now.

His Rain Shadow.

Chapter One

October 1894

Smoke, like an eddying black caterpillar, spiraled endlessly past the excursion car window. This train was one of the three needed to transport the performers, orchestra, cowboy band, staff, tents, props, wardrobe and livestock. Rain Shadow grew tired of watching the variegated red and gold trees of western Pennsylvania reel past and closed her eyes. The steady lurch of the locomotive chugging along the iron rails wore on her nerves. She pulled a gold locket from beneath the neck of her deerskin tunic and thoughtfully fingered her only piece of jewelry.

It was time.

Buffalo Bill's Wild West Show had finished a five-month season in Brooklyn and was on its way south to winter quarters, a trek they made each fall. If she were going to prove herself, it was time. She had the entire winter ahead to prepare. When the show opened again in Philadelphia next April, she would shoot the pants off Annie Moses Butler—the famed Annie Oakley.

"Are you hungry, daughter?"

Rain Shadow opened her eyes and accepted an apple from Two Feathers.

He studied her face a long minute. "You are planning your contest?"

"Yes."

"What if you lose?"

She took a bite of the crisp, sweet apple. Losing was something she'd never let herself think about. Covertly studying Annie Oakley, Johnnie Baker and the other sharpshooters, Rain Shadow had developed her skill. Under Two Feathers' tutelage, she was confident her precision and timing had surpassed the others'. "I won't."

His coal black eyes, unclouded by criticism, bespoke indulgence.

How could she make him understand? How could she tell the father who had nurtured and provided for her since childhood that she wanted to give her son a real family? That she wanted Slade to have a home and go to the white man's school the way she never had? If she proved herself a better shot than Annie Oakley, she was certain her remaining relatives would be proud to claim her.

Instead, she touched his arm. "You know I'm not ungrateful. You've filled every corner of my heart with your kindness and taught me everything you know. Both of us are caught between two worlds. You remember the way it used to be, but I plan for the way it can be.

"When I claim my position as champion sharpshooter, I won't leave you. Together we'll learn how to live a new life. Aren't you tired of living one grand performance after another?"

He grunted and pulled a knife and a whetstone from the satchel at his feet.

Rain Shadow watched his dark, scarred warrior's hands sharpen the blade in deft strokes. Of course he was. She knew the alternative would be unbearable for Two Feathers, a Sioux who'd lived by the direction of his guardian spirit—a spotted eagle. Reservation life was like imprisoning the proud, freedom-loving Indian in a cage.

The Lakota loved the earth, and all things of it; the soil itself, and their attachment to it grew with age. Old people sat on the ground to experience being close to a mothering power; many even removed their moccasins to feel the sacred dirt on their feet.

The Indian's way of life was rapidly becoming a thing of the past. Towns and farms and railroads had presumptuously erased the hunting grounds. The sounds of birds, gourd rattles and ceremonial chants were usurped by tin-horn saloons, clanging steel and the rumble of wagon wheels. The white man's song of progress was louder than the red man's Sun Dance. Rain Shadow had often wondered if it was her white-eyes heart that lent her foresight.

More than grateful to Two Feathers, she loved him as the only parent she'd ever known. He was a man trapped between two cultures. The entire purpose of the Wild West Show was to recreate a piece of the Old West as it had been, and Two Feathers was as happy with the show as he could be anywhere; he no longer had a home and a people. For now the show was the only place she belonged, as well.

Rain Shadow's thoughts shifted to her seven-year-old son on the train ahead of this one. She wanted a full life for Slade. If he were to succeed, he must be given every opportunity to learn and grow and prosper in the white man's world.

He needed a family. She would find him one. Somewhere she had grandparents, aunts or uncles, cousins maybe. Using the locket as her only source of identity, she'd asked in every city and town the show had toured. Having been unsuccessful at locating relatives on her own thus far, she would let *them* find *her*. As soon as her story made the newspapers and the dime novels, whatever family she had would seek her out.

It was only a matter of time.

The bell over the shop door tinkled. Anton Neubauer glanced up to discover Estelle Parkhurst storming into his store.

"*Mr.* Neubauer." Ruddy-faced and out of breath, she marched to the counter behind which he sat on a stool.

On the glass in front of him, a myriad of tiny gears and springs lay—pieces of the clock he'd been working on for the past hour. "Mornin', Mrs. Parkhurst. What can I do for you?"

"You can teach that son of yours some manners for one thing," she huffed. "And for another you can replace the window on the alley side of my office."

"Again?" Anton slid his new spectacles from his face and pinched the bridge of his nose. "I'm sorry about the window. I'll talk to Nikolaus about it."

"Talking seems to have little effect on the boy. He's only six years old, yet he's allowed to run wild in the streets. What he needs is a firm hand and strict guidance!"

"Playing in the alley is hardly what I'd call running wild, Mrs. Parkhurst. I can't expect him to stay cooped up in here with me when I have work to do on Saturday."

"Well, then you should leave him with one of his aunts. The child needs supervision."

Anger rising, Anton stood. "Look. My sisters-in-law both have children of their own to look after, and they take care of Nikolaus plenty as it is." He checked an exasperated sigh. "I said I'd replace the window. Nikolaus is just a boy. It's only natural for him to throw things when he's playin'."

The woman puffed out her ample bosom like a banty rooster. "If he throws one more thing through my window, I'll report you and your boy to the authorities! Do yourself a favor, Mr. Neubauer. Find that child a mother."

Slack-jawed, Anton watched the door close behind her. The bell tinkled musically. He dropped to the edge of the stool. "Tell me something I don't know, ya old pickle puss."

Intuitively, he turned in the direction of the back room. His towheaded son kicked the doorjamb with the tip of his scuffed shoe.

"Hi, Papa." Nikolaus thrust his lower lip forward, and his shoulders sagged. A streak of dirt across one cheek completed the irresistible look of little-boy innocence.

"Hi, Nikky."

"You gonna whup me?"

"C'mere." Anton knelt on the wooden floor.

Mutely, hands stuffed in the pockets of his faded denim overalls, Nikolaus trudged to his waiting father. His round blue eyes filled with tears. "Sorry."

Anton's chest tightened with tenderness and guilt. Hanging around the confining shop was difficult for a child with all the energy of a lightning bolt. For weeks he'd been promising to take Nikolaus hunting for a wild turkey. He pulled the child against his wide chest and hugged him hard, struck as always by the changeless and unbounded love his son inspired. "I know, son."

"It was just an ol' hunk of cinder I found in the alley. I didn't think I threw it hard enough to bust the glass."

"You've got quite an arm there. You'll be a good *mosche balle* player when you're a little bigger." The boisterous game was a favorite activity among the male population of the Pennsylvania Dutch community. A good *mosche balle* player was revered by all.

"Really, Pa?" Nikolaus drew back excitedly.

"Really. I'd better tell Franz and Jakob to watch out."

The bell over the door tinkled, and father and son exchanged glances resignedly. Pickle Puss Parkhurst again? Anton stood. One of his brothers closed the door behind him.

"Jakob!"

"Why're ya surprised to see me? You knew I was bringing Lydia's eggs into town today."

"Uncle Jake!" Nikolaus ran and flung his arms around the legs of the man who looked much like his father.

Jakob ruffled the boy's pale blond hair with a huge hand. "Look what Aunt Lydia sent for you."

The child accepted the small bag and drew out a sugar cookie.

"Why don't you take 'em in back and play with your horse collection for awhile?" Anton suggested.

"'Kay."

They watched him run into the back room. Anton sat and gestured to the other stool.

Jakob straddled it and splayed a large hand on the glass counter. His eyes, less intense, a frostier blue than his brother's, sparked with humor. "Who's the lucky girl tonight?"

"Hmm." Anton put on his spectacles and poked at the clock parts with a long finger.

"C'mon. Your bride shopping isn't exactly a secret. Seems you'd be quite a catch for these local gals. Last week Helena McLaury, the week before that Sissy Clanton... I hear the widow Schofield even had a few spins around the dance floor with you last month. Whatsa' matter, did she step on your toes?"

"This isn't funny, Jakob. I need to find a wife, and none of the women around here are passable."

"Sissy is under thirty and has all her teeth. What's wrong with her? And next to my wife, the widow Schofield makes the best apple dumplin's in all of Pennsylvania! What're you being so picky about?"

"I didn't see you marrying any of them. You picked your wife from that unlikely Harmony Society at Accord."

"She has a sister." Jakob's bright blue eyes sparkled with mischief. "Right pretty, too."

Anton shifted his weight, and the stool squeaked beneath him. "I don't care if she's drop-dead beautiful. Just so she's mild-mannered and...domestic. She has to cook and sew and be a mother to Nikolaus."

"And a wife to you."

Anton shrugged. "Nikolaus needs two parents. A family." The rest wasn't important. He didn't have to love this wife. He wouldn't love her. Not after Peine.

Never again would he allow himself to be vulnerable or stick his neck out begging for hurt. He wanted a soft, demure woman like Annette or Lydia, his brothers' wives. Sissy Clanton wasn't so bad; in fact, he was seeing her again tonight. All week long he'd tried to picture the three of them—himself, Nikky and Sissy—living in a house together as a family. He would work the farm with his father and brothers, as always. Winters he'd fix watches and clocks for extra money, and Sissy would take care of the house and the laundry. Nikky would go to school.

He wouldn't make a fool of himself over Sissy Clanton the way he had over his first wife. Beautiful Peine, moody, discontented...and obsessively in love with the brother sitting across from him. Jakob hadn't reciprocated.

No, Sissy's beauty wouldn't blind Anton as Peine's had. He wouldn't overlook her faults because of his love for her. And he wouldn't let her get too close to him.

He could visualize the clean house, the tasty dinners, evenings around the fireplace with Sissy mending his shirts while he played checkers with his boy. Each detail focused as clear as a bell. What dealt him trouble was imagining taking Sissy to his bed. How could he—

The door burst open, the bell clanging in protest. "Anton! Jake!" panted Tom Simms, a local farmer. "A train derailed down by Ed Jackson's place! People and animals are hurt bad. Livestock—and buffalo—are running wild. They need help!"

Anton peeled his spectacles from his ears and shouted after Tom, already out the door, Jakob on his heels. "I'll take Nikolaus to Mrs. Parkhurst's." He sprinted to the doorway. "Buffalo?"

"Yeah," Tom hollered over his shoulder, running toward the next store. "This ain't just any ol' train. This here's Buffalo Bill's Wild West Congress of Rough Riders!"

The scene Anton came upon a short time later was one he'd tell his grandchildren about. A small herd of elk huddled beneath the dappled shade of an elm, cropping grass like cattle. He drew his horse up and gestured for Jakob to look. They watched in puzzlement for a moment until three brown and white spotted ponies thundered past, and the elk loped off toward a stream.

Sounds reached them before they saw the devastation. Animals shrieked in pain and terror. Men shouted, and echoing gunshots rang out.

An endless string of black railroad cars lay twisted haphazardly across the gently sloping ground like a child's forgotten toy. Mortally wounded horses and longhorn steer writhed on the ground, and two Indians dressed like cowboys fired bullets into the animals' heads, ending their misery.

Able passengers led the wounded to a designated area well away from the teetering cars. Occasionally, an animal or person escaped an overturned railcar unaided.

Overwhelmed, Anton slid from his horse. Behind him someone moaned in pain.

"We need more help." Doc, a beefy Norwegian, dragged his bag across the grass to the next patient. "I sent the Von Goethe boy for another doctor, but it'll be dark before he can get here."

"Neubauer! Over here!"

Anton loped to where the townspeople had formed a team and joined them. Dividing, they methodically checked each car for trapped survivors.

The afternoon passed, and three men were discovered dead—two whites and an Indian. Those in need of a doctor had grown to an alarming number. Toward the rear of the train, a metallic sound caught Anton's attention. He followed the noise to one of the overturned stock cars and climbed the bottom of the car, heedless of the grime already covering him. Squatting at the opening, he peered down.

A young red pony lay dying. Its exhausted body jerked reflexively, one hoof occasionally striking a tin bucket. A cage of chickens had spilled open; feathers and strutting chickens were everywhere. Anton paused, blinked the sting of perspiration from his eyes and wiped sweat from his temple with his shirt-sleeve.

Another sound from below.

Human.

Feet first, he lowered himself inside the car, swung suspended for a moment, then dropped to the metal side with a loud clash of his boots. Squawking chickens disbanded in a dozen directions. He climbed a mountain of feed bags, many burst or split, and discovered tumbled crates, scattered harnesses, snaffle rings and bridle bits. Beneath the rubble, he spotted a hand. Anxiety sparked a cold shiver through his overheated frame.

It was a small, dark hand. A sleeve. Shoving aside a saddle, he made out an Indian boy, his leg pinned beneath a trunk. The boy lay unconscious, dark fingers of blood tracing his brow. Anton lifted the trunk, and the boy groaned. Immediately, something inside him locked in on the boy's pain, and he touched the narrow face tenderly. Just a little boy... a boy like his own.

Running his hands over the child, he checked for wounds, finding none save the cut on his head. The boy's leg, however, rested at an unnatural angle.

Out of crates, he built a stairway of sorts, and kicked open the car's trapdoor. The child was longer than Nikolaus, but surprisingly lighter. Both arms occupied, Anton scaled the shaky pile and crouched in the opening, taking great care not to move the injured leg more than he had to.

Anton reached the doctor's makeshift quarters, and the boy awoke, pain contorting his face. He grimaced and fought tears, then fell back and shuddered.

"Doc!" Anton yelled, then he squeezed the child's thin shoulder through his buckskin shirt. "The doc'll fix you up. It'll be all right. Hold on. Doc!" Gently, he lowered the boy to the grass.

"Hang onto your britches, Neubauer. What've you got here?" Doc gave a cursory examination. "Leg's broke. We'll hafta set it."

Anton jerked his head up. *We?*

The doctor took a vial and a syringe from his bag. "What's your name, boy?"

The child's black eyes widened, and his dark skin paled. He stared at the needle and swallowed. "S-Slade. What're ya gonna do with that?"

"Make you sleep so we can fix your leg."

Admiring the boy's composure, Anton took Slade's chin firmly in one large hand and turned the boy's face away from the needle. He was barely older than his own son. Nikolaus would be screaming his head off in pain and fear. Slade met his gaze and held it. His Adam's apple bobbed twice, and he jerked as the needle pricked his skin.

Sleepy lids drooped over black, black eyes. "Grandfather will be proud," he muttered before losing consciousness.

Anton nodded. He'd be proud if this were his boy.

Annette pulled a coverlet up under Slade's chin and turned to Anton, her tawny eyes filled with sympathetic tears. "I wonder where his parents are? Did he ask for them?"

In the lantern light, Anton studied the dark-skinned boy, so small and alone, asleep in his bed. "He mentioned his grandfather."

"His grandfather could be one of the injured or..." His sister-in-law's voice trailed off. Tendrils of russet-colored hair had come loose from the love knot she always wore, and curled prettily around her face. She had prepared rooms, freshened linens and assisted the men in bedding down their unexpected houseguests.

A motherly lady with a shoulder injury occupied one bedroom. Two Pawnee Indians, one with a head wound, the other with his foot stitched up, rested in another.

When Anton had offered to bring the boy home, it had seemed only right to bring a few others, too. Butler residents and neighboring farmers had taken home as many Wild West passengers as they could. The huge old farmhouse he rambled around in with his father and son held extra beds, and could easily accommodate three more people.

In the morning he and his brothers would head back to help bury the dead livestock, a staggering prospect.

"Tomorrow I'll ask around for his grandfather."

Annette nodded. She knelt over the pallet on the floor and ran her fingers through Nikolaus' pale blond hair, her sweet face reflecting her love. She had helped Anton care for Nikolaus since Peine's death when he was barely a year old. "Didn't take your little *Deutschmann* long to fall asleep after all. He's fascinated by Slade."

"Pretty exciting having an Indian sleeping in your pa's bed," Anton said, grinning.

"You'd better get some rest, too, Anton." She smiled and stretched on tiptoe.

Anton leaned forward, accepting her sisterly kiss on the cheek. She smelled of lilac water, as always. "What about you? Your family will be up early."

"I'll head home as soon as I clean up the kitchen a bit."

The door's soft click behind her roused Slade, and he sat up quickly, wincing.

"Whoa, pardner," Anton whispered. "It's all right. Lay back down and rest." The boy's fathomless, obsidian eyes revealed a combination of pain and fear. "Remember me?" Anton asked in hopes of soothing him. "I brought you home. Doc left some medicine to help you sleep tonight."

He fed Slade a spoonful and patted the child's hand comfortingly. Practically the same age as Nikolaus, and yet so different. He was dark and slender where Nikolaus was fair and robust. He had prominent cheekbones and full, bow-shaped lips. Though opposite in every way, he was as handsome a child as Nikolaus.

Anton pictured the two side by side, Slade half a head taller. What would they say to one another? Would Slade take an interest in Nikolaus' carved horses? How would they entertain him while his leg healed? Anton touched the boy's narrow hand. How would he comfort him if he couldn't find his family?

The little guy had obviously had a traumatic scare when the train derailed. Anton couldn't help wondering about those long, terrifying minutes. Had he been knocked out, or had he lain in pain until he passed out? He imagined Nikolaus seriously hurt and separated from the family—from him. He would be frightened, just as this boy was, even though he'd probably try his best to conceal it. Anton's chest tightened.

"Mister?"

He met the drowsy gaze. "Anton."

"How's my pony?"

Anton studied the tiny cut above Slade's eyebrow, avoiding direct eye contact. What could he say? A hard knot of sorrow lumped in the pit of his stomach, and he met the waiting gaze. "Your horse died, son. We buried him."

The drug Doc had administered seemed to have dulled the pain in the boy's eyes. "Thanks."

Thanks? Wordlessly, Anton nodded.

Slade's black-lashed eyes closed. His narrow chest rose and fell rhythmically. What kind of boy was this? What kind of family did he come from? Anton couldn't begin to imagine a life in the Wild West Show. How was Slade schooled? Was he learning the same things as Nikolaus? Anton gave a brief prayer of thanks that the boy had not been killed, and prayed, too, that his grandfather or whatever family he had was still alive.

Slade slept.

Anton rifled through a stack of dime novels, selected one with Buffalo Bill on the cover and settled into the chair. The book was an exciting story of an Indian attack, but one he'd read before. Minutes later, his eyes closed.

An undefinable whisper of fabric or soft leather against the floorboards woke Anton. He sat up with a start, the book falling to the floor.

An Indian—right out of the pages of the dime novel—hesitated just inside the doorway. Black hair parted in the center and braided in one thick rope lay against the front of a fawn-colored deerskin tunic. The Indian wore pants of the same soft skin. Moccasins had made the faint sound. The garb could have been worn by either male or female.

The wearer was definitely female.

She was probably a little over five feet tall, softly curved and strikingly lovely.

Anton stood.

Her hesitation was nearly imperceptible. She took a deep breath, the graceful swells of her breasts lifting beneath the soft material, the braid rising and falling. She stepped closer and looked up.

Anton stood better than a foot taller. Her almond-shaped eyes were deep violet in color, dark-lashed and liquid-velvet soft. Stepping closer, he took sleepy stock of her gentle, tanned features, the ebony arch of her brows and the perfect bow of her upper lip beneath a slim nose. *She wasn't an Indian!* Caught by surprise, he tried to clear his brain. "Ma'am?"

"I'm looking for my son." She glanced toward the sleeping children. "Your wife let me in."

"Slade?" he asked, ignoring her mistake. The boy did have a family!

"Yes." Relief flashed across her features. "He's here?"

"In the bed."

In an instant she was at the boy's side. The bed barely
sagged beneath her weight. She peeled the coverlet back and
sought his injuries, touching Slade everywhere. Alarm suffused her expression.

Sensing her panic at the boy's stillness, Anton reassured
her. "Just his leg. He's sleeping sound because of the medicine Doc gave 'im." Anton stood at the end of the bed and
spoke softly. "Bone's broken. We set it, and he'll be good
as new when it mends."

She said something softly in a language he couldn't understand and pressed her lips to Slade's forehead. Touched
his face. Buried her nose in his hair.

Her maternal caress roused some bred-in-the-bone instinct in Anton before he'd had a chance to dull it. A long-
buried fragment of hurt erupted, and he looked away.

In the dead-of-night silence, he detected her ragged
breath. She didn't appear old enough to be Slade's mother.
Older sister, maybe. Aunt. But not mother. Her pitiable fear
and tender reunion, however, gave away her parentage.
Anton swallowed and dared to peer back.

She stood and faced him.

"Anton Neubauer, ma'am." He stepped forward and offered his hand.

Without hesitation, she placed her small palm in his.
"Rain Shadow."

His callused hand engulfed hers. She willed her fingers
not to tremble, the way she did when she took aim at a target and squeezed the trigger. His handshake was warm and
gentle. She caught her breath. He smiled, and his features
changed from intense to friendly in an instant. The apricot
glow of the lantern revealed entrancing smile lines in the lean
cheek nearest the light. His thick hair reflected golden
highlights, and his eyes...were they blue? Rain Shadow

shook herself. "I'm afraid I scared a few years off the poor doctor's life."

"*You?*"

"He'd just gone to bed, and I nearly pounded his door down. I tried all evening to find my son. No one—" her voice faltered over the words "—remembered seeing him."

Never in her life had she been so frightened. Slade was her flesh and blood, her world, her everything. Losing him was unthinkable. Rain Shadow prided herself on her competence, on her ability to remain undismayed under pressure. The near panic she'd experienced at Slade's disappearance seemed foreign.

Anton nodded sympathetically. "There was so much confusion, it's not surprising."

A soft rap sounded at the half open door. The woman who'd introduced herself as Annette poked her head inside. "Have you eaten, miss . . ."

"Rain Shadow. No, but thank you. Don't go to any bother."

"It's no bother. I'll bring you a sandwich."

"No—"

Annette vanished into the hallway.

Anton shrugged and gestured to the chair. "Sit down?"

"No. Your wife is very kind, but—"

"My sister-in-law."

"I can't stay."

"Oh." Anton regarded her with surprise.

She surveyed the unfamiliar room, studied her son sleeping in this white man's bed and was consumed with an urgent need to take Slade far away as quickly as she could. They didn't belong here. "I'm grateful you took care of Slade, but I'm here now."

"Well, sure . . ." He folded his arms over his broad chest and leaned against the edge of a chest of drawers. "You're here now. You can take care of him."

"No, we can't stay. We have to leave."

He dropped his arms. "Why?"

Why? She couldn't explain the panic that remained in her soul. She just knew she had to get both of them away from this man and his disarming concern. "Slade is my son. I'm responsible for him, and I will care for him. You've been troubled enough."

"Look, ma'am." He shoved his weight from the chest of drawers and touched her upper arm. "Sit down."

Against her will, Rain Shadow backed up to the chair, and her knees buckled. Through her deerskin tunic, her skin tingled where he'd touched her.

"I don't mean to be rude or nosy, but where would you go even if you could? That's a nasty break, and Doc said not to move him for a couple weeks, at least. After that, he still can't walk. I don't think you want to take a chance on doing something that could damage his leg for good."

A trapped, claustrophobic sensation twined inside her chest, and for one wild instant she wanted to snatch her son from this man's bed and run. She didn't want to be dependent on him, on anyone. She owed her life to one person—Two Feathers. At least she'd given him something in return. She'd been the daughter he had lost. He'd taken her into his lodge and cared for her. And as the years had gone by, the roles had reversed. She'd become the provider, the caretaker. It was as it should be.

She worked hard in the show, earned her way, her pay and respect, depended on no one but herself. If only— What? If only Anton Neubauer hadn't sought help for Slade and generously taken him home? Would she rather he'd left her son to lie in pain until she'd gotten there? If only she'd never allowed Slade to ride on the train ahead with his pony in the first place! If he'd been with her, this never would have happened.

"Ma'am."

She glanced up. Anton Neubauer sat on the foot of his bed, wide shoulders hunched, corded forearms resting on his knees, his long tanned fingers entwined loosely. Begrudgingly, she accepted his logic. She had no choice but to accept his hospitality for her son. "I will pay his room and board."

One corner of his mouth turned up. "This isn't a hotel."

"All the same, I'll provide for him."

"And rob me of doing my Christian duty?" He shrugged. "I'm insulted that you think I expect payment for human kindness." His gentle voice belied any insult.

Was he a do-gooder, then? He didn't seem the type to take pity on every stray that came his way. "I will pay."

"You'll pay." He nodded his fair head good-naturedly, and she allowed her muscles to relax.

Annette arrived with a sandwich and a glass of milk. Rain Shadow took the plate and glass and thanked Annette, who turned and left. Uncomfortable beneath Anton's gaze, she took a few bites. She couldn't help wondering what he saw as he gazed at her. Will was the only white man she'd ever been halfway close to. She had no knowledge of or experience with a man like this.

She stood, set the plate down and sensed the tall stranger's eyes on her as she moved to the bed. She touched Slade's cheek with her knuckles, ran her fingers through his dark, silky hair. Sinking to the bed's edge, her gaze wandered to the bedside table. A gold pocket watch lay on an embroidered white scarf, its chain forming a lazy *S* in and around a few silver coins.

She spotted the dime novel lying open on the floor where it had fallen when he'd awakened. On the cover was an artist's rendition of Will Cody fighting a Cheyenne war party. Her attention was drawn to an oval-framed sepia-toned photograph on the wall—a wedding portrait, though from this distance she couldn't make out the faces. A blue chambray shirt hung on the knob of a narrow door.

An unexplainable sense of voyeurism gripped her. She was an intruder, sitting among this man's private possessions, perched on his... bed. Everything here was his. His family. His house. His home.

"You must be tired," Anton said. "I know I am."

She turned her upper body and faced him, a nagging resentment flaring. This situation wasn't his fault, she told herself, but he'd involved himself. "He's never been separated from me before."

"Well, you're together now."

She realized, at last, that he expected her to stay in his room, too! "I can't stay here!"

"Why not?"

She stood. "I can't stay here," she said again and glanced around uncomfortably. Outside of one or two hotels in London, she'd never slept indoors. The idea was foreign.

"You'd leave him here alone with me, then?"

"I—" She frowned at Slade's slight form on the huge bed, and knew at that moment how a trapped animal felt. Of course she couldn't leave him alone here. "No."

Anton stood, bent at the waist and plucked the book from the floor. The ticking of his pocket watch on the table amplified the silence of the room. The children's breathing was audible. "Why don't you lay down there beside him... just for tonight? Tomorrow we—you can figure out what to do."

Trapped. She had no other choice. Her lodge was packed in the number-ten excursion railcar several miles away. "My father won't know where I am. He stayed in Butler for word of Slade.''

"I'll get a message to him. He can stay here, too."

Two Feathers had never slept in a house in his life. He slept on the ground near a fire as he had since his birth. She couldn't imagine him spreading his furs on these wooden floors. The thought was ludicrous. "He'll need to camp with the others who are guarding the cars and the animals."

Anton tossed the book on the chair seat. "It's settled, then. I'll send word. What's your pa's name?"

"Two Feathers."

He nodded. "I'll carry my son down to the parlor. We'll sleep there."

His son? Where was his wife? Rain Shadow could see no evidence of a woman sharing the room.

"If you want a nightshirt, grab one from the second drawer of the chest." He knelt and easily scooped his sleeping child, pallet and all, into his arms. "If Slade wakes up, give him a spoonful of this." He nodded to the corked bottle on the chest of drawers. "See you in the mornin'."

"Jack!" She suddenly remembered her pony waiting patiently outside.

"Ma'am?" Anton paused and raised his sandy brows in puzzlement.

"Jack. My pony. He's outside."

"I'll put him up in the barn for you."

"I'm obliged." *I don't want to be, but there's not much I can do about it tonight.*

The door clicked shut.

Rain Shadow glanced around the room, avoided the portrait on the wall and stifled the turbulent emotions vying for prominence in her mind and heart. What was it about Anton Neubauer that threatened her so?

For the first time she realized how exhausted she was. With inbred stealth, she slipped off her moccasins, lay atop the coverlet and comforted herself by touching her son's hair and cheek.

Slade was alive. That was all that mattered. Everything—everyone—else she could deal with. With that determination her body relaxed, and eventually she slept.

Chapter Two

The morning was unseasonably warm for late October. Anton stripped his shirt off and tied the sleeves around his waist. Raising his right arm and swiveling it in the shoulder socket, he tilted his head to the side and worked out the kink between his shoulder blades. Buffalo required enormous graves.

The smell of overturned dirt snagged a memory. He'd plowed acres of fertile ground each spring, and the earthy smell always carried the promise of new life, a new season. This time the scent stirred the recollection of a dismal day nearly ten years ago—before Peine, and before Jakob had married Lydia. Franz and Annette had buried their tiny baby boy in the family graveyard on a rise behind the house.

A fresher memory, buried deeper than any other, bobbed to the surface. The pain scissored through his chest as it always did when he remembered. Peine was buried on that same rise. A crisp fall day with acrid ash floating on the autumn air, he'd dug his wife's body from the charred ruins of the barn.

"You gonna lean on that shovel all day?"

Anton realized Jakob must have spoken twice, but since his brother was off to the left, Anton hadn't caught the question the first time. A near fatal case of measles as a child had left him deaf in that ear. Letting go of the memories, he scooped a shovelful of earth and flung it at Jakob. Jakob dodged; the dirt hit Franz and clung to his perspiring chest.

Franz jerked his gaze up to his older brother. He snatched a dirt clod from the pile at his feet and let it fly. Within minutes, others joining, the game became an impromptu contest of *mosche balle* with one bizarre deviation: more than one ball was in play. The nearby sound of men grunting as they lugged another buffalo toward the pit they'd dug brought the game to an end. The perspiring men picked up their shovels and resumed their gruesome task.

Anton couldn't remember the last time he'd missed a Sunday church service, but even Reverend Mercer had turned out to help this morning. They dug, dragged and buried. And all the while Anton's thoughts returned to the boy in his bed . . . and to the boy's mother.

The more he thought, the more convinced he was that the boy wasn't Indian, either. Black hair, black eyes, teak-colored skin—quite possibly from the sun.

Anton's memory unfolded the young woman in vivid detail. The garb, her hair and skin—even her silent walk was misleading. Everything about her suggested Indian ancestry at first glance—everything, that was, except her eyes. Her eyes...bewitched. This morning as she'd returned from tending her pony, he'd stepped off the back porch.

"Mornin'."

"Mr. Neubauer."

"How was Slade's night?"

"He woke several times. I gave him the medicine twice."

Once again her hair hung braided in a long, black rope, the end tied with a leather thong from which intricate silver leaves hung. She regarded him solemnly, the morning sun catching blue-black highlights in her hair. Her most unusual feature, her eyes, were almost exotic, the color of a stormy sky at sunset. Anton had to force himself to think about what she was saying.

"If your sister-in-law will be kind enough to sit with Slade later this morning, I'll bring my things from the train."

He'd tried not to let his surprise show and nodded toward Franz and Annette's smaller house, only a few hundred feet to the west of the main house. "I'll stop over before I head out. She'll be coming to tend the others anyway, so I'm sure she won't mind."

"Thank you."

"Surely." He'd moved aside, and she'd gone into the house.

Now, shoveling dirt over a hairy carcass, he wondered what her position in the show was. He'd never been to a performance of the Wild West Show, but he'd read about it and seen photographs. He had listened to several men this morning, and their jobs ranged from singers and musicians to blacksmiths and cavalry soldiers. She could be a seamstress or a cook. Or perhaps her husband was the showperson.

Anton shook himself. What did it matter anyway? She would be gone as soon as Slade's leg healed.

The question slunk back like a fox worrying a mongoose: where *was* her husband?

Anton gave his enormous bay his head and galloped up the drive toward the barn. Attention drawn to the dooryard, he reined the animal in, leaned across the saddle horn and studied the barbarous sight from beneath the brim of his dusty Stetson.

A tepee stood in his yard.

Centered in the dooryard, it was almost as tall as the second story of the house and painted with geometric designs and hunting scenes. Anton noted smoke curling out of a hole in the top, where several poles were lashed together as supports. An occupied tepee.

Nudging the bay into a walk, he circled the hide structure. For the love of Pete, who had set it up here? The family of one of the Pawnees in the upstairs bedroom? Annette and Lydia must be going out of their minds now that a band of Indians had invaded their homestead. His thoughts raced ahead to everyone who would see the outrageous dwelling in their yard. A realization struck him: they had an autumn barn dance scheduled next Saturday night!

He slid from the saddle and whacked the horse's rump, and the General galloped toward the barn. Anton stood before the closed flap. How did a body knock on a tent? "Hello?"

Movement sounded inside. The flap opened, and Rain Shadow stepped out. "Mr. Neubauer."

"You!" He couldn't help noticing the cream-colored doeskin dress she wore, quills and beads gracing the front. The soft leather clung to her petite body's every curve. "What's going on?"

"What do you mean?"

He gestured. "The tepee and all, I mean."

"I got my things this morning, as I said."

"Yeah, well. I didn't know you were gonna set up your..."

"Lodge? Your father said it was harmless here."

"You discussed it with my pa?"

Her tempestuous lavender eyes narrowed under graceful jet brows. "Is there a problem?"

Behind him, the springboard rolled up the drive. Uncomfortable under her gaze, he turned and watched his father lead the team into the barn. "Something wrong with the house?"

"Pardon?"

"Why couldn't you stay in the house? I'm guessing you figure to stay out here?"

"I've put your family out enough already, Mr. Neubauer. And I prefer my lodge."

"But it's extra trouble for you to come and go taking care of the boy."

Rain Shadow half smiled and shook her head, her black braid brushing the front of her dress in an intimate caress he tried not to notice. At the same time, he thought how unfair it was that the first woman to catch his attention in all those sensually riveting little ways couldn't have been Sissy Clanton.

"Hardly. I'm used to more activity than a little walking."

Determinedly, he kept his gaze nailed on her amethyst eyes, ignoring the way her bow-shaped lips curved up provocatively at the corners. "But there's frost on the ground at night. You'll get cold out here."

At that she laughed outright. Her teeth were the perfect foil for her rich black hair and honey-hued skin. "As long as we can make a fire, it's warm inside. The hides hold in the heat, just like they did on the buffalo."

"What if it rains or snows?" Anton gestured to the smoke escaping the off-center opening.

She pointed to the two lightweight poles holding the smoke flap open. "By moving those, the flaps adjust to compensate for wind and weather. The lodge faces east, and the greater slant of the front braces it against wind from the back."

Anton shifted his weight. He could hardly argue his position with, "What will the neighbors think?" How pompous! But how would he convince her to pack up this eyesore and stay in the house?

"All settled?" His father stepped up beside him, his question directed at Rain Shadow.

"Thank you, yes. I gathered firewood this afternoon."

"There's a whole pile out behind the house," Anton offered, and wondered why his usually dexterous father stepped on his foot and elbowed him in the ribs.

"Good, good," Johann continued as though his son hadn't spoken. "Doc been around yet?"

She shook her head.

"Well," the older man said with a shrug. "I reckon he's still busy tending folks hurt worse. He'll be by shortly."

Rain Shadow nodded.

"Anton, do you think this is a snake hole over here?"

He followed his father to a spot on the ground where he saw nothing out of the ordinary.

"You know," Johann said and rubbed his chin. "I'll wager it helps her feel safe havin' her own place to stay. She might be white on the outside, but inside she's an Indian. This tepee is part of their culture. She and Two Feathers would no more move into our house than an eagle would build a nest in the barn rafters."

Anton glanced over his shoulder at the young woman in the beautifully decorated dress, and his exasperation simmered. So his pa approved of the squatters and their enormous backyard irritation. His arguments were for naught.

"I guess that wasn't a snake hole after all." Johann's faded blue eyes revealed a sparkle of mirth. He appeared to be enjoying the whole situation enormously.

Anton clenched and unclenched his jaw. All right. The tent stayed. But he didn't have to pretend he liked it.

He stalked off toward the barn. "I have cows to milk."

Dawn spread its first golden rays through a stand of eastern hemlock's sparse boughs, and a pair of thrushes called to one another. Two Feathers' breath hung in the brisk air. Morning was his favorite time of day. From the rise behind the house, he surveyed the Neubauers' wooden lodges and animal quarters. To the west, meadows and woods stretched as far as his no longer youthful eyes could see; to the east, acres of fields plowed under. Rich, fertile soil. Land and crops blessed by Wakon Tanka.

Here there was game: pheasant, turkey, and ruffled grouse. He'd seen signs of possum, rabbit and squirrel. A person living on this land could support himself indefinitely. It had been two days since he'd heard the piercing whistle of the iron horse, two restful moons since he'd listened to men roll dice and play cards until the sun rose.

How long would it be until the farmer's medicine man proclaimed the injured ready to move out of the house? Colonel Cody was overseeing the restoration of the train, and it would soon be time to ride it south. Slade would not be ready to leave with the others. Rain Shadow had already spoken of her plan to stay with her son. If Two Feathers left without them, would she catch up soon as she'd planned? A wary sensation brought unease to his spirit. He didn't want to go without her.

The sun appeared over the horizon, a glorious tangerine sphere. He raised his palms toward the earth's sustenance and chanted.

As he finished the prayer, Johann Neubauer ambled up beside him. Two Feathers appreciated the pungent aroma of the pipe the silver-haired man held between his teeth. Smoke curled past his faded blue eyes as he squinted at Two Feathers.

"Nothing like a peaceful mornin'." Johann took his hand from a deep pocket in his wool jacket long enough to adjust the pipe.

What kind of spirit sense did the old man have? Two Feathers eyed him.

"Your daughter gets up mighty early, too."

"We have always risen to greet the sun."

"Nice girl."

"Fine sons you have. Land to call your own. You have been blessed."

Johann nodded. "I have."

"Living with our children beside us is how the Indian chooses to live."

"Yep. We've got a lot in common."

"Many seasons have passed without your wife?"

"Many. I always pictured us growing old together. Watching our sons grow into men." Johann shrugged. "God didn't have the same plan."

Two Feathers heard the pain in his voice, knew Johann's joy was half because he had no woman to share it. "I, too, lost a wife." Strange that he should reveal his sorrow to a near stranger, but sharing it seemed right. "And a daughter."

Johann nodded in empathy.

"Rain Shadow took their place in my heart."

No doubt Johann's curiosity was unsatisfied, but he remained politely silent.

"We are much alike." An inexplicable bond had formed between them, Two Feathers realized. They both loved the land and respected life. Both had raised their children alone. Both were kindred spirits. "I go to catch trout for breakfast. I would be honored to have you join me."

Johann's seamy grin was lopsided. "I'll fetch my pole."

The hall clock struck a few times, but Nikolaus didn't bother to count. It was early; his grandfather had just left the house. Nikolaus crept stealthily to the doorway of his father's room.

"C'mon in."

The voice from within startled him, and he straightened, slowly pushing the door open."

"What's your name?"

"Nikolaus."

Head and shoulders propped up on stark white-cased pillows, the Indian boy laid down the catalog he'd been thumbing through. "Hi, Nikolaus. I'm Slade Two Feathers."

"You a real Injun?" Nikolaus edged to the foot of the bed.

"Nah. Just in the show. My grampa's full-blooded Lakota Sioux, though."

"My grampa's German. He can talk it, too. Can your grampa talk Indian?"

"Sure. This your house?"

"Yup. My room's down there, but there's a lady with something busted in my bed. I been sleeping down in the parlor with my pa." He rounded the foot and perched on the bed's side. "Does your leg hurt?"

"Sometimes," Slade replied with a shrug. "Mostly today my butt hurts from lying like this."

Nikolaus widened his eyes at the other boy. "Does your ma let you say that?"

"What?"

"What you said."

"That my butt hurts?"

"Yeah."

Slade shook his head with the superior wry humor his one-year age advantage lent him. "'Course she lets me say it. I ain't a baby."

Nikolaus' wide blue eyes sparkled in admiration. "I could sneak in my room and get my horses if you wanna see 'em."

"Sure."

"Okay!" He bounced off the bed and turned back before he reached the door. "D'you wanna be friends?"

Slade appeared to consider the possibility. At last he broke the expectant silence. "I got lots of friends, what with the show and all the places I been and all, but I guess I can have one more."

"Aw'right!" Nikolaus raced through the doorway with a whoop.

The doctor showed up shortly after noon the next day. Rain Shadow waited anxiously as he tended the patients in the other rooms, proclaiming them well enough to be transferred. Encouraged, she followed him into the bedroom Slade occupied. The man walked with a marked limp, his movements abrupt. After a terse examination, he placed his instruments in his black bag.

"He's doing fine." His voice was gentler than his gruff appearance and demeanor led her to imagine.

Encouraged, she asked, "May I move him out to my lodge?"

"Not just yet. That was a nasty break, and the least movement the better for healing."

He would have to stay. Her spirits fell. She'd planned taking him out of the Neubauers' house. The imposition didn't rest comfortably. She wanted Slade in the security and familiarity of their lodge.

She met her son's ebony gaze. He was bored and hurting. His toes had swollen and turned black and blue.

The doctor picked up his bag and left the room without a farewell.

Rain Shadow stared after him, her slim hopes dashed. The trains were leaving for winter quarters in a few days. She and Slade would not be on one. What was this going to do to her plans? Guiltily, she swallowed her selfish concern. Slade's well-being was most important, of course. She'd speak with Two Feathers about going on without them. She frowned at the unpleasant thought.

This was merely a snag in her tightly woven plans. She bolstered herself, smoothing Slade's black hair away from his forehead. She could roll with the punches. She would practice every day; she didn't need the fancy setups, and as soon as Slade's leg improved they could take another train. She'd still be ready for an exhibition and contest with Annie in the spring. It was simply a matter of time.

That evening Rain Shadow arranged tin plates in a semicircle near the fire, comfortable in her lodge, pleased to have a familiar task to perform. Annette had been relieved to spend time with her own family, and preparing a meal for the Neubauers was small payment for the care and lodging they had provided for Slade. This was her element, something she knew, something she did well and took pride in.

The fact that Rain Shadow was unable to move Slade to their lodge still nettled. She would be obliged to the Neubauers for an uncertain length of time, not only obliged but forced to spend time in their home. She was torn between her discomfort in their house and wanting to be with her son.

The flap parted, and Two Feathers entered.

"Father," she said in greeting. Her heart grew warm as always by the familiar sight of his craggy face.

"Daughter." He stepped to the right as was the custom and took his place before the fire. "Slade rests."

She glanced toward the flap. "The Neubauers?"

"They follow."

She nodded and retrieved baked sweet potatoes from the coals. A sound outside brought her head up.

"Enter," Two Feathers welcomed.

Johann appeared first. He was a tall, handsome man like his sons. His skin testified to years of sun and weather, deep smile lines bracketing the corners of his faded blue eyes. At Two Feathers' gesture, Johann took a seat near the fire.

Anton and his son entered together. Anton wore a fresh white shirt, its sleeves rolled back over his corded forearms. His flaxen hair was damp and combed from his face in sun-streaked waves. He glanced around the inside of the lodge, and his scrutiny brought Rain Shadow's defenses into play. She couldn't help wondering what he was thinking. In comparison to his home and room, their things no doubt seemed meager to him, but on the move, as they were, they had no need for more. She had never gone hungry or without clothing. Will Cody had great respect for the Indian population, and treated and paid them well. She and Two Feathers had traveled with the Wild West Show since its first performance in Omaha eleven years ago.

Anton's cobalt blue gaze rested on her, and she had to force herself not to look away. He seemed to take stock of her as he had the lodge.

She'd never had occasion to care what someone else thought of her. She'd always been accepted for her ability as a horsewoman and sharpshooter. Anton Neubauer knew none of those things about her. He saw only a woman. She had to deal with him on a level she wasn't prepared to examine.

"Sit," Two Feathers invited.

Leading Nikolaus to a spot near his pa, Anton watched Rain Shadow dish food onto tin plates. Mouth-watering aromas had set his stomach to rumbling as soon as he'd entered the tent. The chickens cooked on a spit over the fire were golden brown. He hadn't eaten chicken like that since he was a boy.

The young woman worked gracefully, with deft, efficient movements, serving his father first. The doeskin garment she wore lent a soft, feminine appeal to her already pleasing shape. Long fringe at the hem and armholes swayed with her every movement, caressing honey-colored skin. Her knee-high moccasins appeared worn and comfortable, the tops visible only when she knelt and the fringe parted.

"Thank you." Anton accepted the plate and biscuits she handed him. Nikolaus, echoing his appreciation, sat in awe of his surroundings and the two strangers.

She served her father, then took her food and sat near him. The two sat companionably side by side, knees touching, as though they'd shared many meals together. The old man she called her father was unquestionably Indian, handsome in a dark, compelling manner. He carried himself straight, his chin high, the proud mannerism of a man who knew his worth. His copper-skinned face, wrinkled from years beneath the sun, was thoughtful and deliberate.

Two Feathers was dressed as many of the Indians had been dressed that morning; deerskin pants, a flannel shirt and a vest. A kerchief banded his forehead, holding his flowing black hair in place. Beads and bears' claws hung from a leather thong around his neck.

Rain Shadow lifted her gaze from her plate and stared at Anton questioningly. He realized he hadn't tasted the food. Biting into the generous portion of breast she had given him, he chewed and looked up in surprise. He'd assumed she'd cleaned one of the birds that ran loose in their dooryard. "This isn't chicken!"

"It's grouse. Don't you like it?"

"Yeah, I like it," he assured her quickly, noting the edge to her voice. "It's just that I thought—I figured . . ."

"That I stole your chickens?"

"No!" He glanced at her father, then his. Both ate placidly, refusing to look up.

"You assumed they were your chickens," she said, her chin lifted.

He hadn't actually given it a whole hell of a lot of thought. The chickens were there; they ate 'em. A fact of life. "It wouldn't have been stealing."

"They aren't my chickens."

How had this silly conversation gotten out of hand? "Well, it's good." He demonstrated by taking another bite and chewing.

The wild sweet potatoes were tender and delicious, and she served them each a handful of roasted nuts. She must have gone foraging today, and her father had obviously trapped the birds. Briefly, Anton considered telling her he appreciated how much trouble she'd gone to, but her reaction to his last comment silenced him.

After the meal, Two Feathers produced a long pipe from one of the many bundles around the perimeter of the tepee. He tamped tobacco into the bowl and lit it. Johann accepted the pipe in turn.

Anton studied their portable dwelling while Rain Shadow cleared away the remains of the food. Three remarkably large trunks were stowed on one side. Each had a lid, several drawers and locks. Robes and blankets made up one pile. Jugs, baskets and a few pans were stacked neatly alongside lanterns and several wooden crates. Just inside the opening was a sizable stack of firewood, and hanging from the interior was a ragged-edged hide with tiny pictures and symbols spiraling in a line from the center outward. Those easily recognized were horses, birds and tepees.

"It's a calendar," she offered.

He turned his gaze on her. Quickly, she lowered her eyes to her task.

"Smoke?"

Anton studied the pipe Two Feathers offered.

"You won't insult him if you don't smoke," Rain Shadow said softly.

"Can I try it, Gramps?" Nikolaus squirmed into Johann's lap, his eyes wide with excitement.

"'Fraid not, Toad," his grandfather replied with a chuckle. "Leastwise not till you grow a few whiskers."

"Aw." He frowned, disappointed. "You try it, Papa!"

Not wanting to breach etiquette, Anton accepted the carved pipe despite Rain Shadow's words. He puffed a few times, decided it wise not to inhale the smoke and passed it back.

Two Feathers wore a craggy smile at the corner of his full mouth.

"Can I be escused to go play with Slade now?" Nikolaus asked his father.

"*May* I be *ex*cused."

"May I be excused?"

"Yes, you may. Mind your manners and thank..." Anton felt his face grow warm and cursed himself for allowing her to make him feel like a youth. He made himself say her name. "Rain Shadow."

"Thank you, ma'am."

"You're welcome. I'll go with you. If Slade's awake, he's hungry." Rain Shadow picked up a plate she had prepared.

Johann and Anton thanked her for the meal. "Any time you'd like a chicken, you're welcome," Anton offered, thinking to save them some effort. They had no kitchen, and it was a long way into Butler for supplies. "There are vegetables still in the ground out back of the house, too."

"We have no need of your chickens, Mr. Neubauer." Her purple eyes flashed, and she shimmied gracefully past him, fringe slapping against her calves. "We eat what we catch, and it's good enough for us."

"I didn't mean—"

She was gone.

"Well, for..." He stared after her. That woman was as grumpy as an old grizzly with a thorn in its foot. Two Feathers met his startled expression with a knowing gaze.

"I didn't mean to insult anybody," Anton said. "I thought it'd be one less worry."

"I am not offended." The Indian puffed at his pipe.

Perhaps not, but the woman was definitely offended. Why did she interpret his every word as a gibe? Better for him if he kept his distance from her. And his mouth shut.

He stood and stretched his legs. It had been a long, tiring day, and daylight would beckon before he was ready. "After you say good-night to Slade, we'll get you to bed, Nikolaus."

"How 'bout a game of checkers before bed, Pa?"

"It's pretty late."

"Just one?"

Anton looked into his son's vivid blue eyes. He knew he didn't give the boy the attention he deserved. The thought reminded him that he needed to do something about that.

Tomorrow was another early start, and Anton hadn't been sleeping soundly. Another night on the sofa in the parlor wasn't the rest he needed. He wouldn't sleep that well anyway, so he may as well indulge in a game of checkers.

"Okay. Just one."

"Yippee! 'Night, Gramps."

Anton watched Nikolaus scamper out. Last night's plans with Sissy Clanton had been disrupted. He hoped she'd received his message. She'd know he'd been busy with the train, so he wasn't really worried. Next Saturday night's barn dance would be time enough to put his search into action. He had to find Nikolaus a mother. The sooner the better.

Another dawn broke, and Rain Shadow crept silently from the room where Slade slept so as not to disturb the Neubauers. Nearing the foot of the stairs, a young voice called to her from the parlor. "Where ya goin'?"

She raised a finger to her pursed lips and whispered, "To find breakfast."

"Oh," Nikolaus replied disinterestedly as he padded barefoot to meet her at the staircase. "Oatmeal's in the bin in the pantry."

"I'll find my breakfast in the woods."

The sleepy cast fled from his expression. "You mean huntin'? You going huntin'?"

She nodded, smiling at his eager expression.

"My papa said he'd take me huntin', but he's been awful busy."

Casting a wary glance at the boy's long father sleeping on the short sofa, she motioned for Nikolaus to join her in the kitchen. Anton had been put out of his room and probably wasn't getting the rest he needed after the strenuous days he put in. All the time he could spare from his work had been taken up with helping the show people, and the least she could do was take Nikolaus hunting so Anton could sleep.

"Get dressed quietly and come with me. You can carry the game back."

"Aw-right!" Her expression silenced him, and he bounded from the room.

The echo of rapid gunfire brought Anton off the sofa with a start. He stumbled over the blanket wrapped around his knees and caught his balance. Trying to orient himself, he realized Nikolaus wasn't on the pile of blankets near the fireplace. Shots rang out again—six in rapid succession.

Tugging on his denims, he ran out of the house and down the wooden porch stairs. "Nikolaus!"

Six more shots volleyed across the landscape. Cocking his head to concentrate with his good ear, he honed in on the direction they'd come from and ran. "Nikolaus!"

"Here, Pa!"

Anton raced toward his son's voice, cursing silently each time he stepped on a stone or twig. The ground sloped toward a stream, then flattened into a broad shady area along the bank. There, with the early morning chill pinkening their cheeks, he found his son and the woman, both booted and hatted, their like expressions faintly apologetic.

Dressed in a pair of leather pants and a waist-length fringed jacket, Rain Shadow slid her revolver into the holster, which rode her hip comfortably. Strips of soft leather entwined one long braid. Her wide-brimmed, flat-crowned hat was trimmed by a colorful beaded band.

"Sorry if we woke you," Rain Shadow said. "We were out in the woods for so long I figured everyone was up by now."

He didn't reply.

"Pa, look what Rain Shadow can do! She shoots these acorns right off the log!" Nikolaus ran and placed a row of acorns along a fallen tree from which the bark had long ago decayed, leaving a smooth, silverish log. Several fresh gouges lined the top. He ran back and stood a few feet from her. "Show him!"

"I think that's enough for this morning." She turned as if to move away.

"No. Go ahead. I'd like to see."

She gazed at Anton uneasily, noted the golden stubble he'd grown overnight. His fair hair was mussed, his shirttails hung outside his dungarees, and his long, bare toes curled into the dewy morning grass. His mood didn't appear pleasant.

"All right," she said, deciding. Quick as lightning, she turned, drew and fired six shots.

Anton's stunned gaze shot from the gun she automatically reloaded to the bare log. A few more nicks graced the top.

"Good Lord," he said to no one in particular.

Nikolaus giggled with delight. "Watch this, Pa."

The boy knelt and picked up a walnut from a small pile at his feet. Swinging his arm in a wide arc, he flung the nut into the air.

Rain Shadow raised the revolver in a flurry of swinging fringe, and the nut exploded into fragments.

The shot echoed in the crisp morning air.

Anton's clear blue eyes lowered from the cloudless sky and settled on her face. She was accustomed to various reactions from men, the most common the discomfort that a woman shot better than they. Deliberately, he subdued an expression of awe.

"Look what else!" Nikolaus ran to a canvas bag under one of the trees and tugged the fabric open. "Turkeys, Pa. Two of 'em!"

She could almost see the color of Anton's eyes darken to an intense, angry blue. His posture rigid, he knelt and peered into the bag beside his elated son. "Turkeys, huh? Well, what do ya know?"

"I'm gonna help clean and cook 'em, too. You're gonna eat with us, aren't ya?"

Rain Shadow watched him wrestle with his feelings and disguise his anger for his son's benefit. "Am I invited?"

Nikolaus raised an inquiring face to her.

"Certainly. Everyone is invited."

Anton stood. "You shot the grouse yesterday?"

"Yes."

"Where did you learn to do this?"

"Practice. I've been around sharpshooters since I was your son's age."

"She knows Annie Oakley, Pa."

"That a fact?"

She tied her holster thong, tugged the drawstring bag closed and handed it to Nikolaus. "I'd better get back to Slade."

Anton fell in step behind her, picking his way across the ground. Resentment flared, glowing hot as he watched his son trot adoringly alongside her, toting the lumpy bag. His jealousy was irrational, he knew, but he'd intended to take Nikolaus turkey hunting before she ever came along. Guiltily, he realized it had been weeks since he'd made the promise. If he'd had more time. . . .

Hell, there was never enough time. The crops were barely in, and preparations needed to be made for winter. When he had a wife, she could take over some of the tasks, and he'd have more time for his son.

He should have been the one to take Nikolaus hunting, rather than that—inadvertently, he watched the snug seat of her leather pants as she moved silently ahead of him—rather than that gun-toting, ungrateful . . .

He'd been outdone by a woman. No, a mere snip of a girl!

Rain Shadow had none of the qualities necessary to snag a husband. She compared unfavorably in all areas to his sisters-in-law—well, almost all areas, he conceded, and wrenched his gaze from her rounded backside. Lydia and Annette dressed demurely, moved with ease and comfort in a kitchen and wouldn't know the first thing about shooting a turkey.

When he found a mother for Nikolaus, she for sure, he swore, wouldn't be digging his father position out from under him. She would know how to behave like a woman!

From the top of the bank, Nikolaus squealed with delight and hopped up and down. "Pa! Pa! Hurry!"

Realizing he'd lagged behind, Anton limped toward them, wondering what his son found so thrilling.

"Look, Pa! It is him, ain't it, Rain Shadow? It's Buffalo Bill, Pa! Look!" Nikolaus dropped the game and raced toward the yard.

Eight or ten riders approached the house on prancing horses. Ahead of the party, astride a black horse with white socks and blaze, in thigh-high black boots and wide-brimmed sombrero, was, indeed, the famed Buffalo Bill Cody.

Chapter Three

Closing the distance to the house, Rain Shadow paused near a rope swing hung from the bough of an ancient oak. A squirrel disturbed from his ruthless gathering scampered into the branches overhead and chattered down at her. Ignoring him, she watched Will and the other riders approach the house. Nikolaus raced past her, intent on reaching the bigger-than-life Buffalo Bill first.

Anton walked around her, and she shot into step behind him. As they drew near, she observed his expression. He took stock of the horses with their hand-tooled silver and turquoise-studded saddles, as well as the opulently dressed men who rode them. *They're show people,* she bit back, as if their finery required explanation or excuses.

"Princess!" Will caught sight of Rain Shadow and doffed his wide-brimmed hat, waving it in enormous arcs. His magnificent black horse raised its forelegs and stood for impressive minutes on powerful hind legs.

"Gosh." Slack-jawed, Nikolaus stared at the extraordinary sight.

"Will! Hank!" Caught up in the excitement of seeing her extended family, Rain Shadow waved. "Come on, Nikolaus! Let's greet Will."

They covered ground rapidly, Anton at their heels. Will Cody slid from his saddle and swung her up and around in a bearlike embrace. She clung to him, a bittersweet emotion aching in her chest. The show was leaving tomorrow. She was staying behind.

Will seemed to sense her distress. "How's Slade?"

"He'll be fine, but he can't be moved for a while yet." She released him and they strolled arm in arm a few steps from the others.

"Two Feathers told me," Will replied, genuine concern in his voice. "That's why we came out before the train leaves tomorrow." He smiled his handsome smile, his once-dark mustache and goatee shot with streaks of white. Though from time to time Rain Shadow resented him for not agreeing with her own aspirations in the show, his magnetism and her love for him made it difficult to stay upset.

She understood his position. He had Annie Oakley. Annie was his big draw, and wisely he played her up. She was the little lady, or as Sitting Bull had dubbed her, Little Sure Shot. Will referred to her as Little Missy.

Rain Shadow was his Princess—his Indian Princess. She drew audiences, too, billed as Princess Blue Cloud. Will preferred that she keep her performance centered on knives, hatchets and bareback stunts on Jack, playing on her uncanny Indian appearance and abilities.

She'd been cast in this role, and no one would ever see her differently unless she broke loose from the mold. Sometimes she wasn't certain who she was. It wasn't nearly as simple as white on the inside, red on the outside. She was white, but she'd been raised by an Indian in an era when the Indian's home and culture were rapidly being destroyed. She loved Two Feathers and respected his heritage, but for Slade's sake she wanted recognition as a white.

Remembering her manners, she broke away and introduced Anton and Nikolaus to Will, six-foot-five-inch Buck Taylor, King of the Cowboys, Johnny Baker and the other well-wishers.

Hank Tall Bear, dressed in his usual leather vest and fringed pants, grinned like an ornery brother. "Princess, your beauty grows with each setting sun. I will have to offer your father many more horses for you next time."

She laughed spontaneously. The brawny-chested Indian was a fellow actor. In the show they enacted a marriage proposal and wedding ceremony, complete with the exchange of goods and ponies, Two Feathers decked out in a father's headdress and she in white ceremonial garb.

Johann appeared on the porch, and introductions began again. The entire Neubauer family gathered for the momentous occasion of having the illustrious Will Cody on their property, and the size of the group drove everyone into the enormous kitchen. Franz and Annette's oldest, five-year-old Clara, was in competition with Nikolaus for the seat with the best view of the famed Buffalo Bill.

Rain Shadow watched Jakob's pregnant wife, Lydia, a tall, dark-haired beauty, produce biscuits, jams and jellies, and serve them to the guests. Annette made pot after pot of coffee. The two women moved with grace, perfectly at ease in their wifely roles. She tried to imagine herself performing the same task, entertaining company in a kitchen, but the thought unnerved her. Gingham dresses, starched white aprons and hair arranged in upswept knots caught and held her attention. The two women visited as they effortlessly made the guests welcome. Rain Shadow decided she'd just as soon look a bobcat in the eye than test her own domestic ability.

The consummate storyteller, Will needed no encouragement to elaborate on stories of his days as a scout, including working for Custer. A famed buffalo hunter, he'd led royalty on glamorous hunts. With the children's undivided attention, he told how his beloved son, Kit Carson Cody, had been captured by Gypsies. At the tender age of four, he had marked the trail and escaped.

"Where is Kit?" Nikolaus wanted to know.

Will did his best to keep his expression from revealing pain. "He caught scarlet fever a year later and died."

Having heard the stories dozens of times, Rain Shadow watched the rapt expressions of those listening. Johann's faded blue eyes misted over with the news of Kit's death. Lydia rested her hand on his wrinkled one, and Rain Shadow was intrigued by the interaction between father-in-law and daughter-in-law. Johann gripped Lydia's fingers gratefully.

The tale of subchief Yellow Hair snared the family's attention. *De Witt's Ten Cent Romances* had called the Indian Yellow Hand, which Will assured them was not so. Poor Yellow Hand had died so many times in so many places and in so many different accounts that the truth ran a sorry last for legend material.

Truth of it was, Cody assured them, eight hundred Sioux and Cheyenne had bolted from their reservation. Will and *Hayowei,* Yellow Hair, rode face-to-face, surprising one another. Both fired. Will's bullet went through Yellow Hair's leg, killing his pinto pony. Yellow Hair's bullet went wild. Cody's horse stepped in a prairie dog hole and stumbled.

"Looked pretty bad for me," Will said, "but I managed to jump clear. On my knees, I took aim and fired Lucrezia Borgia—that's my buffalo gun." Both arms raised in pantomime, he squinted down the barrel of an imaginary rifle. His enthralled audience held their breath. "*Hayowei* fired, too, but he missed me. My bullet went clean through his head."

"Did ya scalp 'im, Bill?" Nikolaus asked, and Anton looked decidedly uncomfortable.

"I did," Will replied. "I sent his scalp, war bonnet, shield, bridle, whip and arms home to St. Louie, and a friend put them in his clothing store window."

Annette and Lydia exchanged looks of thinly veiled horror.

Will quickly changed the subject, relating his days with Texas Jack, Bill Hickok and Sitting Bull. Will Cody was a master showman, whether commandeering hundreds of whites, Indians and animals in a street parade or Wild West performance or just sitting around a camp fire or the Neubauers' kitchen table.

The morning grew late. Franz and Annette left first with Clara and their sleeping baby, Regan. Jakob and Lydia took their leave next, carrying their two sons, Seth and Titus.

"Thanks for the hospitality." Will stood and donned his fringed coat. "I'll say goodbye to Slade now and we'll be on our way."

An awkward hollowness arose within Rain Shadow while Slade received goodbyes from his friends. Besides her and Two Feathers, these men were her son's only family.

"We'll be watching for you," Will said, and embraced her shoulders firmly. "Take care of each other. If you need anything, wire me."

"I will." She hugged him back, fighting the thick tears in her throat. He was the closest thing to an uncle or grandfather she'd ever known.

He brought his gloved knuckles up under her chin and forced her to look him in the eye. "Keep your chin up, Princess. I'm going to go ahead with the plans for the exhibition."

She blinked at him in gratitude. He knew how important her desire to prove herself was. "I'll be there."

From the Neubauers' enormous porch, she waved the party off, an unbearable ache squeezing her heart. She felt herself shrink and diminish as she watched her companions ride off. She was out of her element here with the Neubauers, away from her people and her culture, and she didn't like the feeling one bit. "I'll be there," she whispered with a shiver.

Two Feathers unfolded a blanket he'd left near the door and wrapped it around her shoulders. "I want to stay with you and Slade, Rain Shadow," he said.

"Are you sure?" she asked him. "You can still leave with them tomorrow."

"I have no desire to see the winter quarters this season. It is peaceful here." He folded his arms over his chest. "I want to stay and hunt."

She laid her hand on his arm briefly before he stepped off the porch and moved silently toward their lodge.

Deep in thought, she didn't hear the door open and close behind her.

"Won't be long before you can join 'em."

Anton's voice sent a ribbon of sensation spiraling down her spine and through her limbs. She turned and discovered the front of his jacket inches from her face. Were those words meant to comfort her, or was he reassuring himself that her intrusion would be brief? So close was he, she caught the arresting scent of wood smoke in his hair and clothing.

Stepping away, he settled his Stetson over his shock of hair. "Best tend to chores."

She watched him walk toward the barn, anxiety unsettling her. Her conflicting feelings didn't sit well at all. She was saddened by the departure of her show family but

grateful that Slade was alive and well, and that as soon as his
leg healed, they would catch up with the others. This other
feeling...this almost delightful uncertainty was the one she
couldn't define. The sentiment clouded her senses when
Anton Neubauer cast his intense gaze on her...spoke near
her ear or stood near enough to envelop her with his arresting male scent. That feeling could only mean trouble.

After the winter snows melted and the rivers filled their
banks, she would take Annie Oakley's title from her. When
that happened, fame would turn up her family. Her resolve
strengthened.

Finding them was all that mattered.

A brisk wind promised winter, shaking the red and gold
leaves from the sugar maples. Their stark branches fingered heavenward against a gray sky laden with low-hanging
clouds. Johann and Two Feathers removed buckets from the
trees and carried them to the house, intent on boiling syrup.
Passing them with a wagonful of dead timber, Rain Shadow
tugged up the collar of her buckskin coat and waved. Nikolaus ran alongside. "What are you doing?"

"Going to chop wood."

"Can I help?"

"I'd be happy to have your help. I need to check on Slade
first."

"Slade's reading Clara," Nikolaus informed her.

"Reading her?"

"Yup. Reading her about birds."

"Oh," she replied with a grin. Her son loved to read.
She'd taught him herself. During her childhood days on the
reservation, her education had been less than adequate,
books and supplies outdated and in short supply. Teachers
were generally young and inexperienced, moving on as soon
as possible.

When she and Two Feathers joined the show, she bought and borrowed books, studying when not practicing. She'd read the classics to Two Feathers by lantern light, huddled next to camp fires across the continent. Speech and education were important if she and Slade were to fit into the whites' society.

Nikolaus helped her unload the wagon and put the horses away, then they systematically reduced the tree limbs to manageable chunks. He peered down a slender stick like Buffalo Bill taking aim with Lucrezia Borgia, and she laughed at his antics. Anton called to Nikolaus from the barn.

"What?" Nikolaus called back.

"Did you pull those nails out of those boards like I asked you?"

"I'm helping Rain Shadow, Pa!"

"That's not what I asked." His long legs swallowed the ground between them in purposeful strides. "You had a chore I set you to this mornin'."

"Sorry, Pa. We oughta be done in a hour."

"Nikolaus!"

Nikolaus peered at his father, his wide blue eyes growing wary.

"I'm sorry," Rain Shadow said quickly. "I didn't know he had chores when I said he could help me. I'll help him with the boards when we're finished here."

Anton turned on her, his frosty blue eyes snapping. "What're you doing this for, anyway? There's a whole pile of firewood next to the cabin behind the house!"

His well-directed words effectively cut through the pleasant mood Nikolaus had helped her achieve. Since the night before, she had tried her best to keep an optimistic outlook. She held his aggravated gaze and wondered why he was so obtuse. "That wood is not mine."

"And this is?"

A spark of anger ignited. "I gathered it. I'm cutting it."

"On my land. With my ax. And my son's help."

Her emotions reeled under the cruel blow. He made it seem as if she were taking advantage of him, though she had no choice. She would not be indebted to this rude man! "I will pay you for the wood, Mr. Neubauer," she snapped back. "I'll pay rent on the ax and the land, and wages to your son."

Nikolaus' attention bobbed back and forth between the two adults' obstinate expressions.

"Nikolaus, head into the barn." Anton jerked a thumb and watched his son break into a run before turning back to her. "I don't want your money," he scoffed.

"Just what do you want?" Not about to be intimidated by his formidable height, she pulled herself up straight and pinned him with an undaunted stare. "I don't like being here any better than you like having me, but there's nothing I can do about that now. I guess I have to remind you that you brought Slade here in the first place, and I thanked you for that. Obviously, your concern is for him, and I'm a boil on your backside, but believe me, I try to stay out of your way!"

He pointed a long finger under her nose. "It's my son's way I want you out of. I'm tired of your interference."

Interference! She'd thought to do him a favor by entertaining the boy. Nikolaus' company had been a blessing to both her and Slade. Obviously, there was no pleasing this man. Her defensive stature relaxed. With obvious disgust, she slapped his finger from under her nose. "I thought I was helping."

He snorted. "If you want to help, go in the house and launder the bedding. Do some baking and make us something for supper. Your friends all left this mornin' and Annette won't be doing those things now. She has her own family to worry about. Make yourself useful."

Aching with inadequacy, Rain Shadow averted her gaze at last. She could probably manage to launder bedding, but she didn't know the first thing about baking or cooking the Neubauers' food in their kitchen. All her cooking was done over a fire, in a pit or a clay oven. Unwilling to admit these things to the man before her, she nodded curtly. "I will make myself useful, Mr. Neubauer."

Anton spun on his heel and stalked to the barn. He found his son holding a board down with his small boot, trying ineffectively to work a bent nail out. Nikolaus turned at the sound of footsteps, revealing a dirty trail of tears streaking his rosy cheeks.

Immediately contrite, Anton took the hammer from Nikky's much smaller hand and removed the nail effortlessly.

"Nikolaus."

"Yeah, Pa?"

"Sorry I yelled at you. After all, you were working at another chore, weren't ya?"

"Yeah. That's all right. Are you sorry you yelled at Rain Shadow, too? Me and her was gonna stack the wood and then make some stew for Slade. She's good at knowing how to do things. She showed me to be careful with the ax and keep it sharp to keep from hurting myself."

Silenced, Anton stroked Nikolaus' cheek with a long thumb. He had overreacted. He would have reason to be angry if Rain Shadow treated Nikolaus poorly, but just the opposite was true. His jealousy was irrational. For some reason, he couldn't seem to help how he felt. "How about we do these boards together?"

"Okay." They worked silently for a few minutes. "Pa?"

"Hmm?"

"Was my mama anything like Rain Shadow?"

Anton's grip on the hammer slipped, and the tool fell from his hands, landing harmlessly on his boot. "You've seen her picture. You know she had blond hair. Her eyes were green."

"I know. I mean, was she like her in other ways? She's Slade's mama, and she fixes him special food and kisses his head and things like that. Did my mama do that, too?"

The hammer might as well have landed smack dab in the middle of Anton's chest. He picked it up and studied it as if he hadn't seen such an ingenious device before. Peine had loved Nikolaus. He'd never doubted it. She'd given him all her attention and affection. In fact, when Franz and Annette had lived in the big house, she'd used her baby as a reason not to help Annette with chores.

Later, when Jakob brought Lydia to the farm, Peine had made the other girl's life miserable because of her obsession for Jakob. Nothing Anton had ever said or done could match Jakob's words and accomplishments. Jakob had gone to college in Pittsburgh. Jakob was more handsome. Jakob was perfect.

Perfect. Peine had never let Anton forget he wasn't perfect. His family had accepted his hearing loss, they compensated, they forgot. His wife had criticized, mocked and reminded—ruthlessly.

And the scar....

Unconsciously, he touched the spot on his shoulder where he'd been gouged while fencing with barbed wire. A slightly raised, V-shaped scar was imperceptible through his layers of clothing. Peine had hated that scar.

She'd been lovely, of that there was no doubt. Her fair skin was clear and delicate, her gold hair luxurious and shiny, her body lush and warm. But on the inside....

He'd never really known her.

"Pa?"

"Your mama was beautiful, Nikky." Anton knelt and held his son's shoulders in both hands. "And she loved you very much. She rocked you and kissed your head and fed you special food." He ruffled the blond hair.

Nikolaus threw his arms around his father's neck. "I'm glad. But I miss having a mama like Slade has."

Like a lightning bolt striking without warning, Anton realized his son's innate need for the comfort and security only a mother could give him—a gentle touch, a soft voice, a loving smile and most of all, attention. Anton squeezed his eyes tightly shut and hugged the sturdy little boy.

Chapter Four

From the open flap of her lodge, Rain Shadow watched Anton and Johann empty an enormous coffin-shaped tub in the dooryard. Saturday night. The Neubauers had finished baths in preparation for the barn dance.

The evening was warmer than last, but the stream had been icy cold for her bath. Hair nearly dry, she knelt before the fire and plaited it into two long braids, carefully entwining slender lengths of rawhide she'd meticulously fashioned with quills and beads to decorate her hair without the leather showing.

Her dress was a masterpiece of bead and quill work, geometric designs bordering the calf-length hem and yoke-style neck and running the length of the sleeves. Matching beads swung from the six-inch fringe along the hem. Rain Shadow had worked on the dress while aboard the *Nebraska*, the ship that had carried the show to France. Taking the garment from the trunk and hanging it out, she had been reminded of the voyage and London, and she almost hadn't worn it.

She'd met Slade's father aboard the ship. He was one of the *vaqueros*, then a new addition to the show. She was young. Sixteen. And blinded to wisdom by the handsome South American who'd swept her off her adolescent feet.

He'd professed love. Promised marriage. And then, before they'd returned to America, he'd met a French heiress and married her, instead.

On the voyage home, Rain Shadow had lost every breakfast, lunch and supper into the Atlantic, clinging to the heaving rails of the *Nebraska* and accepting two well-taught lessons: the need to guard her heart more closely and the need to find her own people. Miguel de Ruiz had seen her as less than worthy of his respect. She'd taken the agonizing experience to heart and kept Slade a secret from his undeserving father. She hadn't been Miguel's first choice. He'd chosen a Frenchwoman with a heritage. There was esteem in knowing one's origins.

She placed her hairbrush in the drawer of a trunk and slipped into her moccasins. She carried a threefold stigma now: orphan, Indian and unmarried mother.

For seven years she had searched cities and counties for her family from one performance to the next, relying on the gold locket to trigger a response, hoping that someone somewhere would recognize it or the tintype inside. When that had proven fruitless, she'd come up with the idea of fame as a lure. Slade was going to be treated decently in this white man's land if it was the only thing she ever accomplished in her lifetime.

Rain Shadow stepped from her lodge. She would sit with Slade as long as she could. Perhaps Johann would forget his insistence that she and Two Feathers attend the barn dance and meet the members of Butler County's farming community. It wasn't the dancing; she had danced with the crowned heads of Europe and performed Lakota ceremonial dances in the show since she was a child. No, it was fear. Fear of her inability to fit in with whites when she wanted to so badly.

Slade seemed more restless than usual and begged her to carry him out to the barn for the festivities.

"I would love to, Slade, but you know what the doctor said."

"Does that mean we have to stay here a long time?"

Her gaze flickered around the room. None of Anton Neubauer's possessions remained in sight since he'd temporarily moved into the bedroom across the hall. Nikolaus' wooden horses lined the chest of drawers, and Slade's books and soldiers were piled haphazardly on the bedside table where the boys had discarded them. She was pleased that Slade had a friend his own age, but concerned that if they formed a meaningful bond, it would make leaving difficult for him. What troubled her most, though, was Anton's resentment toward her for befriending Nikolaus, when Anton had obviously formed his own subtle bond with Slade.

"It means we stay here until your leg is mended."

Standing, the daguerreotype on the wall drew her though she'd studied it a dozen times over the past week. This Anton was younger, his face thinner, less intense, his hair longer. Although the image was sepia-toned, his commanding eyes intrigued her. In a dark suit and stark white shirt, a carnation pinned to his lapel, he stood behind and to the right of the woman. The long fingers of one hand gripped a spindle on the back of her chair.

She was beautiful. Soft and fair, a vision of femininity in a shiny, tucked and ruffled, low-necked dress that displayed her luminous white skin and the swells of generous breasts. Rain Shadow unconsciously smoothed the velvety doeskin of her dress across her hips and wondered what had happened to the angelic-faced woman in the picture.

Perhaps she had died in childbirth, not uncommon for a young woman. Poor Nikolaus. Anton's intent gaze compelled her to think of him as a husband...a lover. How he must have loved such a woman!

Perhaps he still grieved. Maybe that was why he was particularly *unpleasant* at times. No one knew better than Rain Shadow how difficult it was to raise a child alone. At least he had his father, brothers and sisters-in-law. It was obvious how Annette, in particular, doted on her nephew though she had two children of her own.

"She's pretty, ain't she?"

Rain Shadow realized she hadn't spoken to Slade for several minutes. "Isn't she, and yes, she's pretty."

"She died a long time ago."

Turning to her son, she feigned disinterest. "Oh."

"Nikolaus says she had yellow hair and green eyes and she went to college."

College. "Hmm." She perched on the bed's edge. "He must miss her a lot."

"He don't remember her."

"I see."

"Just like me and my pa, huh?"

She ran her fingers through his thick black hair, combing it away from his forehead. "Yes."

"Want to play checkers?"

"If you let me win." She groped under the bed and came up with the board.

She'd lost five times when a rap sounded on the door and it swung open. "Excuse me, Slade. I need a—oh."

Anton Neubauer appeared taller and broader than ever without a shirt. Golden hair matted his muscled chest, and his shoulders were wide and dark from hours in the sun. Long, corded forearms were dusted with more gold hair. She'd never seen a man as golden-haired and skinned as Anton. Most men she'd seen had been dark, and Indians were smooth-skinned.

"Sorry. I didn't know you were in here." Midnight blue denims covered his strong legs, and polished leather boots sounded on the floorboards as he crossed the room. "I need a shirt and tie."

Definitely, a matter of opinion.

He shrugged into a stark white shirt and buttoned it beneath their transfixed stares. With crisp, precise movements, he rolled the cuffs over his forearms.

"Gosh!" Slade hiked himself up higher on the pillows. "You look awful fancy. Don't my mama look pretty?"

Anton plucked something from a hook on the inside of his closet door and turned slowly. Heat suffused her cheeks, and she wanted to fling the checkers and bolt from the room. Instead, she tilted her chin and met his ambiguous gaze.

A red string tie dangled from his tanned fingers, fingers she'd just studied with considerable interest in his daguerreotype. He gazed at her from head to foot, lingering on various places in between until her heart beat like a Sioux war drum in those same places. At last he cleared his throat.

"Your mama will have all the fellas begging for dances." His tone had not been sarcastic. She dropped her gaze.

"Really?" Slade bounced on the bed.

"Really." Anton stepped to the mirror above the washstand and slipped the tie over his head. Rain Shadow allowed herself the adventure of watching. Feet planted apart, he jutted his chin out and adjusted the ornamental stone at his throat. The purely masculine gesture struck a peculiar chord deep inside her, its resonant hum pumping liquid fire through her veins.

He opened a drawer, located a comb and tamed his straw-colored hair. She found herself wondering if his wife had watched him with this same fascination, if all women were charmed by the mystique of a handsome man performing his perfunctory grooming ritual.

Immediately, she grew pensive. She had never watched a man like this. The sight provoked, stimulated. The sight was...*intimate*. Did husbands and wives grow accustomed to such familiarity? She hadn't realized she craved the companionable experience until that moment. She took in his broad shoulders and narrow waist, trailed her eyes over his compact buttocks and well-defined thighs, much as he'd looked at her moments before.

Slade let a stack of checkers shuffle through his fingers, and Rain Shadow dragged her admiring gaze to the mirror. In the glass, Anton watched her reflection with the same, intense expression she had seen in the portrait. Something almost painfully warm seared deep into her flesh, quickened her breath and delivered a lambent hum in her ears. She couldn't look away.

"You coming now?" he asked, his voice low.

She wiped her palms on her dress. He'd caught her studying him. Exactly *what* had he seen? What had just passed between them? "I don't know."

Anton turned and faced her.

"Go on, Ma," Slade piped up.

"We weren't finished with our game." She balked, more confused than ever at their silent exchange.

"You weren't trying. I'm getting tired, anyhow."

Out of excuses, she shrugged and simulated poise. "You win."

Anton gestured toward the door, the first gentlemanly act she'd observed in days. She responded, as she did to everything about this man, with an immediate and unsettled feeling of deficiency. She'd go, but she would leave and return to her lodge early. The Neubauers and their neighbors belonged here, rooted to this land. They and their descendants would be here long after she was gone. She didn't belong. She was the autumn wind, a puff of smoke, a fleeting shadow.

Sissy Clanton's dress was a simple yellow calico. An ivory shawl draped her slender shoulders. Gathered from her oval face, her nutmeg tresses hung in gentle waves between her shoulder blades. Sensible small brown shoes peeked from beneath her demure hemline.

Anton handed her a jar of lemonade, and she smiled in thanks, her unpainted lips parting to reveal small white teeth. She had a girlish sprinkling of freckles across her nose that reminded him of Peine. How she'd hated them!

His wife had squeezed lemons, mixed the juice with glycerin and lactic acid and applied it morning and night to prevent them from appearing.

But Sissy was nothing like Peine. She was a complete contrast, passive and unaffected, with caramel-colored eyes and a slow, thoughtful manner of speaking. This was an uncritical woman, he thought with certainty. A woman who wouldn't find fault with his every word, his every act and idea.

"Do you like it?"

"What?" Anton realized he'd been lost in thought.

"I said the lemonade is good."

"Yep." *Bet the beer's better.*

They watched the musicians return to the corner of the barn where the floor had been raised. Jakob, always in demand at festivities, tucked a fiddle under his chin and led them in the Virginia reel.

"Want to dance?"

"Yes, thank you."

He took her empty jar and led her among the throng of dancers, her hand thin and pliant in his. They found their place in a quadrille and matched their steps to the caller's instructions. He bowed; she curtsied and blushed wildly.

He had to ask her tonight. He'd stalled and planned and stalled and considered. What else could he do? He had to make his decision. Nikolaus needed a mother and Sissy was the best choice he had available. She could cook and clean and sew and she was in her twenties—on the shelf in this community. Sure, he was older, but not enough to make much difference to either one of them.

His attention was arrested by the woman in the next quadrille, her elbow linked with that of Lydia's younger brother, Nathan. It was obvious Nathan was enamored of Rain Shadow, and Anton grudgingly admitted that she cleaned up pretty good when she set her mind. Her figure was small, but curved and hollowed in all the right places. She was a graceful dancer, too.

Then she smiled, a smile that would coax the sun up at midnight, and her amethyst eyes flashed with delight. Sissy's smile came to mind, and he struggled not to make a comparison. The woman in the deerskin dress was vibrant, alive and endowed with indomitable energy. Allowing himself to be drawn to her in any way would be a mistake. He wasn't about to let his resolve scatter in the wind because of a woman... or because of his lust—yes, lust.

Her expression when he'd entered his room earlier had confused him. Immediately he'd remembered the scar and anticipated her distaste. Instead, when their gazes had locked in the mirror, a velvet blaze had smoldered within the depths of her violet eyes, measuring, branding, igniting sparks between them. He'd recognized the searing heat in his belly for what it was immediately.

Lust.

The way she looked meant nothing to him. It didn't count that the air became difficult to breathe when she looked at him like that. The fact that she hadn't seemed put off by the scar was of no importance. He'd allowed himself to become vulnerable once before, and his singular concern was to never let it happen again.

Rain Shadow was enjoying herself immensely, and he didn't know why he should resent that. He'd encouraged her to come. Sissy collided with his broad back, a half-completed do-si-do nearly sending her sprawling. He caught her before she fell and righted her with a profuse apology.

"It's all right," she stammered. He could almost feel her attention focus on his hands at her waist. A crimson blush spread upward from her prim collar and suffused her cheeks.

The music wound to an end. Walking Sissy toward the refreshments, he caught sight of Rain Shadow speaking to Nathan Beker. Though the evening held a chill, the interior of the barn combined the warmth of dozens of dancers with a continuously stoked stove.

"Danke, fräulein," the young man at Rain Shadow's side said, breathlessly.

Rain Shadow smiled absently, her attention arrested by the bright blue dress on a woman nearby. She studied the fitted bodice, the gathers at the waist, and allowed her gaze to find another, even prettier dress in the crowd, an intricately tucked and pleated bodice with rows of tiny seed pearls set into the deep rose-colored fabric. The matching belt was simple and complemented the garment perfectly. How did it feel to wear a feminine creation like that?

Her gaze met her father's, and Two Feathers nodded a greeting from across the room.

"A jar of lemonade may I get you?"

Realizing the young man spoke to her, she smiled and nodded, intrigued by Nathan's odd speech. He handed her a brimming cold mason jar, and she thanked him. "Where are you from?"

"Accord, miss."

"Is it far?"

"*Nein*. Several miles."

"But your accent is . . ."

"German. Less diluted than the Neubauers'." He grinned. "A self-sufficient community of believers Accord is. We hold to the language and teachings of our ancestors. Only during the last few years have we been allowed freedom to travel and go to school with outsiders. Attending the University of Philadelphia I am. I am Lydia's brother."

She raised her brows in surprise. Jakob had taken a spell from his fiddle. He and Lydia sat near the wood stove, his arm draped over her shoulder. Lydia's fingers rested on her swollen stomach, and she spoke to him. Jakob smiled and whispered something in her ear.

Sad-sweet regret drew a reflective finger across Rain Shadow's heart. What a blessed child Lydia carried. How fortunate her children and Annette's children were to have two loving parents. There had been no husband to share her pregnancy, no lover to lean into for a shared moment over the miracle of life they'd created together. She would never regret becoming pregnant; in fact, the sun rose and set in her beautiful child, but circumstances were another matter, with regrets aplenty.

Slade uppermost in her thoughts, Rain Shadow excused herself to check on him. The crisp air tasted wonderful after the dry warmth of the crowded barn, and she sprinted across the lawn in the darkness.

Her son slept soundly. The rabbit skin blanket she thought he'd discarded was tucked against his chest. Under her fingers, the fur was soft and worn, warm from the heat of his body. She recalled him as an infant, tucked into its enveloping folds. Two Feathers had trapped the rabbits, and she had sewn them together, grandfather and mother planning for the birth of her child. Soundlessly, she kissed Slade's forehead and pulled the down coverlet under his chin.

The Neubauers' wide porch extended across the back of the house, down one entire side and across the front. Restlessly, she walked its length, returning and gazing across the lawn. Yellow light and gay music spilled from the open double barn doors. Wagons and buggies crowded the drive and one corner of the yard. Horses and a few mules stood staked here and there.

One horse in particular whinnied and fought against a tether. As she watched, he reared violently and pulled the stake from the ground. Pivoting on his hind legs, he spun and broke into a run. As he passed the other animals, they shied away.

Lightly, she jumped the stairs and ran in the direction he'd disappeared. Nearing the corral, the moonlight offered a clear view. Having jumped the fence, the excited stallion pranced and shook his magnificent head before one of the Neubauers' mares. Because of the other horses' behavior earlier in the day, she'd noticed that the mare was in heat. The stallion nipped the mare on the neck, and after an obligatory show of indignation, she turned to accommodate him.

Rain Shadow turned to leave and slammed into a hard chest. Her breath escaped with an unladylike "oof."

Anton grasped her shoulders and steadied her. "Sorry. I seem to be knocking into women left and right tonight."

The scent of his heated skin assailed her senses. He slid his hands to her upper arms. Through her soft dress, his touch was warm, the effect on her pulse swift.

"I was wondering where Tom's horse took off to. I saw him from the doorway." His breath fanned the tiny hairs that had escaped at her temple.

He knew he should release her, but his fingers refused to obey. Instead they wanted to glide down her arms, caress the supple skin beneath her dress, linger at her narrow waist and explore the gentle curve of her hips. He knew he was lighting a match next to a keg of gunpowder, but he couldn't release her just yet. His hands remained gently holding her arms. He raised his eyes and sighted the animal.

"He caught your mare's scent," she said.

An irresistible lure he was fighting himself. "Yeah?"

"Go back to the dancing. I'll return him ... shortly." A strand of midnight-black hair whipped from her braid and streamed in the breeze.

Anton realized she wasn't embarrassed. She accepted the animals' mating instincts as natural. He had to wonder what Lydia's or Sissy's reaction would have been had one of them followed him.

"I needed some air, anyway," he replied.

She nodded and gave him one of those infuriating little smiles. So composed. So self-sufficient. Her dark eyes seemed to focus on his, only to drop immediately to his mouth as if she'd read his burning need.

She smelled wonderful. Not like soap or perfume or talcum, but like rain and trees and sunshine. The scent was his undoing. He lowered his face to her temple—a hair breadth away without touching her—and drew a savoring breath.

Desire uncoiled and slithered throughout his body, a keen sensation he hadn't experienced for a long time, if ever. He'd admitted to himself his appetite for her, but he loathed letting her know how she set his blood on fire.

And then she tipped her head that whisper of distance between them and lifted her face to his. Her mouth was there waiting. . . .

Her breath fanned his lips. He wasn't sure who kissed whom. At first her lips offered the merest touch, like a silk ribbon against skin, so softly did they graze his. Their noses rubbed next, a cautious inquiry while he breathed in as much of her as his senses could take. Her lips parted ever so slightly, and he met them with his own. She came to life in his grasp, an instantaneous fire fed by his ravaging blaze of desire. He stoked her with hot burning lips and hands, pulling her against his body and splaying his fingers across her spine. She knew now. His desire was obvious.

She pressed her flattened palms on his chest, celebrating the soul-scorching kiss with him. Anton pulled his mouth from hers and stared into eyes turned a molten blue-violet in the moonlight. He kissed the corner of her mouth, touched her full lower lip with the tip of his tongue. She inhaled sharply and met his lips with her own, drawing another insatiable kiss from him.

Her reaction was honest, and his blood hummed through his veins. He knew she wanted him, too. "Damn. . . ." Anton straightened, held her at arm's length and wrestled with his shattered determination.

A confused expression replaced the desire in her eyes, and she withdrew from his touch.

"This isn't right. I—I shouldn't have. . ." He inhaled the night air and shook his head as if throwing off the experience. "I shouldn't have let that happen. I'm sorry."

His face held the clean, strong, angular lines of a man— not a boy, and his body testified to the fact, as well. He had a natural virility that appealed to her as it would to any woman. He was not as classically handsome as his brother

Jakob, but he had an aura, an elemental attraction that every woman within eyesight was aware of.

She'd noticed in the barn how he appealed to a woman. He oozed a magnetic, undiluted tone of sexual awareness that beguiled females, young and old, to take a second look.

And she'd succumbed.

Rain Shadow forcibly removed her gaze from his silver-streaked moonlit hair and stepped back as if he were a stick of dynamite. "No need to apologize. Let's just forget it."

Forget it? Anton almost laughed at her ridiculous solution. She turned and walked toward the barn, his scowl following. He realized the hand he raked through his hair was trembling. Forget that kiss? Why not jump off the barn roof and fly while he was at it? He'd just as likely sprout wings as forget that kiss.

What in blue blazes had he done?

Chapter Five

In a secluded corner of the barn, Two Feathers and Johann perched on nail kegs facing one another. A third keg held a checkerboard. Both men's creased faces grew intent on the game before them. A small gathering of white-haired men observed. Slender columns of aromatic smoke from pipes held in clenched teeth curled past squinting eyes.

Anton contemplated the scene with a wry smile, sipped a stein of Ben Karrson's homemade beer and mentally castigated himself. What the hell could he have been thinking of out there?

The farmers clustered beside him discussed crop prices. Annette caught his eye and waved. He returned her smile and watched her walk toward him, the skirt of her royal blue taffeta dress swishing about her ankles.

"Does this old married lady stand a chance to dance with a handsome single gentleman?" Her tawny eyes revealed a teasing warmth.

"Honey, I'd snap up an old married lady like you in a minute if one was available." He offered his arm.

He waltzed her around the sawdusted wooden floor as if the barn were a marble-tiled palace. She smelled of lilacs and faintly of...of babies. He could barely remember a time when she hadn't been part of their family. Franz had married her, his childhood sweetheart, as soon as she'd finished school.

Two years later, Anton had placed an advertisement for a wife in the Pittsburgh *Gazette*. Peine had been his answer. He remembered the letter. Hell, he still had it.

Peine had been to college, raised in a well-to-do family. Her father had been wrongly accused of embezzling funds from the bank where he worked, and the shame had driven Peine's mother to the brink of sanity. Peine had escaped the city. She'd never really fit in here, much as he'd tried to make her feel welcome and loved.

He remembered seeing her for the first time at the train station and recalled his pleasant surprise. The dowdy spinster he'd anticipated turned out a beautiful well-dressed young woman—well-dressed because of the money he'd sent her, he'd learned later. Many facets of her previous life hadn't fit together, but she'd never talked about her past or visited her mother, and the subject proved taboo.

"You're a million miles away." His sister-in-law curtsied gracefully, and the dance ended.

"Sorry. My brain's addled tonight. Thanks for the dance." His gaze cut across the room of its own volition. Rain Shadow held the attention of several children, graceful sign language punctuating her speech. Anton watched for a moment, then searched for Sissy.

He found her visiting with Nathan Beker. "Let's go for a walk, Sissy."

"I'll tell my ma," she replied. "Excuse us, Nathan."

Anton gulped the beer he held and met her outside the doorway, both of them tugging jackets on. "Will you be warm enough?"

"Yes, thanks."

His boots crunched gravel, his breath visible in the clear moonlight. He led the way around the corral where the horses waited to reclaim the barn. His great-limbed bay whinnied and galloped to the rail. Anton raised both hands and scrubbed the animal's neck and forehead with his knuckles. He patted him soundly on the shoulder and stepped back.

"What's his name?" Sissy asked softly.

"General Grant."

"He's friendly."

"Sissy."

"Yes?" Hands stuffed in her pockets, she tipped her head to look at him.

"I've been wanting to talk to you about something."

"All right."

He stubbed the toe of his freshly shined and polished boot in the dirt and wished he smoked.

She waited patiently.

"For a long time now, I've been thinking that I need to take a wife."

She didn't move or say a word, but he sensed her anticipation. She stared back wide-eyed.

"Nikolaus needs a mother. We live in the big house with my pa, and I reckon we'll stay there for a while. Later we'll have a place of our own. You know the way life is on a farm. It's not easy, but we're comfortable. The shop brings me extra money during the winter."

Still she said nothing.

"I'm not going about this right. I can't promise you some fairy-tale courtship or a perfect life, but I can promise that I'd be a good and faithful husband and that you wouldn't want for much." He pulled his hands from his pockets and hung them at his sides. "Would you consider marrying me, Sissy?"

She'd been silent for so long, he wondered what she thought—if she thought. Granted, there'd been no great confession of love, but he'd asked, and she could say yes or no. Damn, if she said no he'd have to go through this all over again with Helena McLaury!

"I'm honored that you asked me, Anton," she said at last, and her voice quavered oddly. "I don't mind not having the fairy-tale courtship, and I know life ain't perfect, but I am wondering about the right reasons. You asked me if I'd consider, and the answer is yes, I'll consider. I'd like to think about it."

Well, hell.... Anton shifted his weight back and forth between his feet and flexed his fingers. Her breath puffed out in tiny white clouds. He knew his was the best offer she'd ever had; what did she have to think about?

He stepped forward, grasped her upper arms through her heavy jacket and pulled her toward him. She came compliantly. He'd give her something to think about.

He kissed her. Her sealed lips were cool and placid.

Kissing Sissy, he didn't think of Peine. He didn't think of the saloon girls he'd been driven to visit in Pittsburgh since his wife's death. He didn't even think about Sissy.

He thought of Rain Shadow, of violet eyes alternately snapping or laughing, of her proud, indomitable spirit and of the erotic sway of fringe against sun-kissed skin. And of hot, treacherous kisses...

Merciful heavens, he thought for the second time that night, what had he done?

Frost crunched beneath his boots early the following morning. Anton dropped hammer and nails into a wooden toolbox and lugged it to the back of the wagon. Belatedly, his good ear alerted him to a set of boots behind him. He turned his head.

Her. Wearing wool trousers smoothed over softly rounded thighs and hips. *Indecent!* A stab of desire seared his vitals. He couldn't help remembering he'd been kissed well.

Boots every bit as sturdy as his encased her feet. She wore a lined waist-length leather coat. No traces of sleep remained on her face; she'd been up for hours. A band of renegades could loot the farmstead, and the family would sleep through it, as accustomed as they'd become to her barely dawn practice ritual.

"What are you doing today?"

He turned to the wagon. "Winterizing stock tanks."

"Coming back here for the noon meal?"

"I suppose so. Why?"

"If not, I'll pack something to take."

"I'll be back." He climbed onto the seat and turned to stare at her when she scrambled up beside him. "What are you doin'?"

"Going with you."

"What the hell for?"

"To make myself useful, as you suggested."

A calf bawled from inside the barn. Anton glared into her liquid violet eyes. "I said cook or clean or do washing, not tag along and get in my way." If she didn't constantly get under his skin, he could laugh at her brass-plated gall!

"I won't get in your way. I'm certain I can do nearly any of your chores as well as you."

He clenched his teeth and picked up the reins. "Get down."

"I want to help with the stock tanks."

"I don't give a sparrow's fart what you wanna do. This is a man's job. Go in the house and do something."

"You said make myself useful. You're every bit as rude about this as you were about that. This is something I can do. Give me a chance."

Anton held a smirk in check. *All right, lady. Don't say I didn't warn you.* "Go get another hammer."

She leapt down.

"And you're going to need a shovel and a bucket!"

She disappeared inside the barn.

Two hours later, Rain Shadow carried the umpteenth bucket of manure and dumped it unceremoniously on the odious pile. Nothing like keeping busy for clearing her mind. Last night she'd been confused. Long after midnight she lay on her pallet, sifting and sorting shaken emotions. Abrasive as he could be, Anton Neubauer drew her like deer to a sparkling stream. She was attracted to him, she finally admitted to herself. Why not? He was pleasing to look at, intelligent and sensitive to his son's needs.

Now she understood his resentment. Against his will he'd been attracted to her, too. He saw her as an Indian. A squaw. A nomad with no permanent home or family. But physically, he was drawn to her.

Rain Shadow remembered the fair beauty in the daguerreotype on his bedroom wall, pictured the elegant low-cut dress, and glanced down at the manure caked to the ankles on her boots. He must feel pretty sullied having given in to his impulse to kiss her last night. In spite of herself, she smiled. She'd never been kissed like that.

She hadn't even known kisses like that existed.

From beneath her wide-brimmed black hat, she watched him shrug out of his coat and toss it on a pile of wood. The blue chambray shirt stretched across his broad muscled back as he sawed a board in half. Bent at the waist, he hammered it into place on the frame he'd built around the stock tank. His body had been warm and solid against hers, his hands. . . .

She regarded them now, one gripping the hammer, the other holding the board in place. They were large and strong, soothing, yet inflaming. She hadn't known caresses like that before. He'd been without his wife for a long time. He was a man with a normal, healthy sexual appetite. She experienced an equally healthy pang of regret. Too bad she wasn't the one to satisfy it.

He straightened and surveyed the pile she'd accumulated. "Ready."

"For what?"

"Now we pack the manure in between the tank and the frame. Keeps the water from freezing."

Inwardly Rain Shadow groaned, but bent to the task. When the space was filled with manure, Anton took boards from the pile and nailed them to the top. He drew a hinged cover from the wagon bed, and together they fixed it to the top.

"Keeps out rain and snow."

She nodded.

"Ready."

What now? She picked up the bucket and shovel and followed him to the wagon.

"Four more to go."

She knocked her boots against the wheel before leaping onto the seat. "Daylight's burning."

He'd thought she would balk at the unpleasant task. He and his brothers had always drawn straws to assign the chore. He'd expected her to tire easily and chafe under his words, but the woman had a fearful ability to stand her ground. And, he admitted, shooting her a sideways glance as the wagon pulled them toward the next pasture, she also had a fearful ability to arouse strong feelings in him.

Working on the third tank, Anton seemed to lose some of his hostility. They talked about winter on the farm. He

warmed to her companionship and discussed his watch re-
pair trade. "Watched my granddad as a boy. I was fascinated by all those tiny gears and springs, and I pestered him
constantly while he worked. He never seemed to mind,
though."

"He was a watchmaker?"

"In the old country. He and my grandmother were bond
servants working off their passage from Germany. He took
up his watchmaking till he staked the farm with a loan."

"That's a proud heritage. You and your son are fortunate."

He looked at her. "I guess so. Sometimes it's hard to see
it that way."

"You take your family for granted."

He shrugged. "Doesn't everyone?"

"No."

He slid his hat off, and the midday sun lit his gilded hair.
His impossibly blue eyes held an unspoken question.

Though he hadn't asked aloud, she answered. "Two
Feathers found me wandering near a massacred wagon train
when I was about three. He raised me as his own child. I
don't remember my family."

Discomfort flickered across his intense features. "I'm
sorry."

Rain Shadow accepted his condolence with a tilt of her
head. "Since Slade's birth I've tried to find my relatives, but
I haven't been successful. In April I compete with Annie
Oakley for the sharpshooter championship. I figure when I
become famous and my story is told, someone will recognize me."

"What makes you so sure?"

"Remember, after the battle of Gettysburg, when a buri-
al detail found an ambrotype in the hand of a dead Union
soldier?"

Anton nodded. "He didn't have any other identification. That picture was on the front pages of all the newspapers. What did they call them?" He tilted his head before answering his own question. "'Children of the battlefield.'"

She nodded. "A woman recognized the picture as one she sent her husband before the battle."

"But how would anyone recognize you after all these years?"

"They wouldn't." She dropped, wiped her palms on her trousers and stepped in front of him. His eyes followed her fingers, dipping inside the front of her shirt. "But my parents' family would recognize these."

She opened the gold locket and displayed the tiny likenesses of her parents. He studied the man and woman. Slowly, he raised his gaze, hesitated a second too long at her mouth and met her eyes. "I wish you luck."

"Thank you."

He bent and hefted a bucket of manure. "We'll go eat when this is done."

She tucked the locket safely inside her shirt.

"Rain Shadow," he said later as they worked side by side. She liked the sound of her name on his lips. "Yes?"

"Would you mind me asking where Slade's father is?"

She straightened and watched him shovel.

"You don't have to answer if it's none of my business."

Uncertain of his reaction, she took her time. "I met him on board the *Nebraska* when I was sixteen. He's a *vaquero*.

"I'm not sure what that is."

"A *caballero*, a South American cowboy. He was in the show that season."

Sixteen? "Oh."

"I thought I loved him." Rain Shadow placed her shovel in the back of the wagon. "I thought he loved me. I thought he was going to marry me."

Anton stacked a few remaining boards beside the shovels. "He didn't."

"He married a French heiress." She didn't bother to add the humiliation and hurt she must have suffered. "She had a heritage and money."

"And you have his son."

She snapped her head up and faced him. "*My* son."

An undefined emotion churned inside him. She hadn't been married. Slade's father had used her. She tilted her pert chin and stared him defiantly in the eye. Something compelled him to reassure her. He spoke the truth. "Your son is a fine lad. You've done a good job with him."

Surprise flickered across her eloquent face. Her stormy gaze filled with quick tears, and she glanced away. "Let's go eat."

Jakob and Lydia joined them for dinner, Lydia having prepared a hot meal of beans and bacon. She cut generous chunks of corn bread and poured thick honey over them. The meal was delicious, the conversation light.

Johann and Two Feathers had spent the morning repairing the chicken coops and outbuildings. After the meal, they lit their pipes. "Tomorrow we butcher." Johann directed his comment to Lydia. "Will you be up to cooking dinner again?"

Lydia smiled and seated herself across from him. "I'll be up to it. I'm fit as a horse and you know it."

The faint irregular cadence of her speech reminded Rain Shadow of Nathan. She was a lovely ivory-skinned woman with a fine-boned face and dark, amber-flecked eyes. She wore her sable-colored hair in a fashionable twist on the back of her head, with delicate ringlets at her temples and cheeks. Rain Shadow studied Lydia's soft hand, fingers resting on the edge of her teacup, then took stock of her own. Four blisters dotted the base of her fingers. Her knuckles were chafed red from the scrubbing she'd given them at the pump.

"How about you, Rain Shadow?" Anton's voice held a teasing challenge. "Will you be up to butchering?"

Little russet-haired Titus sat on his lap, his tiny hands trying to open Anton's pocket watch. Anton's enormous fingers absentmindedly smoothed the child's hair. The sight caught at Rain Shadow's heart. She could picture him sitting just that way with his own son. She met his arrogant stare. "I'll be up to it."

Anton suppressed a grin. Yep, he bet she would. She'd carried bucket after bucket of reeking manure without so much as a wrinkle of her fine nose or a complaint. She'd proven herself a hard worker and a passable companion. The morning hadn't been so bad after all.

Jakob rose and helped his oldest son button his coat. Anton couldn't help watching for Rain Shadow's reaction to his brother, but she observed Jakob insignificantly, and his thoughts turned to the man who'd fathered her child. He remembered the fire in her kiss, the response of her supple body in his arms, and imagined her at the vulnerable age of sixteen. Beautiful. Ripe. Innocent.

She rose and helped Lydia clear dishes. Rain Shadow's trousers smoothed over her hips and thighs like a glove. She wore her shirt tucked in at her narrow waist. Two long, black braids draped across her full breasts, inviting attention. She was still beautiful. She was still ripe.

Her stormy-sky-at-sunset eyes met his, and heat pooled in his loins. But she wasn't innocent.

Miguel de Ruiz stared out the carriage window. He patted the engraved invitation in the breast pocket of his fine

Irish linen suit, drew his fingertip over the wing of his stingy black mustache and surveyed the Boston Common with shrewd contemplation. There were few carriages out this particular evening. He considered it a pure stroke of luck that he'd been introduced to Madelena Avarato so close upon the heels of his arrival in the city. He'd been informed she was one of the brightest debutantes of the season. Young. Attractive. Wealthy beyond imagination. Heir to the Avarato fortune, although she'd never done a thing to deserve it.

Rain-wet bricks rumbled beneath the carriage wheels, and he scrutinized the Back Bay's distinctive buildings. Beacon Street. As he'd imagined, this section of town smelled like money, breeding and arrogance. The first commodity Miguel lacked and was of a mind to acquire, the other two he possessed, or so his former wife had said.

Comtesse Remmington. His narrow lips twisted in bitter self-derision. A title with no money is what she'd turned out to be, and she'd had the audacity to divorce him when she'd discovered *he* was without resources!

The carriage pulled to a stop in front of a two-story brownstone, and Ruiz paid the driver. With slim fingers, he checked the impeccable crease of his trousers, straightened his ruby-studded cuffs and raised the knocker. It fell with a resounding clack on the brass plate.

A butler ushered Miguel into a sitting room where several other guests were conversing.

"Mr. Ruiz!" Madelena rose from the brocade settee and greeted him. "I'm so glad you could come."

"*Encantado.*" Adroitly sliding into the too-familiar role of suave charmer, he kissed the back of the hand she offered.

She blushed, the rosy glow complementing her dark features. Her black hair, shiny and straight, was coiled in an elaborate coronet around her head, a gold comb jauntily winking from her crown. She was of average height, her waist small, her body slender. No generous display of bosom swelled over the top of her bodice, but the diamond and emerald teardrop necklace drew his appreciative gaze to her breast regardless.

"Father hired musicians to play for us after dinner."

He forced himself to look into her zinc-colored eyes. "You must promise me a dance, *querida*."

"Of course. Come meet my mother."

An exquisite turquoise gown did nothing for the shorter, plain-faced woman with dull brown hair and eyes. Ruiz took her hand and flattered her with a lazy smile. Madelena had obviously inherited her father's looks.

"Mr. Avarato." Miguel spoke to the man he'd met the week before at the same function where he'd been introduced to Madelena.

"After we met, I remembered I knew your father, Mr. Ruiz." Phillipe Avarato's elegant black mustache turned up in a smile. "We had business dealings before the war."

Unblinking, Miguel smiled through the tempestuous feelings the mention of his father roused and offered a polite reply. Avarato couldn't know Miguel's father had disowned him years ago, or he wouldn't approve of this liaison with his daughter. Perhaps the Ruiz name and his father's wealth would prove to be Miguel's trump in this game.

Miguel's hungry eyes devoured the opulence of the dining room to his left. Sparkling fine crystal lined the twenty-foot table, and gold-rimmed plates glittered beneath the prismatic chandelier. He stood on an imported Persian carpet, inhaling the elegance that tinged the room. He'd been born and bred to this way of life. Raised among the wealthiest and most affluent people in South America! Schooled for success in the world of the privileged, and someday, he vowed, it would all be his again. Someday soon.

A servant announced dinner, and Miguel took his seat across from Madelena and next to her grandfather, a silver-haired gentleman with a hearty laugh.

"Where are you from, young man?"

"Buenos Aires, sir."

Fredrico Avarato quirked a white brow. "Our family originated near Rosario."

"We are neighbors." Miguel saluted his host with his wineglass, then raised it to his lips.

"You were there during the republican revolution?"

"I had business in Europe during that time," Miguel evaded.

"What is your family's business?"

"Textiles. Leather goods."

The brow rose again in recognition. "Your father owns the largest manufacturing plant in Argentina."

"Our family's business is shipping," Madelena stated needlessly. "I wonder if our ships have carried any of your goods, Mr. Ruiz?"

Relieved of the old man's questions, Miguel disarmingly turned his attention to Madelena. "Miss Avarato, you are not only beautiful, but intelligent."

Madelena's lashes swept her cheeks in an artless imitation of beguiling femininity. Conversation hummed around them, but Miguel offered her his undivided interest. "Father's aide instructs me each week," she said. "Father says I must be informed so that I can oversee the shipyards should anything happen to him or—"

Miguel leaned forward as though hanging on her every word, inwardly weary of the offensive game.

She blushed. "Or my future husband."

Disgust seized his insides. He nodded sagely. "Ah." Miguel pressed a napkin against his lips, careful of his mustache. "Do I know your future husband?"

Madelena laughed and covered her mouth with her napkin. "I'm not yet promised to anyone."

This was the last time. The last time he would prostitute himself for what he deserved in the first place. "No hurry, *querida*. Your father looks in perfect health."

She flashed him an enamored smile. "You're right. There is no hurry. The controlling stock doesn't become mine until I'm thirty."

The wine Miguel sipped turned to vinegar in his mouth. Thirty! She could not be—he slid a critical eye over her features—nineteen! If he married her now, he would have to wait ten years to see his investment pay off! Could he wait that long? He knew from past ventures, a woman's appeal dimmed in a matter of months.

The servants cleared the dessert plates, and he glanced about for an escape.

"Join us for a smoke, Mr. Ruiz?" Fredrico invited.

Relieved, Miguel excused himself and followed Phillipe and the elderly gentleman into a wood-paneled office. The room smelled of leather-bound books and expensive tobacco. Folding himself into an Italian leather sofa, he studied the gold inlay pendulum clock on the desk. The timepiece was worth more than his entire marriage to the *comtesse*.

And Madelena only nineteen! Stupid little harridan. All this at his fingertips, and the heiress was nineteen!

Phillipe seated himself across from Miguel.

"So you've been traveling." Fredrico flipped open a brass humidor.

"*Si*." Miguel accepted the cigar and sniffed the finest Colombian tobacco money could buy. He observed the expanse of the room, noticing the marble fireplace, the portrait over the mantel . . . It would take ten years to obtain all this. *Ten years.*

"I spent some time in Europe, too," Fredrico broke into his thoughts, speaking as he seated himself behind his enormous desk. "Tediously stuffy, isn't it?"

Miguel listened with one ear. His wandering gaze noted the beautiful woman painted in the portrait, jet hair and somber eyes like Phillipe's, revealing a family resemblance. He lit his cigar and enjoyed the rich tobacco flavor. A soft-looking aqua gown bared the woman's slender shoulders, and against her pale chest a necklace, exquisitely captured by the artist's adept brush strokes, caught shards of light.

The necklace riveted Miguel. Not diamond and emerald like the one Madelena wore tonight, but gold . . . a unique filigree clasp and a briolette-cut amethyst stone mined only in Bolivia.

A remote flash of recognition sparked his consciousness. *Gold filigree, a winking lavender stone . . .*

"—a family I met in Paris," Fredrico said loudly, breaking Miguel's concentration, irritating him beyond measure.

He nodded politely and drew on the cigar. Frowning at the portrait, he peered with vague interest across the woman's face and hair, the elegant gown, and was drawn once again to the locket. The elusive memory wavered. Dark hair. *Si.* Dark hair. *Trencilla.* A braid?

Miguel choked on the smoke, and his eyes watered. He stood and gaped at the painting. It could not be.

Ignoring Fredrico's monologue, Miguel strode to the fireplace and gaped.

Recognition flared. It could not be. The locket loomed vivid in his memory. There could not be two such lockets. Its design was unique. The face in the portrait wavered. The

Indian girl had worn it. The appealing young girl he'd met just before the *comtesse*. The girl he had seduced on the ocean voyage.

Rain Shadow.

Chapter Six

What was Rain Shadow doing with the Avarato family's locket? Miguel studied the woman's face, noting no resemblance to the Indian girl. "Pardon my inquisitiveness, but who is the stunning woman in the portrait?"

A flicker of pain passed over the old man's face.

"That is Juanita, my sister," Phillipe supplied.

Miguel returned to his seat. "All the women in your family are lovely."

A black-clad male tapped at the partially open door. "Would you like a fire, Mr. Avarato?"

"Thank you, Esteban," Fredrico said. "You know I take a chill in the evening."

Miguel watched the servant light a stack of prepared firewood and exit. The blaze crackled pleasantly, and he imagined stretching his legs toward the fire and enjoying a bottle of port with his cigar.

"Juanita is no longer with us."

Miguel slanted Fredrico a glance. Had she left or died? "I hear pain in your voice."

"It was many years ago," Fredrico said simply.

Miguel puffed on his cigar and pondered his next words. "I have seen that necklace before."

Phillipe straightened. "You must be mistaken. There are no two lockets like that one."

Exactly. "I am certain. A piece of jewelry like that is hard to forget."

"I had it made for her sixteenth birthday," Fredrico explained. "Tell me, Mr. Ruiz, where did you see this locket?"

His eager expression played right into Miguel's hand. "I could find it again."

"I will hire an agency immediately." The eagerness in the old man's voice told Miguel he had struck pay dirt.

Miguel sat forward. "Do you want the necklace or the woman?"

Phillipe unfolded himself from his chair and stood behind his father. "Mr. Ruiz, this is a painful subject. I think it best if we—"

"No, Phillipe." Fredrico Avarato brushed a trembling hand over his brow. "I wish to talk about her."

"Perhaps I can be of help to you," Miguel prompted.

The old gent studied the portrait, his eyes misting. "Juanita met a young man when she was eighteen. A tailor's son, a man of no position or wealth." His voice was unsteady as he continued. "Juanita was a most unusual girl, uninterested in jewels or clothing like other girls her age. Her tastes were simple. The locket suited her well." He turned away from the portrait of his daughter. "I discouraged her from marrying the man."

Miguel watched him shuffle uneasily in his chair. "As any father would," he encouraged.

"I have wondered a thousand times over in the years since." He placed his hand over his son's on his shoulder. "The foolish young man had dreams of going west and making his fortune. Juanita went with him. I learned they were married and joined an ill-fated wagon train."

"Did your daughter survive?"

"I didn't believe so. But if you've seen the locket. . . ."

"I have seen it." Miguel stood. "Mr. Avarato. Let me do this for you. Let me try to locate the locket and perhaps your daughter if she is alive."

The older man's slate eyebrows rose.

Phillipe stepped from behind his father and perched on the edge of the desk before Miguel. "Why would you want to do this? We are strangers to you and your family."

Miguel nodded as though he understood the other man's hesitation. Make him believe it. Make him buy it. "I know the woman who wears the necklace."

"Tell us who she is, and we will have our own people look into it."

Miguel gave him a half-smile of regret. "Mr. Avarato, I am a man of my word. I am in her confidence, and for reasons I cannot disclose, she lives under an assumed name. If she thought anyone was seeking her out, she would disappear."

"Don't you think we have exhausted every trail in searching for my sister?" Phillipe interrupted. "This issue is best left closed."

"Phillipe." Fredrico placed a hand on the desk. "I am still the patriarch of this family. I understand your concern for me. I have grieved for her all these years, and you think it best I forget." He opened a drawer and took out a key. "I cannot forget."

From another drawer Fredrico withdrew a strongbox and unlocked it. After shuffling through the contents, he held up several papers. "I want to know before I die."

Phillipe's dark gaze slid from his father to Miguel, his impotence in the situation an obvious frustration.

"The passenger list," Fredrico clarified. "No survivors were ever located . . . but communication from the west was poor." He handed the sheets across the desk. "Reward probably means little to you, but I will pay handsomely for any information."

Solemnly, Miguel took the papers. "I will donate the reward to charity." He glanced through the lists. "I may have a problem," he said distractedly. "My cash is tied up right now."

"Your expenses will be the least I can do." Fredrico stood and stepped around the desk. "Please, wait here."

Avarato left the room, and Miguel met Phillipe's piercing gaze. "Do not play my father for a fool, Mr. Ruiz. You will find nowhere to hide if you lead him into a hurtful situation."

"What reason could I have to mislead your father? You must know I would do nothing to lower my esteem in your daughter's eyes." Miguel glanced at the papers in his lap and stifled a smile. His stay in Boston was proving much more pleasant than he had imagined. Researching the wagon train could be done while enjoying the finest hotels and restaurants.

He ran through the possibilities. Perhaps Juanita Avarato had been captured by an Indian and Rain Shadow was her daughter. If Rain Shadow did turn out to be an Avarato heiress, marrying into the family might not be quite as unpleasant or take as long as he had feared.

The Wild West Show would be in winter quarters now, an additional stroke of luck. Will Cody didn't spend the winter with the others, and Miguel didn't need to run into Cody. Miguel's welcome had worn thin by the time he'd met Rain Shadow, and Will had been ready to let him go.

Rain Shadow had succumbed to his charms easily enough once; he'd make sure she would again. And, remembering their shipboard romance, he thought the task would not be an unpleasant one.

* * *

The blazing barn undulated, one moment graphically clear, the next blurred by shimmering orange waves of heat and, tears. Anton watched keenly, helplessly. Horrible, tortured screams raised the hair on his neck and arms. The sound came from inside—from the woman trapped inside the blazing barn. Heat blasted his face and scorched his eyebrows while a cool breeze flirted with his back.

The other sound prickled his scalp, sent shudders along his spine and tore the breath from his lungs: a baby crying.

His feet were lead, the earth a gigantic magnet, securing him to the spot. His hands weighed hundreds of pounds apiece, hanging like window weights at his sides. Blisters erupted on his face, the skin stretched and peeled, and still he stood helpless.

And still the baby cried.

The baby.

Anton bolted upright. The coverlet lay twisted around one ankle, trailing onto the floor. On the night table his pocket watch ticked in the silence of the dark room.

Tick. Tick. Tick.

His baby. The child he had planted inside a wife who'd never loved him. Nikolaus' brother or sister. A child who would have been a few months older than Clara and Seth, Jakob and Franz's two oldest children.

He hadn't had the dream in ages, and he didn't understand why he'd had it now. The dream wasn't always the same; there were a number of variables. Sometimes he could barely walk or crawl, but he never got any closer to the barn. Sometimes he ran inside the building, smoke and flames blinding him so that he couldn't find Peine or the baby.

But the scene never happened the way it had in reality. The screams had been Lydia's; Peine had been beyond rescue. And of course, an unborn baby couldn't cry. And most

importantly, he had tried to save her. He'd fought his
brothers like a wild man, and they had prevented him from
getting himself killed.

Anton adjusted the coverlet and lay back on the pillow.
Tick. Tick. Tick.

There were so many things he hadn't known about Peine
that he wondered if anyone had ever really known her. He'd
never met her parents, seen the home she'd come from or
heard her speak of herself as a child. It was as if she hadn't
existed until she'd come to him. Rain Shadow had been
more direct with her replies to his questions than Peine had
ever been. He hadn't realized the lack of information until
later, much later. Until it had been too late.

Too late he'd admitted to himself her obsession with Jakob. Perhaps he could have spared her. Spared their child.
There were times he mused on what their second child would
have looked like. He'd always fancied a house full of tall,
blond-haired sons as his parents had. Once in a while he'd
look at Nikolaus and picture a brother alongside him, a
towheaded boy a year and a half younger.

Maybe if he'd built them a house of their own none of it
would have happened. Removing Peine from the source of
her disturbing preoccupation may have snapped her out of
it.

But he hadn't. And her unreasonableness had grown—
thrived—fed on her hatred for Jacob's new bride, Lydia.
Tick. Tick. Tick.

Morning couldn't be far off. Anton willed himself back
to sleep. As was often the case when he couldn't sleep, odd
images entered his mind. He dwelled on things he couldn't
fathom why he'd thought of. A picture of Peine rocking
Nikolaus bloomed in his mind's eyes. The only affection
she'd ever shown had been for their son.

He remembered a particular Christmas morning Annette had presented Franz with an exquisite powder blue silk shirt she'd painstakingly sewn for him. Lydia had once used her egg money to buy Jakob a hand-tooled saddle he'd admired. Try as he might, Anton could not recall Peine ever giving him one single thing. Nothing.

She'd even tried her damnedest to keep Nikolaus from him, too, though the child hadn't been old enough to understand her insults or the way she twisted the truth.

She withheld love, respect, companionship. He rolled and punched the pillow into a ball under his head. Lack of those things would never hurt him again. He didn't need any of them except Nikolaus, and he had him all to himself now. That thought stimulated the memory of his son running alongside Rain Shadow.

An irrepressible vision kindled warmth and a powerful yearning: Rain Shadow had kissed him as Peine never had. The way no one ever had.

And he'd liked it.

Obviously, he'd been without a woman too long when a callused, gun-toting snippet who fancied herself an Indian could set his skin on fire! She must be the reason he'd had the dream; working beside her wasn't like toiling with one of his brothers.

She'd told him to forget that kiss, and he was trying.

Lord, he was trying.

She'd borne a child out of wedlock. That should be enough to keep any man distanced. Sixteen years old. Land sakes, she'd been a mere child! What kind of man would take advantage of an innocent young girl and then marry the first well-to-do woman who came along? A gold digger, that's who. And she'd been left to face her father and society and raise the child herself.

Anton gave up on sleep and rolled to his feet. This was crazy. He'd asked Sissy Clanton to marry him, and he should be envisioning Christmas mornings with her, wondering if she would be a good mother and wife. Instead he lost sleep over a tetchy, unfeminine little menace who wore pants and a Smith & Wesson and shoveled cow dung like a man!

As Anton lit the lantern, the match burned too short, singeing his finger. He cursed into the silence, and his irascibility felt good. Ultimately satisfying. And safe.

"Whoa! Them horses have to start a stampede. Let's say this one's mine." Positioned on the floor, his good leg curled with sole touching the knee of his side-thrust splinted leg, Slade demonstrated by standing a wooden horse on its hind legs.

"Just like Buffalo Bill, huh?" Nikolaus reared another carved figure on its wooden legs and whinnied his best horse imitation.

"Hush up or they'll come in here and see me out of bed!" Slade warned in a loud whisper.

Nikolaus hunched his shoulders up to his ears and pulled a face.

"You want 'em to find out it don't hurt as bad as I let on?"

"Nope."

"I can probably stay on till winter if they don't find out. Got any more puzzles like that one we did yesterday?"

"Yup. Got a whole pile in my room."

Slade's dark eyes lit with eagerness, which immediately turned to regret. "I wish I could go in your room. Do you have a big bed like this one and furniture and all?"

"Yup." Absently, Nikolaus scratched his neck inside his shirt collar. "Hey." The hand fell to the wooden floor.

"Maybe when everyone's working after lunch, we could sneak down the hall."

"Yeah? How am I going to get there? It really does hurt some, you know. I can't stand up or walk or nothin'."

Nikolaus' blue eyes scanned the room. He jumped to his feet. "I got it! You sit on this rug." He slid the braided oval rag rug from the other side of the bed to where his friend could see it. "Aunt Annette's got these floors waxed so slick I can drag you clean down the hall!"

Slade's expression lit with excitement. "Aw-right!"

Two Feathers ignored the curious stares of the few townspeople gathered on Butler's boardwalk that afternoon and tucked a brown paper-wrapped parcel under his arm. Johann met him in front of the livery.

"Get what you wanted?"

Two Feathers nodded.

They climbed onto the seat of the springboard waiting near the hitching post. Johann settled his dun-colored hat so that the brim shaded his eyes. "I've a hankering for some of Lydia's fresh pie. What d'ya say we make a stop? I got her a sack of flour and some nut meats we can drop off."

His Indian friend's smile creased the corners of his wizened eyes. "I, too, have a gift for Lydia."

Johann cocked his head and peered at Two Feathers.

"I have a favor to ask of your son's wife." Two Feathers placed the package at his feet and enjoyed the leisurely sway of the springboard as the horses drew them toward the Neubauer homestead. The package contained thread and needles for Lydia, and dress fabrics for his daughter.

He'd raised Rain Shadow. He understood her. He'd seen her secret admiration of the clothing the other women wore and knew she was afraid to express her interest. Not only did she wish to spare his feelings, but he sensed her uncertainty over her position. She would like to be like the white women, but she feared failure.

It was the only thing he'd ever known her to hesitate over.

He'd watched her as a girl, fearlessly learning to ride standing barefoot upon the back of a dappled pony. Many times he'd patched her knees and elbows and watched her leap back on until she got it right. It took unwavering confidence to throw a hatchet at a target six inches from his head, but she had done it hundreds of times. Her own worth was of more value to her than money or property. She longed for security and comfort, but trusted only herself to provide them.

Two Feathers beheld the stand of beech trees on the horizon, a covey of crows darting through the branches and streaking into the sky like sparks from a fire.

"Much different here than where you're from?" Johann asked.

Two Feathers studied the sky before replying. "Different, but the same in many ways. When I was a young brave the Dakotas were my home. There was game...and beauty. Wakon Tanka owned the land and the sun and the sky and shone his face upon it. Now men say they own the rivers and land and sky because they have pieces of paper."

Johann handed him the reins and drew his pipe from inside his coat. Thoughtfully, he tamped tobacco into the bowl and lit it. He'd always appreciated his heritage, been proud of parents who'd come from the old country as bond servants and earned this land that now "belonged" to him and his sons. Looking through Two Feathers' eyes, he was an intrusion himself. His German parents had come here to practice religious freedom as had hundreds and thousands of immigrants, but what had that done to the Indians' freedom?

"I'm sorry," he said at last. What could one old man do to change the loss of an entire nation?

He met Two Feathers' eyes, and an understanding passed between them. They were old men, and it was pointless to hate or resent or pine for what was lost. The future belonged to the young, and each had a valuable stake in his children and grandchildren.

"Your son looks at Rain Shadow like she is the sun he has gone many summers without."

"Your Rain Shadow looks at my son like he's a piece of Lydia's pie."

The two men laughed heartily, the sound carrying across the open countryside.

Rain Shadow needed to blend into the white man's world, needed to find a spot for herself and her son. She tried so hard and looked so far that she'd missed the obvious. Two Feathers would help her see it.

Ever since that first stormy evening many summers ago, she had demanded little for herself, yet given unsparingly. Rain Shadow's happiness meant more to him than the show. More than anything under the sky. She was his daughter. His Rain Shadow. He would do his best to give her the desires of her heart.

Lydia was overjoyed to help Rain Shadow with the dress patterns. They spent an afternoon cutting and basting the fabrics Two Feathers had selected. Annette dropped by and offered material for undergarments, as well, and the three sewed drawers and something Lydia called a shimmy. Rain Shadow finished them herself, stitching and hemming by firelight.

While she worked, Two Feathers contentedly smoked his pipe and dozed. She couldn't imagine her flesh-and-blood father caring for her any better than Two Feathers had. He

was a kind and honorable man. She loved him unquestionably, and at times almost felt guilty for her curiosity over her
parents. She could never have proceeded with her plans if he
had not understood her desire to locate her family and to
blend into the white man's society.

Alone in the lodge the following afternoon, Rain Shadow
tried on her favorite new creation: a high-necked white
blouse followed by a sleeveless shirtwaist of blue and white
checked taffeta silk. The full skirt had taken nearly three
yards of material and was trimmed with five vertical bands
of white taffeta. Rain Shadow spun until the skirt blos-
somed out in a full circle, like a flower twirled by its stem.

She combed the braids from her hair with her fingers and
brushed its length until it crackled. With unusually clumsy
fingers she attempted an upswept style, but the heavy black
tresses fell across her shoulders.

Caressing the skirt with flattened palms, she wished she
had a mirror. Brush and hairpins in hand, she peeked from
the tent flap. No one in sight. If she ran now, she could use
a mirror in the house before anyone spotted her.

The kitchen was deserted as usual. In her hurry, she
dropped her hairbrush on the stairs and had to hop down
after it.

The door to the room Slade used was closed. "Slade?"

"Yeah, Ma?"

She entered and studied the two boys. Her son sat back
against the pillows, and Nikolaus popped up from the other
side of the bed and stared at her. Both of them breathed as
though they'd run a foot race. "What are you two doing?"

"Playing."

"Why are you out of breath?"

"We was seeing who could hold their breath the longest.
Mama, you look pretty!"

"Were seeing who could hold their breath the longest, and thank you."

She stepped to the mirror over Anton's low chest of drawers and surveyed the different woman staring back at her. Why, she looked like any one of the young women who'd been at the Neubauers' barn dance! Except for her face and hands, tanned as they were from going unprotected in the sun. Now able to watch her hands, she attempted another coil on the back of her head, and this time it stayed.

"Where you going dressed like that?" her son asked.

"I'm not going anywhere. I was practicing."

The boys laughed, as if women in general were silly.

"Are you hungry?"

"Nope."

"Does your leg hurt?"

"Yeah, but playing with Nikolaus helps me forget."

"Thank you, Nikolaus."

The boys exchanged glances.

The checkered skirt billowed ahead of her with each step down the stairway, her knees jerking the fabric upward in funny bumps. Underclothing was a new and odd feeling. What was the white man's expression about trying to make a silk purse out of a sow's ear? If she felt this strange, how would she appear to others?

The enormous kitchen was the perfect stage to spin in a circle and feel the material swirl around her legs and calves. A wonderful chill breeze caught her dress as she sprinted down the porch steps and across the dooryard.

More lighthearted than she'd been in weeks, she spotted the rope swing dangling from the ancient oak and scampered toward it.

"Rain Shadow?"

One hand on the rope, she swung around.

Anton strode toward her.

"From a distance I thought you were Annette."

Self-consciously, she fingered the high collar of her blouse. A gust of wind flattened her skirt against her thighs. Daring to meet his eyes, she found him studying her face. Did he think she was trying to be something she wasn't? "Well, what do you think?"

Her heart slammed against her rib cage as she waited for his reply.

"The dress looks nice." The wind ruffled his sandy hair. "A big change, but pretty." *I think if you were Sissy Clanton I couldn't wait to marry you. I'd throw you down right here on the grass and wrinkle your pretty dress.*

Relieved, she smiled.

"Aren't you cold?"

"No, I just came from the house. The boys were behaving strangely."

"Strange for boys or strange for humans in general?"

Just under his irritable surface a sense of humor lurked. She smiled.

Her waist was so narrow he could span it with his hands. A strand of black hair whipped from its loose coil and streamed in the breeze. Definitely an improvement over those trousers and boots. His gaze automatically slipped to her feet. Beaded moccasins completed the ensemble, and he smiled to himself, somehow assured that the woman he thought he knew hadn't completely disappeared.

"I don't have any shoes."

Her full lips were naturally the color of a summer rose, and the crisp air had kissed a complimentary pink tint into her cheeks. Looking at her wasn't healthy. He had enough problems without adding an indefinable attraction to this little peach. Abruptly, he turned. "I have work to do."

She backed onto the wooden seat of the swing and watched him walk away from her, wondering how she'd fallen short. Was wearing this dress like trying to turn pigweed into an orchid? That niggling shred of insecurity wouldn't go to sleep. Why hadn't her family ever tried to find her? Was she somehow unworthy of her true heritage?

Rain Shadow looked at her moccasined feet beneath the checkered skirt, symbols of the two people she was inside. What if her people never claimed her? What if she and Slade were the only family they'd ever have? The breeze seemed colder now, less friendly.

She stood. It *wouldn't* happen that way! Why was she suddenly doubting what she'd been so certain of before she'd come here? Determinedly, Rain Shadow pushed the negative thoughts from her mind. It was only a matter of time. She headed for her lodge, the swing swaying forgotten behind her.

Doc limped away from Slade's bedside and washed his hands in the water Rain Shadow had provided. "I think you can move him to your tent now." He turned and picked up his leather bag. "Not in and out and all around or away yet 'cause it's still hurting him, but you can take him out since you're itching to."

"Thank you, Doctor. Slade, isn't that good news?" She brushed his hair from his temple. "You can move out to our lodge!"

Her son slumped against the pillows, his chin digging against his chest in a dark pout, and stared at a spot on her vest. "Yeah."

"What—wait a minute," she said with a frown. "I'll see the doctor out."

At the door, she thanked him, pressing a roll of paper money into his hand.

"It's more than we agreed on," he objected.

"Barely. You had a long ride several times a week to see Slade. I want to repay you for your time."

He nodded and ambled down the porch steps to his buggy.

Whatever was the matter with Slade? She intended to get to the bottom of his sulkiness. Why wasn't he pleased at getting better? She ran up the stairs, her booted feet sounding her return. "Slade." Rain Shadow perched on the high bed's edge. "Why aren't you happy about the doctor's news?"

He shrugged. Nikolaus slipped from the room.

"I've missed sleeping in our lodge. Not that I minded staying inside with you, but this isn't our home."

His obsidian gaze shot to her face. "I wish it were."

She sat, silenced. Hurt.

"I like it here, sleeping in this big bed and playing with Nikolaus. Sometimes we pretend we're brothers."

A dreadful ache closed around her heart. She studied the narrow face of the son she loved with all her heart, the son she wanted to give the best of everything and watch grow up to be independent and fulfilled. "We can't stay here forever, Slade. It's better if you don't let yourself like it too much. We will leave when your leg is well."

"I know." He bunched the coverlet into a knot at his hip and pounded it with his fist once, twice, three times. "But would it hurt to make it last as long as it can before we have to go? I know this ain't our house—"

"Isn't our—"

"Isn't our house and Nikolaus ain—isn't my brother, Ma. I just want to act like it while we're here. Like acting out the attacks on the settler's cabin and the stagecoach. It's not real, but it's fun. When it's over, we can go back to our real life just like in the show."

Powerless, Rain Shadow read the hunger in her son's eyes. Just as she'd feared, he'd grown attached to the Neubauers and their stable life. Maybe she needed to face what she would do with their lives if no family claimed them. Maybe if this was the only shred of familial security Slade would ever experience, it would be cruel of her not to allow him the temporary pleasure.

"Rain Shadow!" Anton's voice echoed up the stairwell. "Somebody here to see you!"

She hugged Slade soundly. "I'll be back, and we'll finish our talk."

Braid bouncing against her breast, she descended the stairs. On the first landing, one dusty booted foot on the bottom stair, his expression unreadable, Anton gripped the handrail and waited, face raised. Sun streaked through the high window and gilded his hair and skin. Tall and lean, shirtsleeves folded back over corded forearms, the sight of him made her think of solid things, of home and security and waking up in the same place every morning. She was struck by how appealing he was in his golden way, like sunrise on an autumn morning. How well she understood Slade's envious dreams of staying here forever.

She stepped lower, and glossy black boots came into view, followed by long slim legs and torso in a tailored European suit. Shiny black hair cut precisely around his ears, the guest turned his elegant head.

Rain Shadow's heart stopped.

She clutched the banister as though she were sinking into a quagmire. Dread roared in her ears. Unblinking, lips parted, she stared into the swarthily handsome features and midnight-black eyes of Miguel de Ruiz.

Chapter Seven

She forced one booted foot ahead of the other. Anton's wary blue gaze gauging her expression, Rain Shadow willed composure into her limbs. Her heart, however, refused to obey, pounding against her ribs at an astounding rate. *Miguel!* What was he doing at the Neubauers'? Why had he come? And—her heart missed a beat—what if he saw Slade?

Anton stepped aside, and she stopped on the landing, protectively between the man below and her son upstairs. The son he wasn't aware of. Only she and Two Feathers knew the boy's sire. And—she shot a quick look at Anton. She'd told Anton.

He looked expectantly from her face to Miguel's.

It was Miguel who spoke first. "Rain Shadow. You are lovely!" He reached for her hand, but she stepped past him, ignoring the gesture.

"What are you doing here?"

"Would not introductions be appropriate?" The rolling *r*s in his mellow Spanish accent raised the hair on her neck.

She realized how strange Anton must think her behavior. "Miguel de Ruiz, Anton Neubauer."

"Mr. Neubauer. I am pleased to make your acquaintance.

"Ruiz." Anton shook the hand offered.

"I have come a long way to see Rain Shadow. Would you be so kind as to allow us privacy?"

"That'd be up to her," Anton replied.

Rain Shadow nodded, but didn't meet his eyes. "It's all right."

Anton hesitated in the doorway. "Have a seat in the parlor."

She led the uninvited guest into the suggested room. He seated himself on a couch. She stood, boxed in and guarded, impatient with his polite facade. "What do you want?" she demanded once Anton's back disappeared.

Miguel unbuttoned his jacket and made himself comfortable, crossing long black-clad legs at the ankle. "I want only to see you. I wondered if you were well."

"After all this time." It was a statement. Almost an accusation, and she hated herself for it.

"I understand your bitterness," he said, drawing a long finger across the line of his mustache. "You have every right to be angry with me."

"I don't need your permission for anything," she said, and crossed her arms over the front of her vest. Her gaze wandered about the room.

"The years have been kind to you," Miguel said, his persuasive voice low and emollient. "You are beautiful. Just as I remembered you from so long ago."

"What do you want?"

He gave her a wounded look, one that wrenched her gut and stabbed fear into her heart. She'd seen the look more times than she could count—on her son's face.

"I want only to see you, *querida*. To know you are well."

She bristled at the endearment. "Now? After all this time, why now?"

"I did not forget. I cannot forget what we had together."

She let her arms fall to her sides. "How is your wife?"

"The *comtesse?* She is quite well."

Was he going to get to the point? Damn him! *Say what you want and get out!*

"She is in Naples right now, I believe."

Rain Shadow paced the floor near the doorway. "I can't imagine why you're here. Butler, Pennsylvania, isn't exactly the social seat of the East."

"I deserve your sarcasm. What I did was wrong. I know that now." He stood and stepped in front of her. "I should have married for love. I wronged you, and in the end I wronged myself. I was young."

"You were a hell of a lot older than I was!"

His black eyebrows shot up in surprise, but he fixed his expression quickly. "You are right, of course. I can only beg your forgiveness." He reached toward her and curled long, dark fingers around her elbow.

Repulsed, Rain Shadow jerked away. "Why are you here?"

Obsidian eyes filled with unexpected pain. "I need to make amends for the past. I have been through a lot since we parted. I learned valuable lessons."

She studied his fine-bred features, black, black eyes, narrow nose and shapely mouth. She'd once thought Miguel the most handsome of men. No longer. Eyes she'd girlishly considered love-laden were arrogant. Lips she'd thought eloquent spoke only self-serving words. He was polished and smooth, well-dressed and fine-mannered, and she'd foolishly thought herself in love and allowed him admittance to her young heart and body. He still sounded sincere, but now she knew better.

He wanted something. Last time he'd wanted entertainment on a long ocean voyage. This time? He could be dangerously persuasive.

She turned her back on him. "Leave."

"Rain Shadow, I want to—"

"I want you out of here now."

"Is there someone else?"

She swung and faced him. "And if there were?"

He looked decidedly uncomfortable and glanced around the room, as if noticing it for the first time. He nodded over her shoulder to the dining room beyond. "Him?"

In the kitchen, Anton shot an annoyed look at the noisy metal coffeepot boiling over the flame on the stove and cursed his bad ear. The everyday sound was an annoying distraction.

He'd sensed her apprehension, known instinctively that all wasn't right. How had he grown attuned to her in such a short time? He couldn't have left her alone in this house with that snake if his life had depended on it. He stepped nearer the dining room doorway.

Ruiz was too polished. Too slick. Did he know about Slade? Rain Shadow wouldn't have told him, but could he have found out some other way? And what if he did know? Anton sensed her fear and was afraid for her, as well.

His first look at the man, gracefully lowering himself from a majestic black stallion, had speared intense dislike through his vitals. Black-browed eyes had turned toward him, and the feeling had intensified. *Slade's father.* Not a doubt in his mind. He'd thought Slade's dark hair and skin Rain Shadow's until now.

The whole idea sickened him. He poured a scalding cup of coffee and cursed Ruiz. Though Anton stared out the window at a good portion of the shady porch and the side yard beyond, his mind reeled with pictures of the swarthy South American's long-fingered hands and wolfish mouth on Rain Shadow. How could she have let that—that oily vermin touch her?

And how could Ruiz, after tasting a flower like her, have married another woman? Anton knew what it was like to touch her. Had she responded to Ruiz the way she had to him? She'd no doubt given more to that unprincipled he-goat in their brief encounter than Peine had given him in their entire marriage! She'd probably given Ruiz more than Sissy would ever give him in the forever years to come. . . .

Rain Shadow's voice rose in the other room, and he strained to hear with his good ear.

"You're not welcome here. Leave!" Her words carried, clear and insistent.

"Permit me a few moments of your time," Ruiz entreated calmly. "To get these things off my—"

"I said get out!"

"She's tired of your company, Ruiz." Anton spoke from behind her.

"I mean no harm. We need to talk."

"I'll see you to the door."

Ruiz' dark eyes flamed with menace, and then as rapidly as blowing out a candle, the glare flickered, replaced by a disillusioned furrow. "I am sorry to upset you," he said to Rain Shadow. "It was not my intent. Perhaps there is something you could ask of me that might prove my sincerity."

Anton sensed the strength it took for her to keep her aplomb. She said simply, "Leave."

He followed Ruiz outside. Ruiz plucked up his wide-brimmed hat, settled it on his head and mounted. He rode gracefully, urging the horse into a light-limbed gallop without visible command. Only a cloud of dust remained when Anton turned back to the room.

She perched on his father's chair, looking small and alone and—angry. Her luminous violet gaze met his, and he remembered her belligerent claim when he'd asked about Slade's parentage. "*My* son," she'd said defiantly.

She'd told him the truth candidly. And she frankly dared him to think less of her for it. She could have invented a dead husband to give her respectability, and no one would have been the wiser. But she'd chosen to live her life honestly, no matter what others thought of her. He'd been so caught up in seeing her as soiled that he hadn't looked beyond his own feelings and recognized hers. Now he realized his callousness, and her attitude commanded his admiration.

Her fear struck a vulnerable spot. Her pride kept him from acknowledging it. He stopped in front of her, discerned the tremble of her fingers in her lap.

"Thank you for staying," she said at last.

"A man can have a cup of coffee in his own house if he wants."

"You know who that was."

"The *vaquero*."

She nodded.

"Does he know?"

"No!" She stood, quickly dragged her palms down her trousered thighs and shook her head. "No."

Rain Shadow watched Anton shovel a hand through his hair. She'd experienced immeasurable guilt and shame years ago, called herself a fool and wallowed in regret. Two Feathers had helped her see that she couldn't change the past. What was done was done. The future was all that counted.

So she'd recovered and planned. All she could do was become someone she could respect. She'd spent seven years accomplishing that and she wasn't going to throw it away now! Why did she care what Anton thought? She had enough worry with Slade hurt, the contest coming up and now Miguel's arrival. His appearance festered old wounds, unearthed fears and feelings she thought she'd conquered.

Miguel de Ruiz had used her. Lied to her and left her for a better prospect. He wanted something again, and the possibilities terrified her.

"He mustn't know. He has no claim! No rights!" she shouted, and her slender body shook with rage.

Anton nodded, understanding.

Rain Shadow's strong, independent spirit rebelled at the prickling sensation in the back of her throat. Horrified, she turned her face sharply away and willed herself not to weaken. Her eyes filled with tears, and she tried to blink them back. A single tear escaped and trailed down her cheek.

"He's not worth it."

Anton's gentle voice and words touched her soul and dislodged another defensive stone in the wall she'd constructed around her tender susceptibilities. She pressed her lips together to keep them from trembling. "It's not only him," she said at last. "I'm afraid for Slade."

"Well . . ." He sounded almost uncomfortable with her emotions, yet he replied. "He's worth it. Go ahead."

She balled her fists at her sides and pressed her mouth into a straight line. Slade was hers and hers alone. She'd borne him in her lodge, a Pawnee medicine woman attending. She'd provided his food and shelter and taught him to read and write and ride. And she had plans for his future—their future. Plans that didn't include a slick-talking *vaquero*.

Her composure broke, and she dissolved into tears. Anton's strong, hard arms closed around her, one hand bringing her head to his chest, the other pressed into her lower back, holding her flush against him. Gratefully, she wrapped both arms around his waist and clung, her sobs muffled by his shirtfront.

His fingers kneaded the back of her neck, burrowing into the hair at the base of her braid. After maintaining her emotions for so long, she exhausted her tears quickly, hating herself for the vulnerability yet reveling for the first time in the admission of her humanity. It felt unbelievably good to have someone to lean on, someone warm and solid. Someone she could trust in this uncharacteristic moment of weakness.

And somehow, instinctively, the conviction that Anton was different, that she could trust him, gave her the freedom to accept his reassuring embrace. She absorbed his strength and relished the steady, comforting beat of his heart against her temple.

Her tears ended, her senses filled with Anton: the faint and familiar scent of leather and horses, the warmth of his hand on her spine and his body against hers, his hard chest and thighs, the damp fabric of his shirt beneath her cheek, his breath against her forehead. Undeniably male evidence pressing into her stomach told her he'd been aware of her for some time. Without separating them an inch, she raised her head and gazed up.

She remembered the kiss. The kiss she'd told him to forget. She could see in the gentle blue eyes boring into hers that he hadn't forgotten, either. A forbidden and uncalculated hunger strained between them. The impact was sudden, jarring and deep. If he hadn't been holding her, she would have buckled.

The hand at her spine glided upward, dipped into the curve of her waist, spanned her rib cage and began another downward journey. The fingers at her nape caressed, his thumb rubbing, consoling, rhythmic circles soothing her distress.

Slowly—very slowly, so that, had she wanted to, she had time to pull away—he lowered his face to hers. Her breath, caught in her chest, hurt. His breath fanned her lips, and a piquant shudder slid down her spine. His warm lips covered hers, tentatively at first, gauging her response. Gentle wasn't enough for either of them. Immediately, his mouth grew hard and demanding. He angled his head and held her face in his rough palm, his thumb beneath her chin securing her for his sensory assault. She returned the kiss, bringing one hand up to frame his jaw, as if she could cup the keen pleasure in her palm and prolong it.

She tasted tears and coffee and satiny desire and knew instantly that years of practiced reserve and independence hadn't prepared her for Anton.

Beneath her hand, his heart changed from a slow, even tempo to an urgent throb. He tested her lips with the tip of his tongue, a warm, wet inquiry. Rain Shadow inhaled sharply, and his hand at her neck was poised as if to hold her should she withdraw. She didn't. She couldn't. She needed this moment, this kiss, this man.

She caressed his jaw, enjoyed the rasp of his cheek against her palm, brought her thumb against the corner of their fused lips. He turned his face just enough to bite her thumb.

Passion washed through her, her pulse drumming in places she instinctively pressed more intimately against him. Persuasively, Anton rubbed his tongue against her mouth. Heart thundering, she parted her lips, and his tongue swept inside, hot and delving, shocking her with the pleasure he created. She returned the bold kiss, pulling herself on tiptoe and snaking one arm around his neck for a secure hold.

The logic of her mind warned that the blood and thunder pounding through her veins stemmed from her recent scare. She clung to Anton like a weak, frightened woman. She should stop this abandonment of good sense. Douse the glowing embers now before they blazed out of her control.

But her body denied the warning, fanned the fire and refused her time to collect herself. His combination of textures—sandpaper jaw and satin hair, rock-hard body and pliant, sweet-fierce lips—assailed her senses, touched her to the quick, and she caught the flame.

Anton pulled his mouth from hers and, breathing raggedly, burrowed his face into her neck. He nipped the tender flesh along her throat and under her ear, waves of sensation shuddering along her arms, tightening her breasts. Eyes closed in acute pleasure, she craved him, more of him, all of him. She wanted him too much. More than she wanted his protection or his kindness, she wanted this fever pitch of sensation that seized her with urgency. His mouth, hot and exciting, returned to nip her chin, suck at the corner of her mouth.

He pushed her leather vest aside and unbuttoned the top buttons of her shirt, pressing kisses upon her chest. Silvery shivers tingled across her shoulders and down her arms. Ignoring good sense, she framed his face in her hands and tipped her head back. She felt his warm fingers brush against her energized skin as he undid the remaining buttons and opened her shirt.

The air's silken kiss pebbled her nipples. Anton pressed his face between her breasts, inhaling deeply. Against her delicate skin, his cheek and chin seemed delightfully rough, his lips exquisitely hot and moist, his hair incredibly soft and cool. Awash with sensation, Rain Shadow buried her fingers into his hair and held fast. Forcing herself to breathe, she couldn't help the tremulous moan that escaped her lips.

The sound brought Anton to his senses. She was aroused. Every bit as aroused as he. He couldn't indulge the weakness in his armor when he saw her tears and held her in his arms. He couldn't indulge the craving desire that had spurred to life with his first look at her honey skin and

stormy amethyst eyes, fueled to fever pitch with her hungry
kiss and the heart-stopping sight of her small, brown-tipped
breasts. He couldn't indulge, and didn't need this ache in the
pit of his stomach, the trembling want in his limbs or the
hankering of his hands to touch more of her—all of her.

Almost ashamed, he released her abruptly and stepped
back. Rain Shadow wilted onto the chair. He had to turn
away from her gaping shirt, her glistening, swollen lips and
the unguarded look in her eyes. Silence filled the room,
yawning uncomfortably between them. What was he allowing to happen? "Will you be all right?"

"Yes—" she tried to say and had to start over. "Yes."

"I'll do whatever I can to help you keep him from finding out. Do you think he'll be back?"

"I don't know," she whispered, deeply affected by his
touch, his kiss. Did he think she behaved that way with all
men? Was he disgusted? Judging her? He headed for the
door. "Anton?"

He looked over his shoulder. She'd buttoned her shirt.

I didn't know I could feel that way. What had begun as
consolation and comfort had snowballed into passion and
desire neither of them was prepared for. "Keep your eyes
open."

He nodded and was gone.

Frustrated, Miguel left his mount in a copse, sidled up a
bank and pulled a spyglass from his jacket. Nearly half an
hour passed before the hay-hired man loped down the porch
stairs.

Miguel seethed.

The farmer was a complication he had not anticipated.
The old Indian he could have handled. The old Rain
Shadow he could have handled. This Rain Shadow, this self-
assured spitfire, was not the same sixteen-year-old girl he

had seduced aboard the *Nebraska*. This woman was more than he had expected—or wanted.

And the man? Was he the reason she had stayed in Pennsylvania? Neubauer exuded a possessive attitude as though he were. It could not hurt to know what he was up against. He collapsed the spyglass and made his way to his horse. He would go to Butler for his things, change clothes and pick up food to last a few days. He swung into his saddle, urged the animal forward and surveyed the landscape. He searched out a good place to camp unobserved, then headed for town.

He should be back before sundown.

"All right, Slade. I've decided you can stay in the house as long as you're welcome to."

"Aw-right!" her son whooped, and bounced a good eight inches above the bed.

"Calm down before you hurt something."

He settled himself beneath the covers, his excitement barely contained. "How about you, Ma? Are you still going to stay here with me?"

She smoothed the shirt she had folded and placed it on the bureau. She had planned to move out to her lodge tonight, but Miguel's appearance had changed her mind. Slade wanted to stay in the house, and it was the safest place for him. Yesterday she would have thought nothing of sleeping in her lodge with Slade in the house, but now she didn't want to separate herself from him, especially all night. Even the thought of Two Feathers sleeping alone terrified her. She would tell him of the danger, and perhaps he could be persuaded to sleep inside. "Yes, I'll stay with you."

"Good. What's for supper?"

"How about a hot, thick stew?"

"Uh-huh! Will you ask Nikolaus to come up?"

Minutes later, Nikolaus pounded up the stairs. "What'd she say?"

"We're staying in the house."

"Aw-*right!*"

"What's she doing now?"

"She has some rabbits to skin. I want to watch her."

"What do you wanna do that for?" Slade threw the coverlet back.

"I dunno. Just do." Nikolaus rubbed his toe repeatedly into a crack in the wood floor.

"Well, I got something better for you to watch."

"What?" He scrambled onto the foot of the bed.

Slade tossed the remaining covers back, exposing his splinted leg. He tugged the oversize shirt he wore up his thigh and unwound raveled strips of bandaging.

"What are you doin'?"

"You'll see." He found the end of another strip at his knee and removed it the same way. A third at his ankle came off, and the splint fell away, still in two fairly solid pieces. His narrow leg was white and wrinkled, the skin dry-looking.

"Oh, ugh!" Nikolaus screwed his freckled face into a grimace.

"It's okay. Watch this." Supporting himself with slender arms, Slade scooted to the bed's edge and balanced on his good leg. The other he touched tentatively on the floor. Reaching for the footboard, he took a few limping steps away from, then back to, the mattress.

"Gosh!" Nikolaus stared in awe. "Does your mama—"

"'Course she don't know, and we ain't gonna tell her."

Nikolaus plopped back on the bed and smiled at the ceiling. "'Course we ain't."

* * *

Rain Shadow adjusted the blanket beneath her head for the hundredth time. For the last half hour she'd been thinking of the pile of pillows on the bed above her. Slade didn't need all of them.

In the inky darkness, she crept around the foot of the bed. Pillow in hand, she paused, stilled by unmistakable sounds coming from outside, though the windows were closed and the curtains pulled. The horses in the barn were restless, the chickens setting up a squawk in the pen behind the barn. A fox or a stray dog?

Her heart beat double time. She hadn't been able to convince Two Feathers to sleep in the house. *Could be Miguel.*

Silently, she slipped into her trousers and shirt and buckled on her holster. Grabbing a coat from the back of a chair, she tiptoed from the room.

Dark cloud cover obscured the moon. She could barely see her breath in front of her face. She allowed her eyes time to adjust and surveyed the dooryard, peering toward the shadows near the outbuildings. She reached the barn door, and her pony whinnied a greeting. "Easy, Jack," she whispered. "Whatsa matter, boy?" She slid into the stall and calmed him with a soft nicker in his ear.

Anton's massive bay bobbed his head. Rain Shadow climbed over the rail and scrubbed his forehead with her knuckles. "Shush, now, General." The other horses calmed at her touch, too. She peered carefully into each stall and checked the opposite side around the grain bins.

A noise came from the direction of the tack room.

Slowly, cautiously, she made her way toward the doorway. Even the barely audible sound of hay beneath her boots was deafening to her ears. Rain Shadow eased her gun from the holster and held it ready, inching toward the doorway.

Outside the tack room, she flattened herself against the rough-hewn wall and strained her ears for any sound. Her heartbeat. Her breath. Nothing.

Holding her breath, she slipped through the doorway and flattened herself against the wall on the other side, the barrel of the gun poised into the air next to her cheek. In the pitch black, hair rose on her arms and neck. *She wasn't alone.* Her sixth sense was acute, her hearing keen. To her right another person breathed. Someone taller.

Heart pounding, she waited. The other person, still as stone, obviously knew she was there. Perhaps he didn't know who she was. If Miguel was night prowling, what would he be doing in the barn?

All at once, the person lunged—not toward the door as if to escape, but directly toward her—and she took a sideways leap. A rock-hard body struck her and knocked her from her feet, the gun skittering across the floorboards. A hand spanned her throat easily, cutting off her breath, and superior weight crushed her hips and legs.

The other hand groped at her shirtfront and closed over her breast. Immediately, the heavy body stilled. He had to feel her heart thudding. She needed to breathe. The hand molded her breast in quizzical palpation.

"Rain Shadow?"

Relief washed through her. *Anton!* She tried to nod.

He released her throat, and she sucked in a grateful whoosh of air. The hand at her breast withdrew. He sat at her hip. "Good Lord, woman, you scared ten years off my life!"

"M-me?" she rasped, lying flat on her back staring into the darkness. She slapped at him with a limp wrist. "Seems to me you had the upper hand! How—" She coughed. "How do you think I feel?"

A low rumble met her ears. He was laughing! "You felt pretty good to me!"

She pulled herself to a sitting position and kicked him in the darkness.

He laughed outright. "You gotta admit it's funny. I never went through so much to get my hands on a woman."

She felt herself flush, imagined for a moment the shock he experienced when his hand found her breast. She managed a chuckle. "Who did you think I was?"

"Who did you think I was?"

The question sobered her quickly. "Why did you come out here?"

"I heard the animals."

"Do you think there's someone out there?"

"Not now. I checked all around before coming to the barn. Just as I got inside I heard you at the door and ducked in here."

"Let's ride out," she suggested. "Just to be certain."

"If you want to."

"I do." They stood. "You know, this wasn't funny at all. I could've shot you."

"What the hell were you doing with that gun, anyway?"

She groped across the floor until her fingers closed over the barrel. "And what did you plan to use to defend yourself? Your caustic wit?"

"Get Jack."

She waited impatiently while he saddled his horse. Within minutes, they led the horses off the drive, mounted and walked in ever-widening circles around the house and outbuildings. A slice of moon appeared and offered them a measure of guidance. They paused, and Rain Shadow sniffed the air. "I smell a fire."

Anton lifted his nose toward the night sky. His saddle creaked beneath his weight. "Do you think he's out there?"

A camp fire, no doubt. Miguel de Ruiz was as persistent as he was persuasive. And he wanted something. She studied the black shapes of the trees to the west, and a shiver ran up her spine. "He's out there."

Chapter Eight

Thumps and bumps sounded in the room overhead. What in the world was Nikolaus doing up there? Rain Shadow stared in frustration at the Anchor Brand wringer mounted to the barrel washer and fed the sheets through one last time. The front of her shirt was soaked. She'd rather be out in the barn oiling harnesses with the men, but since she and Slade made more work, the least she could do was launder the bedding. She couldn't expect Annette to do Slade's washing, since she already washed and ironed for the men. Lydia cleaned house once a week and kept baked goods in the pantry.

Grateful for the opportunity to leave the house, Rain Shadow hung the sheets on the clothesline. She glanced over her shoulder at the Neubauers' home. The family members were all comfortable in its confines and worked together like gears of a well-oiled machine. She wondered how many meals had been shared at its enormous kitchen table, how many laughs had echoed through its waxed and polished halls...how many fires had been built in the stone fireplace...how many babies had been conceived and born on the lofty feather beds....

The absence of a woman in the house didn't seem to harm the aura of warmth and security. At one time all three sons' wives had lived in the big house. She remembered the picture of Anton's wife, a lovely blonde with a lush, corseted body. How he must miss her. Anton was so alive, so strong and male. Her pulse throbbed at the thought, and her fingers stilled on a clothespin. Desire had been stamped all over his face the day before. He'd wanted her. She'd seen it in the fierce blue glow in his eyes, felt it in the heat of his hands and the coiled tension in his hard muscles. He'd been without his wife for a long time.

And she wanted him.

He was a rock. Anton loved his family and farm. A man who stayed in one place, who'd lived and worked the same several hundred acres since he was a youth. As permanent as the land itself, he was a wonderful, loving father, a hardworking, bright, dauntless man. He buried a sense of humor and possessed a tempestuous, full-rigged temper that sometimes got the best of him. His concern for her, a side she hadn't seen before, was apparent in the way he'd found things to do around the house and yard all day. He worried about Miguel returning.

A curious discomfort closed around her heart. Annette and Lydia said Anton had been looking for a new wife. They guessed he had it narrowed down to one or two. The young lady with the nutmeg hair? Rain Shadow recalled her pressed and proper dress. Sissy certainly wasn't as flamboyant as his first wife, but a good choice. Yes. She had roots. A family.

What did it matter to her? She plucked the wicker basket from the ground and carried it to the porch. He might desire Rain Shadow, but he'd made it plain that the idea was offensive to him. Could she blame him? No. She was an orphan raised by Indians, an unwed mother of a seven-year-old boy. What did she have to offer him?

"Hello?"

She turned and realized he'd called to her more than once. She waved.

Anton strode toward her with an easy, long-legged gait. "What are the boys up to?"

"Last I checked they had everything out of your closet so they could pretend it was Nikolaus' office. He's a marshal today, you know."

"He knows better than that."

Uncomfortable with his displeasure, she sat the basket down.

Anton shrugged, relaxing. "What have they got to do, stuck inside all day, anyway? No harm done. I probably need to get rid of some o' that junk, anyhow." He studied her. "You're going with us tonight? The Thanksgiving celebration in Butler?"

"Oh, I don't know. Your family needs an opportunity to get away from us for a while."

"Well, if you don't go, I don't go."

"Why not?"

"You know why not. I'm not leaving you alone with that polecat slinking around out there."

She stared at him. For the first time someone besides Two Feathers wanted to protect her. Only a few weeks ago she would have bristled. Her independence was as vital to her survival as water and air. Today, however, his concern wrapped warm arms around her heart. She reveled in the sensation, and further understood Slade's desire to meld himself with these people, to belong. The warm, solid feeling of well-being was something neither she nor her son had ever known.

"Thank you, Anton," she whispered.

Her words and the soft shimmer that suffused her eyes caught him off guard. Everything this woman did and said and stood for caught him off guard. He'd been prepared for an indignant display of self-reliance, not for the unguarded look of trust. He trailed his gaze from her face to the snow-white sheets billowing from the clothesline, back to the damp shirt clinging to her breasts. *Saints preserve him, she'd done the laundry.*

"You'll go?"

"I'll go. And I'll take Slade. I'll make a travois to carry him on."

Without comprehending his satisfaction, Anton nodded and headed for the house. For some reason it had become important that she remain near him. Wouldn't anyone feel the same duty?

He didn't understand her compliance, but he knew better than to look a gift horse in the mouth. In a way her acceptance almost frightened him more. She was so brave, so independent, that for her to give in to his precautions, her fear of Ruiz must be great. He would have to stay alert. He'd brought them here. Now he was responsible for them.

Ruiz bathed and changed clothes at the boardinghouse. Two nights of sleeping on the cold ground were more than he cared for. In that time he had learned the comings and goings of the Neubauers. Learned that Rain Shadow slept in the house rather than in the tepee with the old Indian. And learned that there was a towheaded little boy who made trips to the privy and appeared on the porch occasionally. Whose child? Could the child belong to her and the tall farmer? No one in the show had been willing to offer any information when he had searched for her at winter quarters.

Inadvertently, he had learned of the contest scheduled for April. Many of the reports indicated she stood an excellent chance to win. If so, she was well on her way to fame, and a cut of the action could be his.

Before he left Boston, he had traced the former investigations done on Juanita Avarato, following them up with his own visits and letters. There was no doubt in his mind that Fredrico's granddaughter had been killed on that wagon train without giving birth to a child.

Knowing as he did that Rain Shadow held the locket in her possession, it only stood to reason she had acquired it by other means. Perhaps one of the marauding Indians had stolen it from Juanita's body or belongings, traded it to another tribe, and it had somehow come to Rain Shadow. The possibilities were endless.

Miguel still had two options. To take the locket and bargain with it, or convince Rain Shadow to play the role of Juanita's daughter. In any event, Avarato would want the necklace, and Miguel planned to benefit from the sale.

For the time being, however, he would amuse himself with the local lovelies at the farm boys' celebration this evening. There was time enough to let the pieces fall into place. Perhaps he could learn some more about the Neubauers and Rain Shadow's relationship to them. It could prove to be an interesting evening.

Arno Friedrich volunteered his stable for the celebration. Swept clean, the building still smelled of horses. The central corridor, wide enough to turn a team and a buggy, provided space for the dance floor, grooved planks that the men dropped into place with practiced ease. A scattering of sawdust, a platform laid for the musicians, tables set up for food, beer kegs, punch, and the festivities were under way.

"Mama, I can't see good from here," Slade complained.

"You can see as well as you need to." Rain Shadow brushed the wrinkles from the pallet she'd laid for him at a stall's entrance. "We're not taking the chance of having someone accidentally step on you and hurt your leg. Nikky and I will bring whatever you need. Are you hungry?''

He pouted.

She shrugged and straightened, smoothing the damask skirt over her hips. She fervently hoped she didn't look as out of place as she felt in the deep blue skirt and high-necked white blouse. She'd stuffed the toes of the high-topped leather shoes borrowed from Annette with newspaper. Wanting to belong to this world, she would no doubt trip over her own feet and make a fool of herself.

Her gaze caught the young woman carrying a picnic basket toward a table. Sissy. Her spice-brown hair was gathered from the sides and hung in long, lustrous waves down her back. Her stylish blue and white checked dress showed off an embroidered bodice, a row of lace standing up around her slender neck. The cuffs, too, were trimmed with matching lace, drawing attention to her delicate white hands.

Rain Shadow watched Sissy remove cookies and pie from the basket. She glanced at her own hands and frowned at the tiny calluses at the base of each finger. How did these women keep their hands so soft and white? She wasn't allowed time to consider.

Fiddle and harmonica music filled the stable. Franz Neubauer bowed before her and extended his arm. She smiled at Anton's gregarious brother and linked her arm through his. He led her through a Turkish trot and a reel before escorting her from the floor.

"Thank you." He smiled with another gallant bow. "You're looking especially pretty this evenin'."

Tom Simms became her next partner, and after that the single men took turns dancing with her. All were friendly, and one or two were good dancers. She decided to enjoy herself.

Pretending disinterest in the string of dance partners vying for a turn around the floor with Rain Shadow, Anton caught Sissy's hand and led her to one of the tables heaped with food. "Hungry?"

She placed a few cookies on her plate while he piled his with sandwiches and potato salad. She followed, and he picked their way to a row of available folding chairs lining the wall. "I haven't seen you lately, Anton."

"I've been busy."

She nibbled at a molasses cookie. "Will you come have dinner with my family one night this week?"

The sought-after blue skirt and white blouse twirled by.

"Sure." He pictured the fawn-colored fringed dress. Sunkissed silken skin. Brown-tipped—

"How about Wednesday?"

"Wednesday would be nice." He looked into Sissy's caramel eyes. Would Sissy kiss him in broad daylight? Would she breathe hard and fast when he pressed his face to her breasts? He thought of the manner in which he'd coupled with his first wife—quickly, because she didn't like it. Hard and fast, because she'd goaded him until he was angry. In the dark; his body disgusted her.

How would he bear it again? Was he wicked for wanting so much more? He glanced at Sissy's hands, delicate and sprinkled with freckles. Would she touch him in the ways a man yearned to be touched? Small but strong tanned hands had burned themselves into his lusty imagination. Lord, have mercy! Was he torturing himself until he'd never be satisfied with any woman?

He shook himself and resumed eating. He was marrying Sissy to take care of Nikky, and she definitely met all those requirements.

"Wanna try a piece of my mince pie?"

"Sure." He watched her move away, trying not to compare the way her hips looked in that dress to another's slim shape in a pair of snug wool trousers. He forced himself to look away and surveyed his brother Jakob on the musician's stand, fiddle tucked under his chin. A tall figure entering the stable caught his attention.

Damn!

Rain Shadow eyed the cold drink table over Erich Spengler's shoulder. Anton cut in, and her lanky partner bowed out. Anton took one of her hands in his and placed his other hand at her waist.

"He's here."

She met his intense blue gaze. Realization dawned, and panic quickened her pulse.

Her steps faltered. Anton urged her through the motions. Alarm rising in her throat, she glanced around.

"Over by the door to the forge."

She scanned the wall and spotted him. Dressed in dark brown slacks and a ruffled white shirt, Miguel de Ruiz stood out among the farmers. He held a jar of foamy amber liquid and spoke to the man next to him. His onyx gaze swept the dancers, discovered her and held her in view.

"What's he doing here?"

Anton squeezed her hand. "Drinking beer and chatting, near as I can tell. No laws against that."

Rain Shadow's breath grew short, and her chest constricted. "Slade," she whispered. "He can't see Slade." She attempted to pull away, but Anton's grip held her fast.

"Relax. Soon as I saw him come in I had our pas take the boys for a buggy ride." Anton took her chin between his thumb and forefinger and forced her to look at him. "Don't say anything about his leg for five seconds. Which situation is more dangerous?"

She nodded her agreement, and he released her face.

"Just act natural for a while longer, and we'll leave early."

"He has no right." Anger rose until her body trembled.

Anton wanted to pull her against him and ease her fear. Instead he increased the pressure of his hand at her waist and watched her luminous violet gaze rise to his.

"I told Slade the truth," she said as though he'd asked her. "That his father left without marrying me or even knowing about him."

He nodded. "I would've expected that."

"But how would he feel if he knew his father was here— close enough to see?" she asked, fear injecting a husky quaver into her voice. "He'd want to meet him. He doesn't know what kind of a man Miguel is. He's too young to understand!"

Anton took both her hands. "Let's go outside."

"But—"

"It's all right. Come on." He led her past the tables of food and drink, past a few curious glances, into the chilly night air. They stood out of the wind beneath a lean-to near the corner of the building.

"Telling Slade the truth took courage. I haven't had the guts to tell my son about his mother yet. I know he should hear it from me, though, not from someone in town when he's older and can understand. I'd like it if he never had to, but someday he will."

"That's different, Anton. She's dead. She can't hurt him."

"She's already hurt him."

She turned away. "What's that got to do with—"

Anton grabbed her shoulder and turned her toward him. "What if this was your pa? Think about it. You who wants to find your family at the cost of everything else."

"You don't know what you're talking about."

"Don't I? What if you had a chance to meet your pa when you were seven years old, but Two Feathers took it on himself to decide, 'No, that wouldn't be good for her,' so you never got to know him at all, good or bad?"

She breathed decisively through her nose, her lips taut with anger. Wind flapped the canvas over their heads, and the chill crept into their clothing. She hated him for putting it like that! An uncontrollable shiver shook her shoulders.

"You don't know what you're talking about," she repeated.

"I want you to see it from a little boy's eyes for a minute, just in case Slade's curious. Ruiz is dangerous. You have every right as Slade's mother to decide what's best and protect him. You're a good mother."

She wouldn't cry again! She wouldn't! She raised her chin. "Thank you."

"You may not be able to protect him, though. He might find out and wonder why you kept his father from him."

Damn him! He was right!

His form loomed tall and broad in the darkness before her. Close enough to touch. Close enough to feel the warmth emanating from his body. Close enough to step forward and fold herself into his steadfast arms. He was a comfort too easily obtained. It would be too easy to lean on his strength, too easy to grow accustomed to his protection and solidarity.

With deliberate restraint, Rain Shadow stood where she was. Soon she would be gone, gone from this man and his strong arms and his enveloping family. She and Slade and Two Feathers would make a new life, and Anton would marry Sissy Clanton. Why did that recurring thought plague her?

Rain Shadow needed to hold onto herself, needed to remember everything she'd worked for and wanted. She was tough as boot leather, and Miguel de Ruiz wasn't going to stop her from getting what she wanted or come between her and her son. She would tell Slade that Miguel was here.

Gravel scraped outside the lean-to. The acrid scent of a cheroot blew into the enclosure.

"What are you hiding from?"

Together they stepped out and spotted the orange glow of his cigar. He'd been wise enough to pull on a coat.

"What do you want, Ruiz?" Anton draped his arm around Rain Shadow's shoulder protectively.

"I do not see how it is any of your business, plowboy."

Anton stiffened. "I'm makin' it my business."

"Ah, he's 'makin'' it his business," he said to Rain Shadow, mimicking Anton's clipped speech.

"There's nothing for you here," she said quickly. "Why did you come?"

"I tried to tell you the other day when you would not give me the chance, *querida*."

"And I told you, I'm not interested. You might as well be on your way."

He sucked the cheroot till the embers glowed. The smoke turned Rain Shadow's stomach. "Where is the *nino?*"

Her heart slammed against her ribs like a loaded wagon hitting a brick wall. "Who?"

"The black-haired Indian boy with the broken leg. I heard about him. Are you hiding him?"

A waterfall roared inside her head. Over the rushing sound, she made out Anton's voice. "Look, Ruiz. Why don't you just move on? I'd hate to have to get the good townspeople to remove you."

"You would not want to make a scene." He flicked the end of his cheroot into the yard. "Is he mine?"

Rain Shadow forced her voice to work. "Who?"

"The boy. Is he mine?"

"You're unbelievably conceited. Of course he's not yours."

"His age is correct."

"He's not yours," she said convincingly because she meant it.

His laugh sounded more like a sneer. "You and the widower had better get back inside before his other girlfriend sends out a search party."

"Thanks for the warning."

"I must wonder why you have a respectable girl in there but you are out here with the squaw."

She was fast, but she wasn't strong enough to prevent Anton from leaping away from her. His fist cracked against Miguel's jaw with a pop that sounded like a rake handle breaking. Miguel landed unceremoniously in the drive. He scrambled to his feet and lunged. Anton sidestepped, caught Miguel's coat front and flung him away. He crouched and circled the dark man.

"He is ill-tempered, *querida*. You belong with me. My skin is dark, too. I would not hide you in the shadows like he does. He is ashamed of his desire for you."

Shame washed over Rain Shadow in a hideous, black torrent. How foolish she'd been to ever trust this man! He was contemptible!

A low growl erupted from Anton's throat. He lashed out with one long leg and caught Miguel in the stomach with his boot. Miguel groaned and fell to his knees on the black ground. Anton rushed at him, pummeling his face with a solid right, then a left.

Miguel pivoted away. In moments he recovered, staggered to his feet and poised himself. A silver glimmer of steel glinted in the moonlight.

"Anton, a knife!" Instinctively, Rain Shadow reached for the knife she always wore in her boot, her hand meeting only the short top of Annette's shoe. She didn't have her knife!

Miguel crouched and feinted. Anton circled warily. Miguel lunged and Anton deflected the knife, thrust his shoulder into Miguel's chest and shoved him backward. Miguel staggered. "Are you hot for her, widow man?" he panted. "She is a warm-blooded feline, is she not? Not good enough to marry, however. You will marry the cool miss in the gingham dress." He laughed. "No surprises."

Before either of them caught their balance, Anton had one enormous hand around Miguel's throat, pinning him to the ground. Rain Shadow hedged around the two scuffling men, mindful of their flying legs as they grappled for an upper position. They rolled, Miguel coming up on top. She rushed in, grabbing the back of his coat and yanking.

"Get back!" Anton shouted, enraged. Another sound escaped him, this time one of pain, and he cursed violently.

"Anton!"

"Get back!" He groaned. The terrible sound sent her running toward the stable door.

"A gun!" she demanded of the group of men sitting inside the doorway. "I need a gun!"

"What'sa matter, little lady?" a gray-bearded gentleman asked, peering over the tops of his spectacles.

"I need a gun. Now!"

"Arno, you got a gun?" Doc asked quietly from a checkers game behind her.

The stable owner started to rise. "On the wall opposite the forge."

"Is it loaded?" Rain Shadow asked, spinning.

"Yes, ma'am."

Skirts flying, she took off at a run, dodging dancers. Seconds later, the crowd parted and stared, but the music continued. Rain Shadow tore across the room, cocking the Remington. The old men were the first to follow her out the door.

"Miguel, you black heart! Get off him, right now!" she shouted into the cold night air. She fired the rifle into the sky, the shot echoing between the buildings. Closer, she was surprised to see Anton leave his prominent position in the scuffle and stagger backward. "Get out of here, or my next shot won't be aimed at the stars!"

Deliberately, she cocked the rifle. "And I hit what I aim for."

Miguel stood slowly. "He is not for you. You will be sorry."

"I'm already sorry."

The old men and several dancers gathered outside the stable, the curious crowd growing.

"You have not seen the last of me. I have some information you will find extremely interesting."

She lowered the barrel from its skyward position. "The next time I see you I'll aim for your heart. Or whatever passes for one."

Miguel edged toward the corner of the barn. "This information concerns a briolette-cut gemstone. Think about it, *querida.*"

A minute later, atop his magnificent stallion, he leapt the corral fence and galloped away into the night.

Holding his shoulder, Anton plopped ungracefully onto his behind on the hard-packed drive. Amazingly, he chuckled.

Lowering the rifle, Rain Shadow ran to him. "Are you all right?"

"Do I look all right?"

She knelt beside him. "You're bleeding!"

"And you thought I wasn't human." He flopped on his back.

"Get the doctor!" she shouted over her shoulder. Two Feathers appeared at her side. "Father, bring the travois I made for Slade."

The crowd moved in for a closer look.

Doc knelt on Anton's other side. "Bring a lantern!"

Erich Spengler held a kerosene lamp over Anton's feet. The left side of Anton's shirt glistened crimson with blood. Rain Shadow unbuttoned it with trembling fingers. Doc peeled the fabric away from his shoulder.

Unconsciously, Anton waved his right hand toward her. She grasped it and resisted pressing her lips against his knuckles. "I'm sorry," she whispered. Had Miguel's words infuriated Anton so because they were true? Hadn't she thought the same things herself? Hadn't she suspected he was sickened by his desire for her? This was all her fault. "Can you hear me?"

Eyes shut, mouth slack, he nodded and pressed his thumb into her palm.

"Let's take him home and clean this up," Doc said, interrupting her thoughts. "You okay, missy?"

She nodded. Above Doc, the glow of the lantern illuminated a face. A pale oval face, framed by nutmeg tresses. Sissy.

Chapter Nine

Pale, freckled hands smoothed the blanket and tucked the coverlet under Anton's chin. Rain Shadow watched Sissy fuss over Anton's long, sleeping form and turned away. Picking up the gory rags, she dropped them into the already bloodstained basin of water. Of course Sissy's hands were soft and smooth. She hadn't boiled cheesecloth in soda water to make rags. She hadn't wrung out blistering hot dressings and soaked them in carbolic acid to disinfect Anton's wound. She hadn't washed the doctor's instruments and placed them in the hot oven.

No! While Annette and Rain Shadow prepared dressings, Sissy hovered in the bedroom doorway, reluctant to watch Doc clean the wound. Jakob sat on Anton's legs for the suturing, Rain Shadow snipping lengths of catgut and threading the needles.

Now, after swallowing a third of a bottle of the corn liquor Johann produced, Anton slept. And Sissy fussed. She plumped the pillows behind Anton's head. Rain Shadow swallowed a momentary wave of resentment and carried the basin downstairs.

She dumped the water before looking in on the boys, lying side by side in the enormous bed. To Slade's delight, Rain Shadow had moved her son into Nikolaus' room so that Anton could recuperate in his own bed. Both children turned sleepy heads toward her.

"Your pa's okay, Nikky," she reassured softly, and smoothed his fair hair away from his forehead.

"He ain't gonna die?"

"He's going to be good as new in a few days."

"I was awful scared seeing him laying in that wagon without moving."

"So was I." Terrified was more like it. Filled with remorse and guilt. Anything that happened to the Neubauers was her fault.

"Why did that man stab my pa, anyhow?"

"Yeah, what did Anton do to him?" Slade demanded defensively.

"Well...." Her son studied her with furtive black eyes. "That's something we have to talk about." He trusted her. Depended on her. "That man's name is Miguel de Ruiz. I knew him a long time ago."

She swallowed, her discomfort audible. The boys waited quietly, subdued by the evening's near tragedy. "He said he wanted to..." How did she explain this to children? They were far too young to understand the naive mistake she'd made. Too young to be subjected to a shrewd, self-seeking wastrel. "To be my friend again. But I don't want to see him anymore."

"Why not?" Nikky asked.

She sighed. "He disappointed me. Hurt me a lot. I'd be happy if I could forget him."

Nikolaus sat up and threw his sturdy little arms around her. "I don't like him if he hurt you, Rain Shadow. And I don't like him 'cause he hurt my pa. I don't like nobody hurtin' people I love."

Heart in torment, she hugged him back, remembering the things Anton had said about Nikolaus' mother hurting him.

She didn't like that woman very much for hurting someone she loved, either.

"Ma?"

The disenchantment in Slade's eyes cued her to his next question, inducing dread in her breast. "Yes?"

"Is that man my pa?"

She'd raised a bright boy. She wasn't surprised at his astuteness. She'd taught him the truth was always best, but she was bitterly sorry that this was the truth. "Yes, Slade."

Slowly, Nikolaus pulled from her arms and stared at his friend. "Gosh!"

Rain Shadow's bruised and aching heart went out to each of them. They were friends. One friend's father had stabbed the other friend's father. If she was confused, how must they feel?

"I hate him," Slade stated.

"Slade—" she began, almost guilty for the torrent of relief she experienced at his terrible words. He could have defended Miguel or sought a relationship with the deplorable man. Either of those reactions would have broken her maternal heart.

"I do. I hate him." He turned on his side, away from them.

She had prayed this day would never come. For herself as much as for Slade. How could she tell him not to feel shame for what his father had done? How could she help him understand that he had no control over another person's actions when guilt and shame consumed her, as well?

She was the one at fault. If she hadn't become foolishly involved with Miguel in the first place, none of this would have happened. Anton wouldn't be lying in the other room hurt. Nikky and Slade—

She leaned over her son and kissed his head. No. Slade wouldn't be here at all. She crawled between them in the feather bed, and the boys cuddled into her embrace on either side. What good were regrets now? She would make it up to them. All of them. Somehow.

Miguel de Ruiz had hurt the people she loved.

Anton developed a fever during the night. Down the hall, the woman he'd asked to marry him slept in Jakob and Lydia's former room. It would be of little use to wake Sissy; she'd been unable to look at the wound in Anton's shoulder, and she'd turned as red as a June radish every time her gaze had come in contact with his broad bare chest.

Rain Shadow watched his face as he slept. He'd jumped to her defense. The thought still astonished her. She was accustomed to taking care of herself. And Slade. And recently, Two Feathers. Miguel's venomous words had shamed her beyond tolerance, and she regretted Anton had heard them. He'd never held a high opinion of her, and Miguel's accusations couldn't have raised it. Beneath the compress, the wound appeared red and feverish. She prepared fresh dressings and perched on the bed's edge.

His shoulder was on fire. Rain Shadow bathed his face, neck and upper body with cool water. Her hands were cool and soothing against his skin. Through a haze of pain and fever, her touch inadvertently speared him with desire. Lord, help him, he prayed she couldn't gauge the effect she had on his traitorous body.

He felt her raise the bandage. Waiting for her reaction, he cringed inwardly. His shoulder had pained almost this bad for two nights after a roll of barbed wire had laid it open. Peine had refused to care for him, and he'd been too embarrassed to ask Annette, so he'd cleaned and bandaged himself. How Peine had hated the resulting scar! Now he'd have two on the same shoulder.

He opened his eyes, rolled his head and focused on her. "You still up?"

Her head came up in surprise. "I slept with the boys for a little while."

"Two Feathers?"

"I finally convinced him the lodge wasn't safe. He spread his blankets in your father's room."

He nodded his approval.

"Doc left medicine for you." She worked the cork from the bottle.

"I don't need it."

"You'll have a fever for a while before the wound begins to heal." She offered the spoon authoritatively, and he accepted the dose. "I need to change the dressing."

He wrapped his long fingers around her wrist, but she brooked no argument and peeled the bandage away. Anton waited for her to flinch or for disgust to cloud her features. Instead, she performed the task as if she were caring for her son or cleaning up after a meal. "You saw the other scar?"

"Hmm?" She wrung the cloth and draped the cool towel across his chest.

"The other scar. On my shoulder."

Dark, dark eyes discovered the raised V, and some unsqueamish emotion flickered there.

He ran a dry tongue over his lips and swallowed. The wet cloth soothed. Was it possible he didn't disgust her? "It's not something a lady should look at."

She gave him a puzzled glance. "Why not?"

"Just shouldn't."

"In case you haven't noticed, I'm not one of the fainting belles you're accustomed to. Sioux braves bear scars of courage from the Sun Dance, and everyone is injured at some time or another. Scars aren't repulsive to me—but then I'm no lady."

"Don't say that," he denied, but then thought of her skinning rabbits and gutting grouse. Her eyes told him she was thinking of the cruel things Ruiz had said.

She shrugged her shoulders. "Anton, I'm sorry."

"It isn't your fault."

"Yes. It is. This wasn't your problem."

"If you think I can stand by while Ruiz insults you, think again."

"Why should you care?" She lifted her solemn gaze to his face. "I've done nothing but get under your skin since Slade and I happened to you."

He frowned at her words. Happened to him. He couldn't have said it better. She irritated him beyond reason. She possessed none of the qualities necessary to interest a man such as himself. She wasn't a good housekeeper or a cook. She was more at home in the open air than in a house. She worked in unflattering men's clothing, occasionally donning calico and damask like an adolescent playing dress-up. She was frank rather than coy, unaffected rather than coquettish, mouthy, willful. . . .

Why should he care?

Sissy possessed all the virtues he looked for. She was everything he'd told himself he needed in a wife. He had asked Sissy to marry him. Why then, did *this* woman's innocent touch arouse him?

"While you're on my land, staying—more or less—in my house, it's up to me to look out for you. Why are you in here instead of sleeping, anyway? Why didn't you let someone else do this?" Once the questions were out, he wanted to bite them back. He didn't want her to think he cared. He couldn't care. Caring opened a person up, subjected them to inevitable heart damage, and he was beyond that.

"It's my fault you're hurt. I'll take care of you."

Of course. She felt responsible. She didn't care a straw about him. The weight he experienced pressing in on his chest had nothing to do with her words. He couldn't be disappointed because he'd never expected—never wanted—anything more.

He closed his eyes. His head hurt and his shoulder throbbed. This thinking wasn't doing him any good. Why did he care? He had to forget her problems and concentrate on marrying Sissy. Though his body flushed with excessive heat, the thought left him cold.

The following night his fever raged. Rain Shadow had been grateful for help that evening, but Annette had long since gone home. After checking on Anton during a particularly peaceful half hour, Johann had followed Two Feathers out to the cabin they'd cleaned out.

Sissy brought fresh water.

"Thanks." Rain Shadow took the basin and rinsed clean cloths. "I know Anton appreciates your help."

Sissy raised her wide-eyed gaze. "He'll be all right, won't he?"

"Of course he will. He's fighting the infection right now. He's strong."

"Nikolaus?"

Both women turned to Anton.

"Nikolaus?" he said again.

Sissy stood quietly, clasping and unclasping her pretty hands.

"Nikolaus is asleep, Anton," Rain Shadow soothed.

"Don't carry the lantern into the barn without me." His eyelids flickered as if he could see his son behind them.

Rain Shadow wrung a rag and placed it on his forehead. He slept. Both woman slumped in rockers they carried from other bedrooms. Rain Shadow listened to the tick of Anton's pocket watch on the bedside table and remembered the first night she'd come to this room. The night she'd discovered him taking care of her son. The memory was vivid: his tall, golden form in the lantern light, his intense blue eyes. As his wife, Sissy would hear the tick of that watch echo long into every night. Did the thought occur to her?

"Peine!"

Her pulse stopped. She jumped forward in the chair and placed her hand over her breast until her heart beat again. Sissy, too, sat forward, startled.

"Peine!" Anton shouted in his delirium. Head rolling, he thrashed against the sheets.

"Anton, lie still." Rain Shadow held his good shoulder and pressed him back.

"Oh, God, the baby!" Terror-stricken suffering glazed his voice. Torture. More pain than she could imagine sharpened his voice and transmitted long-endured grief to Rain Shadow's heart. He kicked the sheets off and fought her tenuous hold. "The baby!"

Sissy's eyes filled with helpless tears. Her cheeks blazed crimson.

"Go to bed," Rain Shadow ordered. "I'll stay with him."

Sissy fled.

"Shh, Anton, everything's okay. Just lie back and rest." Rain Shadow struggled with his greater strength and weight, careful not to hurt his injured shoulder. "Shh," she whispered, soothingly. He responded by allowing her to press him against the pillows and cover his nakedness with the sheet. She ran her fingers through his thick, damp hair, rubbed his temples and forehead as she did when she put Slade to sleep. Long minutes later his body went slack.

Raking his hair in rhythmic strokes, Rain Shadow watched his eyelids flicker, hallucinations haunting him.

"Dear Lord, not the baby..." Racking sobs shook his broad chest. "My baby..."

"Anton, what?" she cried against his hair. "Shh."

"I couldn't save her. I couldn't. I couldn't save the baby. I tried." Tears squeezed from beneath his tightly closed eyelids. Anguish furrowed his brow.

"You did all you could." She washed his face, wiped the tears from his cheeks. "I'm so sorry. So sorry," she whispered.

"I think my face is burned."

"No. You're fine." His expression softened, and his hand groped blindly at his side. "You're just fine here with me." Rain Shadow picked his hand up and pressed her lips against the back of his fingers. What horrors did he relive? What bitter agony brought tears to this strong, confident man?

Once again his body relaxed. He opened his eyes and looked at her. "Rain Shadow?"

"Yes."

Within minutes his breathing grew even, and his eyes closed. An hour later she changed the bedding and gave thanks that his fever had finally broken.

"Where is she?"

On her way past Anton's room two days later, Rain Shadow paused in the hallway. "Where is who? Sissy?"

"Of course, Sissy! Who the hell else would I be talking about?" He flounced back against the pillows and winced.

"In the kitchen. Smells like she's baking something."

"Go down there and tell her I'm sleeping. I'll be sleeping the rest of the day. Don't let her come up here and plump my pillows or water the flowers one more time! And tell her I'll choke if I have to look at another piece of mince pie!"

"I think it's apple."

"Apple, mince, they all taste the same."

"Anton, her pies are heavenly. Almost as good as Lydia's."

"Who the hell's side are you on, anyway?" he shouted.

She leaned insolently against the doorjamb and tried not to grin. "Since when have there been sides? Was a battle line drawn while I was out riding?"

Frustration lined his face. "You can go out riding! You don't know what I'm going through! Dammit! I can't take one more day of this bed! And I can't take another minute of her fussin'."

"Seems to me you'd better get used to it. She'll be fussing over you and Nikolaus for a good long time—the rest of your lives."

Anton's expression darkened into a scowl. He'd thrust himself smack in the middle of this quandary. He wouldn't do anything to hurt Sissy, yet how in the sam-hell was he going to live with himself? The more he saw of Sissy, the more he fought the nagging fear that he'd done something he would regret. The doubt would never have grated on him like this if not for—

He frowned at the woman who'd undermined his confidence. "You sure know how to depress a man."

That night the dream taunted him again—at least at first it seemed like the same dream. It wasn't. In this scenario, Anton made it as far as the splintered hole chopped in the side of the barn. But the hole was smaller, and no amount of kicking or hitting or tearing at the wood enlarged it. The opening grew so small his face barely fit. Through it he could see a child trapped inside, a small boy standing still as stone amid the flapping flames. There was no sound from the boy, no screams or cries; in fact, all Anton could hear was the crackle and hiss of the consuming fire.

"Nikolaus?" No, no! Nikolaus hadn't been in the barn that day! Intolerable heat scorched his face, but he couldn't tear his gaze from the boy. The flames flickered momentarily, then dropped to a level that allowed Anton to secure a better view. For one suspended moment, the heat subsided, and the fire almost sucked itself backward. The child's face came into focus with terrifying clarity.

"Slade!"

Anton jerked awake, sitting upright at the bed's edge. *Slade?* Why this startling alteration in the dream? His shoulder throbbed as though he'd moved it too quickly. He raised his arm and winced. A knife fight with a lunatic was probably enough to give the most stoic of men a nightmare or two.

A sliver of light appeared at the door and widened. "Anton?" Rain Shadow glided to the end of his bed on bare feet, her white gown lit from behind like an opaque chimney lamp. The hall light defined every curve and hollow of her smooth-limbed form, displayed the size and shape of her perfect breasts and nearly stopped his heart. His body surged with the gut reaction he'd come to expect.

She scrutinized him. "Anton?"

"I'm all right." *I'd be better if you'd move away from that light.* "Go back to bed." He adjusted the sheet in his lap.

She padded around the side of the bed so that her gown was no longer transparent, and he breathed easier. The cotton looked soft to the touch, the cut surprisingly demure. "The dream again?" she asked intuitively.

Embarrassed but curious, he asked, "How do you know about the dream?"

"You had it several times during your fever." She picked up one of his pillows from the floor. Sissy would have plumped it importantly and tucked it behind him, but Rain Shadow held it. "Lie back. Do you want your medicine?"

"No." He took the pillow from her hands. Reluctantly, he allowed her to press him back, her cool fingers against his shoulder anything but soothing. The dream had cast an ominous shadow across his already gloomy heart. Ruiz had goaded him into the fight that had landed him in this bed with another unsightly scar on his shoulder. He'd been in more than his share of scraps, most with his own brothers, and he could handle himself in a fight. But he'd never fought another person who would gleefully maim or kill him. Ruiz would.

He'd seen it in his eyes that night. Something dark and dangerous. Unmerciful. What did Ruiz want? At first it seemed he wanted Rain Shadow, but—Anton wasn't sure anymore. Was it Slade he wanted? Something Ruiz had said while Anton lay slipping from reality escaped him. The *vaquero* was too close to stumbling across the truth about Slade. He had, in fact, uncovered it, but Rain Shadow had been quick to deny it. He'd gotten close. Too close for Anton to rest easy until something was settled. But what could he do?

The scrape of the rocker against the wooden floor caught his attention. Rain Shadow tugged the chair near, the terror provoked by his dream dissipating as she settled in. "There's something I want to say now that you're better."

From the strip of light that bled in from the hall, he could see little of her features, and he was grateful. Just the memory of her haunting amethyst eyes was enough to unnerve him; he didn't want to shame himself in the light. He had in broad daylight seen her perfect breasts, buried his face there and knew the unforgettable, arousing smell of her silken-soft skin. Knowing all that and knowing, too, that she was forbidden was a desolate sort of pleasure-pain. The darkness lent an anonymity that preserved his determination.

She hesitated and drew a quivering breath. "I heard you because I wasn't sleeping myself. I can't get what happened out of my mind. I'm so sorry," she whispered.

"You don't have anything to be sorry about. I'm responsible for myself."

"Yes, you are, but you're not responsible for Slade and me. You're not responsible to defend my honor or fight my battles."

"Your battles? Good Lord, woman, he provoked me! You were perfectly calm, so he worked on me. I could have handled it better."

"I don't think so." Her head lowered as she studied her hands in her lap. "I think he would have found a way, used any means to stir up trouble."

"Why?"

She leaned back once, twice, the ancient rocker creaking beneath her minimal weight. "I don't know."

He'd seen her fear that first time, the day Ruiz had shown up at the house without warning, and his first glimpse of her vulnerability had lodged in his chest, seized something tender near his heart and pounced on it. The bruise was still sore. Her independence was carefully preserved, her determination well-tended. She guarded the security of her tiny, unlikely family like a badger with a litter.

He stared at the ceiling. Her hand closing over the back of his took him by surprise. "This was my fault. I want you to know how bad I feel. You were nothing but generous bringing Slade here. Getting Two Feathers and I was more than you bargained for, but once you were stuck with us, you did okay. My father hasn't been this happy in years. Maybe never." Her thumb brushed lazily across the backs of his fingers. "Slade, too."

Her touch fanned sparks he did his damnedest to deny. As whenever he was alone with her, a perpetual blaze simmered. *And you, Rain Shadow? What about you? Have you been happy here, too? Don't care about me now. Not now. Don't offer me your respect or touch me as if you need that physical contact as much I do. I want you so badly I could pull you down with me right here, right now, but I've asked Sissy to marry me.* "I've been impossible, and you know it. Don't try to make me sound good."

The ever-present tick of his pocket watch filled the next minute's silence, and though he couldn't see her, he had the distinct impression she smiled. He turned his hand and captured her small one in his palm, wondering when the last time someone had cared for him like this had been. Never. Not since his mother, and she'd died when he was young. What other woman had appreciated anything he'd ever said or done? None.

Was there another woman as poised and proud and bull-headed as Rain Shadow in the entire world? He doubted it. Her stubborn confidence was appealing, but these rare glimpses of vulnerability drew him to her more surely. There must be something he could do. As much as she would object, he had to find a way to protect her. He could picture her hackles rising if he suggested such a thing, but he had to find a way. Ruiz wouldn't get to her or her son if he could help it.

How could he prevent it?

Chapter Ten

Standing on Jack's back, Rain Shadow unerringly flicked tin cans from the fence rail with Smith & Wesson's new model three revolver. The pony routinely circled the corral, obeying commands Anton never heard or saw.

He'd had to give up holding his breath as he watched her ride, bare feet on the horse's rump; he would've turned blue an hour ago. He forced himself to relax, ease the tension from his neck and look the opposite direction. It was good to be outside, though frustrating that his arm still hurt so much. He walked to keep warm, scanning the countryside, wondering where Ruiz was and how long it would be before he returned. As long as that man was out there, his family wasn't safe.

A quarter of a mile north, a wagon was headed for the farm. With his good right hand, Anton pulled out his watch. Three twenty-five. Odd time for visitors. By three-thirty a team pulled Garner Clanton's black buggy up the drive with Sissy perched beside him, father and daughter wrapped in jackets and scarves. Anton disguised the plummeting sensation in his stomach by waving. Back so soon? Johann had just taken her home day before yesterday.

He met the wagon and stood, embarrassed that he couldn't help her down. Her father assisted and turned his ruddy, freckled face to Anton. "I'll be havin' a word with your pa. Know where he is?"

"Barn, last I saw him." Anton watched Garner's red plaid back, then turned to Sissy. "Want to go in and warm up?"

She frowned toward the house for a moment, then shook her head. "No. I want to talk to you."

Oh. Was this the day he'd forced from his mind? Had she come to give him her answer to his proposal? He glanced toward the porch, but decided it was warmer in the sun. "Let's walk."

Brittle leaves crunched beneath their shoes, and Anton wondered which of the Clantons had come with a purpose. The longer the silence stretched, the more he wondered. In the back of his mind, he realized Rain Shadow must have holstered her gun in deference to their callers.

Sissy stopped abruptly. Anton turned and studied her, skin pale in the chill air, freckles dotting her nose and cheeks in sharp relief. Fat sausage curls hung beneath her dark woolen cap. "I've thought and considered like I promised."

Here it comes. He'd asked for it! Why did his stomach feel sick? He'd ticked off her virtues as fast as a seven-day clock wound tight and thought her the perfect choice. Too late for second thoughts. Too late for regrets. Wasn't it? What would he do if she said yes? Kiss her? She would expect him to. He should. He managed a nod.

"I can't marry you, Anton."

He would have to act as if he was pleased, but Lord, how was he going to spend the rest of his life with—"What?"

"Something's just not right. I like you. I like you a lot, and maybe someday—well, I don't know. I just know there's not enough there to start a life on, even for someone like me." She inspected her gloved hands self-consciously.

Well, he'd be— She'd turned him down! He stared at her speechlessly. He knew she'd never had a better offer. He wasn't such a bad catch—never smoked, didn't drink much, worked hard. *Hell.* He'd fathered a fine-looking son, owned hundreds of acres of prime farmland and worked it well. What did she want? The answer came to him with the chill wind at his back. A pronouncement of love. *You've got the wrong man then, little girl.*

"Truth is," she admitted, and brought her gaze to his face, "I have feelings for Nathan Beker. Once he knows I turned you down, he'll court me. He told my papa so." Her pale cheeks took on high color.

Anton stifled a self-derisive snort, his ego as ragged as a chipped tooth. If not for his stinking male pride, what the hell did he care? He'd been tied in knots thinking of committing himself to her in the first place. She'd just let him off the hook, free and clear! He could swim away to bluer waters and never look back. The whole idea hadn't set well from the beginning. The sensation of relief confused him. He shot an involuntary glance toward the barn, unable to stifle the startling thoughts that immediately warmed and exhilarated.

He was uncommitted.

No. *Don't even think of letting any part of your shortsighted body influence your brain, Neubauer.* Maybe Helena McLaury was the better choice after all. He was marrying for Nikky anyway, not for self-gratification, and Nikky hadn't expressed any great fondness for Sissy.

"Well...." He stuffed his right hand in his coat pocket and leaned back on his heels. "It's best you were honest with me. Thanks for that."

"Any hard feelings?"

"None." He watched her gaze skitter away, remembered her perceivable tolerance of his kiss and immediately thought of Peine. His wife had tolerated him much the same. He was too wild, too undisciplined for her taste. Anton knew in his heart that Nathan Beker was better suited to Sissy than he.

Now, Rain Shadow... There was a woman who participated in a kiss. He flung the memory away. "C'mon. Let's get a cup of coffee to warm you for the ride home."

She smiled.

Half an hour later, he waved the Clantons off, his shoulder throbbing. He was glad of the pain, thankful for something to keep the buoyancy from his chest. He turned toward the house, stifling the urge to let loose an earsplitting, Nikolaus-like *Aw-right!*

Rain Shadow tucked Jack's curry brush in a leather bag and slapped his withers. "Now that you're settled, my handsome love," she said to the horse, "I have quail to cook."

Nearly every day since Anton had been hurt, she'd prepared meals, though not consenting to use their stove or oven. Anton had given up on trying to get her to stay in the house but had insisted she go no farther than the corral alone. She resented the restriction. No one had ever monitored how far she traveled or how late she returned. No one had ever come looking for her when she'd been alone for several hours, and accountability didn't rest comfortably.

She wanted to bathe in the stream, but knew Anton wouldn't stand for it. He'd already offered to have their fathers lug and fill the tub the Neubauers used for bathing into their kitchen. Instead, she'd carried water from the well to her lodge.

A small gray and white cat rubbed himself against the top of her boot, and she knelt to scoop him up. Out of the half dozen cats who had the run of the barn, this particular one had grown attached to her. She scratched his ears, and his contented purr rumbled beneath the silky fur.

"That's Runt." Anton pulled the wooden door shut behind him. "First time I saw him, I wondered if he would make it. Last time I saw him he was tormenting one of the late robins."

The cat raised his head and stared through slitted eyes as she scratched the white tuft under his chin. She couldn't imagine staying in one place long enough to give a cat a name or see it grow. Even seeing a bird's nest pointed out how transitory her life was. What would it be like to watch a robin build a nest and still be there when the fledglings first tried their wings?

"Almost done out here?" he asked.

Rain Shadow placed the cat on the straw-littered floor. "I started a cook fire. Tell the boys to wash for supper."

"Will do."

Something about his cheerful reply brought her head up to meet his eyes. The spirited look she read there signaled a change. What had happened? As soon as she'd seen Sissy daintily exit the wagon, she'd been foolishly glum. What was it to her if he wanted to marry that insipid, doe-eyed paragon of domesticity?

He left, and Rain Shadow plucked her hat from a rail post. How would the silly girl ever maintain her prudery as his wife? She'd been mortified at the mere sight of any portion of his anatomy during his recovery. She'd baked and stewed and laundered at the drop of a hat, but Rain Shadow suspected most of those chores were used as an escape to keep her from his room. She couldn't fathom a mince pie satisfying Anton Neubauer's appetite on his wedding night.

"Give the girl a chance," she muttered to herself, skewering her birds on the spit and suspending them over the fire. She crouched and warmed her hands near the flames. Anton, given half a chance, could warm the frostiest resistance.

She knew.

She knew how every callus on his palms felt sliding across sensitive skin. Those hands would thaw Sissy out. She knew the hard-soft bulk of his strength against her aroused body. That exciting pressure would light a spark under Sissy's primness.

Rain Shadow crossed her arms over her breasts and stared hard at the dressed birds starting to turn golden brown. She'd learned more. Much more than he'd ever have allowed had he been able to prevent it, but he'd been indisposed. He was capable of loving deeply and passionately, but still grieved for his wife and—what Rain Shadow had assumed from his feverish ravings—baby. Perhaps the woman had died giving birth to Nikky's younger brother or sister. The fires in his nightmares confused her, so she easily explained them to herself as hallucinations born of his high temperatures.

He'd be an unconventional and stormy lover. That would toast Sissy Clanton's shy uncertainties. *Wouldn't it?* Rain Shadow watched succulent juice form on the crisp skins. The audible hiss as it dripped into the coals brought her out of her reverie. What did she care? She had Miguel to worry about.

"Eating with us?" Anton asked when she delivered the quail to the kitchen, the look in his eyes a direct challenge.

Thus far, she'd managed excuses, but tonight nothing credible came to mind. She shrugged out of her coat and washed her hands. "Where are our fathers?"

"The cabin, I guess. I'd send Nikolaus for them, but I don't want him out alone. They'll show up." One-handed, he set plates around the table.

She stood by awkwardly until he plunked a cutting board on the table and attempted slicing a loaf of bread, then edged him out of the way. "Let me."

Watching her deft slices over her shoulder, his gaze fixed on her breasts, bobbling beneath her thin flannel shirt. Instantaneous desire, never far from the surface, sprang to life. Pulled by a force beyond himself, he leaned forward until his face was inches from her neck and inhaled her clean, outdoor smell. Her hand stilled on the knife. He knew she was aware of his closeness, but he indulged himself, the ferocious itch for her blotting out the pain in his shoulder, the hunger his his belly.

She made the last slice, deliberately laid the knife across the cutting board edge and turned slowly. Her dark lashes lifted from his shoulder to his neck, her eyes at last focusing on his, only to drop immediately to his mouth as if remembering the pleasure they'd shared. The tip of her tongue dipped out to trace her lips...unconsciously? The movement stirred him so that his lips parted and his breath lodged painfully in his chest. *Seductress.*

If only I'd known you first, he thought, regret eating at his gut. *If only I'd known you when I could still feel...still love...still hope.* Peine had never looked at him like this. But then, Peine had known him better, lived with him, experienced his lovemaking and hated his many imperfections.

Each time Rain Shadow provoked his response, he compared it to Peine, to the pain loving her had wrought. Learning the hard way had convinced him he didn't want to go through it again. For the first time, Anton questioned his motives. The distance he needed to keep obviously hadn't been fair to Sissy, and she'd recognized it. Hadn't cheated herself.

Was wanting her but having nothing to give in return fair to Rain Shadow?

Rain Shadow fought the urge to close her eyes and lean into him. Why did he torture her this way? What did he want? They both knew she wasn't what he wanted. And she wasn't foolish enough not to know why. Was he goading her? It would serve him right to call his bluff. They'd reached an almost comfortable coexistence, so why did he risk tipping the boat?

She knew he wanted her. Had known it from the first time he'd looked at her just this way. What did she have to lose? Respectability? He already thought her a woman of loose morals. Crazily, she raised her hand and outlined the silky texture of his upper lip with one finger, his nostrils flaring in response. She traced the lower lip, parting her own and reveling in the power it seemed she held in one slender finger, for his eyes darkened and the pulse at his throat beat wildly.

Encouraged, she flattened her palm against his rough cheek, the tips of her fingers sliding into the silky hair behind his ear. Rain Shadow drew herself on tiptoe and pulled his head to hers, meeting no resistance. His mouth clamped over hers, his tongue fulfilling her unspoken request against her own. He groaned into her mouth, a tortured sound that reached her toes.

She pulled away, her body alive with want. No. This was no joke. This was real and crazy and something she'd be denied because she wasn't Sissy Clanton. She was Princess Blue Cloud, Slade's mother, contestant for the sharp-shooter championship... orphan.

Boot heels clomped on the back porch, and they stepped apart guiltily, Rain Shadow turning her fuzzy gaze to the loaf of bread. Two Feathers and Johann entered with a sidelong glance. They passed an unspoken confirmation between them and silently washed at the sink.

"I'm glad Sissy ain't gonna be my ma."

The fire hissed, and something sounding like a screw rolled on the tabletop in the ensuing silence. Anton studied the clock parts scattered across the scarred table, lamplight glinting off his spectacles.

"She ain't?" Slade asked Nikolaus innocently. "Why?"

"'Cause her and my pa ain't comparable."

Anton cleared his throat and corrected, "Compatible."

"Yeah." Nikolaus sprawled on a quilt before the fireplace. He and Slade were munching popcorn Rain Shadow had popped over the flames.

"What's that?" Slade pressed.

Sitting between the boys, attention arrested, Rain Shadow sensed Anton behind her and employed untapped reserves of willpower not to turn around. Her skin flushed from the heat of the blaze.

"They don't like the same things. Ain't that right, Pa?"

For the first time she could remember, Anton didn't correct his son's grammar. "That's right."

"Sort of like you love popcorn, but she doesn't?" Slade twisted his body to get a better look at Anton.

"Well . . ." he hedged.

A log rolled in the fireplace, and Rain Shadow focused her attention on it.

"It's a little more complicated than that, but that's the gist," Anton said.

"Why're you glad, Nikolaus?" Slade tossed a kernel in the air and caught it on his tongue.

"She doesn't act like a ma and she has too many freckles. Did my mama have that many freckles?"

Rain Shadow held her quivering lips taut at Nikolaus' serious expression.

"No. But, Nikolaus, freckles aren't a reason not to like a person. Sissy isn't a mother yet, so how would she know how to act like one?"

"What *was* a good reason you decided not to marry her then, Pa?"

"Son," Anton said, an exasperated puff huffing out with the word. "You're too young to understand. Besides, some things are personal."

"Did she cry when you told her you didn't wanna marry her?"

"That's personal, too."

"Well, did she, Pa?"

"Nikolaus."

Suddenly the source of his embarrassment struck Rain Shadow. Laughter welled up inside her and bubbled over. She clasped her hand over her mouth too late and convulsed with mirth. *Sissy had turned him down!*

"What the hell's so funny?" At last she turned toward him. He jerked his gold-rimmed spectacles from his nose and stood.

"*I—I'm—sorry.*" His indignant expression provoked another fit of laughter.

"Is my personal life so damned amusing to you?"

She smothered another grin. "Don't cuss in front of the boys."

Vexed, he spun on his heel and stomped toward the kitchen where his father was intent on saving his last two red kings. Anton poured himself a cup of coffee and scowled out the window into the blackness.

"You going to check the animals tonight?" Johann asked.

"I'll do it," he returned.

"It's getting harder and harder to keep Rain Shadow in at night, but we have to be careful. Two Feathers found a cold campsite on the east ridge this mornin'. Ruiz is still out there."

Anton took a scalding sip of strong brew without glancing into the room. "Wish I knew his intent."

Two Feathers grunted in agreement.

"Do you think it's her or the boy?" Anton asked the old Indian.

Wizened black eyes lifted to inspect Anton's face. "What he wants is for his own profit. Of that I am sure."

Anton nodded grimly. "I'm sick of waiting around for his next move like a sitting duck. I think I should go after Ruiz. Turn the tables on him."

"What then? Kill 'im?" Johann asked.

Anton met his father's eyes. Of course not. But there must be something he could do.

Johann tamped his pipe with fresh tobacco. "Or ride into his camp and say, 'Would you mind leaving these parts? You're tryin' me'?"

Anton slammed the mug down on the table in frustration. "There must be some way to discourage him!"

Johann shrugged his shoulders. "Too bad she ain't married."

Two Feathers nodded sagely.

"Married?" Anton frowned at his father as if he was hallucinating.

"Yup. If it's Rain Shadow he wants, a husband would clear that right up. If it's the boy, her husband could sign some papers and have legal rights."

"You sure about that?"

Johann shrugged negligently. "Could check it out easy enough."

His pipe held between his teeth, he focused his attention once again on the checker game. A spiral of smoke curled past Johann's grizzly white brow. Anton grabbed his coat from a hook and wondered at the sheepish look the two old men exchanged. "I'll be in shortly."

He'd lain awake nights with his shoulder throbbing, trying to uncover a solution. Sending her to winter quarters would only relocate the problem, besides removing her from his protection. Ruiz had found her once, he'd find her again. Seeking the law didn't sound helpful. After all, Anton had thrown the first punch in that free-for-all. Ruiz could plead self-defense. He'd thought the situation over, always ending at a road leading nowhere.

But his father's suggestion was ridiculous. Who would marry her? That Tall Bear fellow from the show who'd joked about offering her father more horses?

Anton allowed the rich, pungent aromas of animals and grain to soothe his ire. Helplessness didn't sit easily. He offered Jack a handful of oats and rubbed the bony ridge between his eyes.

"You earn your keep, fella," he said softly, thinking of relentless circles in the corral, Rain Shadow standing surefootedly on the animal's back defying gravity while taking perfect aim at last night's bean cans.

Marry a woman like that? Nobody in his right mind would marry her! Anton fingered Jack's meticulously braided mane. For days he'd mulled over a solution to protect her and Slade from Ruiz. There was no justifiable reason for him to feel he should be the one to find an answer. His common sense told him to let her take care of herself as she craved. Every self-preserving instinct screamed for him to mind his own business. But something else, some illogical voice, overstepped all sense and sanity and prodded him to consider his father's idea.

He kneaded Jack's ear between his fingers and couldn't help recalling the loving words and caresses Rain Shadow bestowed on the animal. Earlier he'd had no means to protect her. If his father was right, he did now. He no longer held a commitment to Sissy. As mad as it sounded, marriage seemed like the all-round best solution so far.

Rain Shadow was surprised to discover sleet needling her cheeks when she stepped off the back porch. The house cushioned noises and weather she was accustomed to hearing inside her lodge. She buried her hands deep in her coat pockets and hurried to the barn.

Anton turned at the sound of the door sliding open and shut.

"Don't tell me I shouldn't be out here," she said defensively. "I'm sick of being cooped up in the house."

"I know the feeling well."

"You mean we have something in common?"

He set a bucket aside.

"Anton, I'm sorry I laughed."

He shouldered past her without comment.

The gray and white cat sidled against the top of her boot, and she smiled, inexplicably pleased with herself. She'd gotten to Anton, disturbed him on a level she'd never reached before. Why the thought warmed her inside she didn't know.

"Wanna ride into Butler with me?" Anton paused on the back porch. Rain Shadow's hair shone blue-black in the morning sunlight, her braid hidden inside her coat. She looked up from a shirt she'd been mending since breakfast. "What about the boys?"

"Annette's asked for them to stay at her place today. And our pas will be close by."

She considered.

"I thought we'd scout the east ridge on our way, check out those campsites."

"When do we leave?"

"How soon can you be ready?"

"Only need my hat and holster." Any other woman would've taken a good hour to prepare herself for a visit into town. Not her. She stabbed a needle into the flannel and stood. "Can you help me carry Slade over?"

"I'll get him. I have to grab a pair of boots." He ran stocking-footed up the stairs, pleased with the improved movement of his arm and shoulder.

Passing Nikolaus' room, Anton glanced in and stopped in his tracks. He stared at the empty bed for a full minute. Voices reached him, and he followed the sound. Entering the usually unoccupied bedroom, he discovered Nikolaus and Slade standing side by side in front of a long, low mirror, obviously chosen for its exceptional reflection of their painted faces. He stepped back against the doorjamb; they hadn't seen him. They spoke in husky, guttural voices, absorbed in a game of war paint and imaginary ponies.

Both wore loincloths. Bear claws hung from their necks, and their faces were masterpieces of ferocious black and white geometric designs, apparently painted by Slade. Anton wanted to laugh and tiptoe out to collect Rain Shadow. The thought disturbed him. When had he ever had the desire to share a moment like this with someone?

A realization hit him belatedly.

Slade stood beside Nikolaus, no sign of his splint. His long, narrow leg was every bit as sturdy as the other, and he was having the time of his life.

Anton leaned against the wall outside the door. Why, those two little scoundrels! How long had this trickery been going on? All the while his mother carried him and worried and slept in this house while wanting to be out in her lodge,

Slade had been pulling a fast one. And Nikolaus! His son had gone right along with the deception! What did they hope to gain?

Time. Time together as brothers. Time Rain Shadow could ill afford. Anton considered going downstairs for her after all. He considered it for about five seconds, padded to his room, stomped his feet into his boot heels and hollered, "You fellas ready to go over to Aunt Annette's for the day?"

Rain Shadow would hit the ceiling if she knew! She'd rant and rave and gather her son and father, pack her lodge and be out of here before the sun set tonight. He couldn't let that happen. For some reason unknown to himself, that damned obligation to protect her from Ruiz grew stronger with each passing moment. He couldn't shield her if she left.

Several thumps and bumps later, he strode down the hallway, paused to straighten a picture on the wall, and entered Nikolaus' room. Painted and feathered, two sets of wide innocent eyes greeted him, Slade's splints once again in place.

Anton thumped his chest. "Me friend. Me take braves to squaw's house make heap good cookies." The boys crumpled on the bed, chortling like conspiring brothers.

A small figure in a flat-crowned black hat and fringed buckskin jacket dismounted, tying a familiar painted pony to the hitching rail. Beside Rain Shadow the tall, blond farmer looped the reins of his bay over the rail next to hers. Neubauer scanned the street from beneath the brim of his dun-colored Stetson, and Miguel receded into the alleyway. The farmer spoke, pulled a watch from his pocket to show Rain Shadow, then kept her under observation until she entered the mercantile.

Neubauer crossed the street with long-legged strides and entered a one story building with *"J.J. Hawkins, Attorney at Law"* painted in block letters on a wooden sign above the door. Miguel leaned against the building and drew a cheroot from inside his coat. It had grown too cold to waste nights warmed by a camp fire, and he'd been waiting days for a response to his telegraphed message to Fredrico Avarato. His cash was nearly gone. A man like him deserved more.

How could he get close enough to convince her after that scene at the farmers' dance? Neubauer would be sorry.

No. Rain Shadow was his target, not the farmer. He must keep that in mind. If he could not come by the locket with her consent, he would secure it without. Separate her from her guard and take it. He puffed on the thin cigar, smoke drifting past his black brows. Before snow flew in this godforsaken place, he would have the locket in hand.

Rain Shadow slung her ammunition-laden saddlebags over her shoulder, her boots treading heavily on the wooden boardwalk.

"Rain Shadow!"

She turned and watched Anton lope beside her. "Finished?"

He nodded, considered offering to carry her bulging leather bags, but instead watched her stride to Jack and shift them from her shoulder to the pony's pack with little difficulty, humiliated to realize he probably couldn't have done as well, his shoulder tender as it was.

They mounted and rode toward the Neubauer farm, the ground beneath the horses' hooves hard from the cold. They cantered in silence for half a mile, the sky a heavy gray blanket above their heads.

"There's something I want you to think about."

Rain Shadow glanced at him, noting the tall, easy way he sat his bay. She raised one brow in question.

"I had a talk with Jed Hawkins back there. He's an attorney."

She waited for him to get to the point.

"He claims if you were married that your husband could sign an affirmation of some sort and Slade would legally be your husband's child."

She gazed at a barren stand of maple trees. "I guess somewhere in my plans for the future I've thought of marriage. I'd like Slade to have a father. A boy needs a man— not that Two Feathers hasn't been a wonderful companion and teacher for him," she added quickly. She gave him a sharp frown beneath the flat brim of her hat. "Why would you talk to a lawyer about something like that?"

His eyes diverted to the horizon. "Our fathers came up with a plan."

"A plan for what?" she asked, wariness in her voice.

"They think if we were married, Ruiz would be discouraged." At her surprised expression, he hurried on. "He'd have nothing to hang around for. You'd be taken, and Slade would have a legal father. His two reasons for staying would be gone."

That fever must have left Anton brainsick! Jack stepped over a hole, and she rocked with his gait. "You can't be serious."

His brows drew together and he scowled at her with a look too dark for such a golden man. "Look, I know I'm not the catch of the county. That's been pointed out to me recently. I'm not asking you to fall all over yourself with gratitude. I'm simply suggesting that you marry me to protect yourself from Ruiz."

"That's the craziest thing I've ever heard."

His lips drew into a taut line.

He wanted her physically, he'd made that obvious, but he certainly held no respect for her as wife material. "Did you stop at the saloon?"

"This isn't a lifetime commitment we're talking about here. We'd marry, Ruiz would go away, and we'd sign some more papers. The marriage would be annulled. You could go on your way, free and clear."

"Is there such a thing?"

"Hawkins assured me."

"Married people just go to a lawyer, sign a paper, and their marriage is over?"

He looked decidedly uncomfortable. "Well, only if they haven't . . ."

"Haven't what?"

"Haven't—consummated their marriage."

Consummated their marriage. The image of that act with Anton burned an indelible picture in her mind. She stared ahead sightlessly. Married. To Anton? Married to Anton and not consummate? Ridiculous. The entire idea was ridiculous. "Our fathers had this idea?"

"Turn me down if you want. I live for rejection."

"Oh, Anton, that's not it at all. Even if marriage did solve my problem, what would you gain?"

"Does everyone need a selfish reason to do things?"

The farm came into view. How would she know? The only man she'd ever trusted besides Two Feathers and Will Cody wasn't an example of chivalry. "I don't need your charity."

"Like hell you don't!"

She jerked her gaze to his blazing blue one. "Slade and I don't need anyone but each other. I've gotten by this far."

"Oh, and you've done so well."

Anger blazed hot in her cheeks. She threw him what she hoped was a shriveling scowl and kicked her heels into

Jack's withers. The contemptible jackass! Who did he think he was? She rode hard, her head lowered over the horse's neck. Jack seemed to love the exercise, and stayed dexterously ahead of Anton's much larger bay.

She vaulted from the horse, yanked her bags and the pad she used as a saddle from his back and turned him into the corral. He'd been trained to walk several turns around the enclosure, a means by which he cooled himself, affording her time to get ready for her next performance.

She ignored Anton as he galloped up the drive and dismounted. He led the General around the outbuildings before turning the bay into the corral.

Rain Shadow carried her supplies to her lodge and started a fire.

"Rain Shadow!"

She ignored Anton's angry voice outside the flap.

"Rain Shadow!" he called again.

She warmed her hands over the flames that sprang up.

Anton flung the tent flap aside and crouched through the opening.

"You can't come in here! I didn't give you permission!"

He pulled himself up straight, looking taller and broader than ever in his sheepskin coat. He'd left his hat elsewhere. "I'm here, aren't I?"

"An Indian would never commit such a breach of etiquette. I didn't invite you."

"Yeah, well, I'm not an Indian, am I? And neither are you. Sometimes I'm not sure what you are—except cantankerous!"

"Get out."

"I'm staying till we talk this out."

"There's nothing to talk about."

"Yes, there is. Think of Slade."

Think of Slade! What else had she done for the last seven years but think of Slade? "Why, you—" She snatched a piece of kindling from the ground at her side and threw it at him.

Neatly, he caught the stick and tossed it on the fire.

Standing, she met his glare. He stepped closer, still looming a foot above her. "Why don't you think of Nikky? Where does he fit into all this lunacy?"

His blue eyes flinched with her words. "Nikolaus would want Slade safe, too."

"Would we live together?" she asked, keeping her voice even.

His gaze wavered and then narrowed. "Isn't that the point? Ruiz would have to think we were happily married."

She crossed her arms over her breasts. "How would we explain a temporary marriage to the boys? It wouldn't be fair to them," she said, thinking how close the two of them had become, how much closer they'd be in a few more weeks. "It would be a mistake." She raised her chin. "I know what you're thinking. I made a mistake once, but I won't do it again."

"I wasn't thinking that."

"What were you thinking?"

The corner of his mouth almost twitched. "That you're thinking about it."

"You're an infuriating man, Anton Neubauer."

"But you'll think on it?"

As much as she hated to admit it, the idea held more promise than anything she'd been able to come up with herself.

"Rain Shadow?"

"I'll think on it."

Chapter Eleven

She was out her mind to consider such a harebrained scheme. Anton was out of his mind to suggest it! Their fathers were way out of line to think of such a plan! By the end of the week Rain Shadow deemed the plot ludicrous and pushed it from her mind. There was something more to worry over.

Thanksgiving. The Anglo-American holiday lush with family traditions only gave her more cause to realize she did not fit in here.

Annette informed Rain Shadow their family always ate together on holidays, therefore she and Slade were taken in under the familial wing and expected at Franz and Annette's. Johann and Two Feathers had shot the turkey the day before, and Rain Shadow had dressed the bird, her only contribution to the festivity, since she didn't know how to do the things Annette and Lydia did. Inactivity had worn her endurance thin. With each passing moment, the Neubauers' house had grown more and more confining.

A change of atmosphere appealed, but the thought of dinner at Anton's sister-in-law's comfortable and solid home pointed out how inept and gauche she really was. The remaining hours passed with dread, until finally Rain Shadow changed into the dress she'd finished hemming that morning.

Franz and Annette's house was only a few years old, sturdily built, decorated with handmade doilies and sepia-toned daguerreotypes. Annette was everything Rain Shadow wasn't; capable, domestic, a perfect wife, mother and hostess. She showed Rain Shadow the house and set her to peeling potatoes while she scurried about the kitchen.

Lydia and Jakob arrived, and Lydia knew just what to do and where things were, busying herself between the kitchen and dining room, at the same time pacifying both her and Annette's youngest children.

"Will you set the table?" Annette asked Rain Shadow when the potatoes boiled.

Rain Shadow nodded and stared hard at the bread crumbs falling to the tabletop as Lydia deftly sliced a crusty loaf. Something hollow ached in her chest, and her hand trembled on her cotton skirt. Annette's shoes appeared in her line of vision, and she forced her gaze up.

"The plates are in the china closet in the dining room, the silverware and napkins in the top drawer." Annette turned to the stove.

Rain Shadow wanted to bolt for the door. She didn't know the first thing about setting a proper table. She felt like a sow in a wren house. Slowly, she stood.

Annette puckered her pretty brow in thought. "I think I counted ten. You'd better count again."

Rain Shadow stepped into a silent dining room, so spacious her entire lodge would have fit in the area. An ivory lace cloth draped the long table; sheer ruffled curtains swagged across the windows. She opened the glass-inset doors of the cabinet and stared at the delicate rose-patterned china plates. What if she broke one? Her hands might shake so badly she'd drop the entire stack on the floor! Two sizes of plates, assorted platters, endless cups, saucers and other strange pieces were displayed before her distressed gaze. Was she supposed to do something with all of them?

"Need a hand?" The familiar voice came from behind.

She whirled to face Anton, her palm flying to her breast. "Oh!"

"Sorry, I thought you heard me." He circled her arm with his fingers. "You're shakin'. What's wrong?"

She glanced into his eyes and away. "You startled me, that's all."

One sandy brow lifted in disbelief. The question hadn't sounded like one of his digs; perhaps he was just being courteous.

"Yes, I can use some help," she replied, knowing her acceptance threw him off guard. "Will you lift the plates down for me?" Words Sissy Clanton might have used. Hearing them from her own mouth, Rain Shadow almost blushed.

Anton reached past her, and she caught the scent of his clean hair and shirt. Only days before he'd watched her heft ammunition-laden saddlebags onto Jack's back, and they both remembered it. There was no logical reason on earth for her to need his assistance. He carried the plates to the table without comment, took the top one and began spacing them around the perimeter.

Gratefully, she followed his unconscious lead.

"Been thinking?" he asked.

She watched his dark hand rest on the ivory tablecloth, and suddenly the sight became intimate. From nowhere came the image of him striding shirtless into the room he'd turned over to Slade, the planes and curves of his tanned and muscular torso defined by the gas lamp. Rain Shadow remembered watching him brush his unruly hair, slip his tie over his head and adjust it before the mirror. She'd wondered then about the intimacy between a husband and wife, wondered what it would be like to share a house...a room...a bed.... Had she been thinking about his offer? "Yes."

"And?"

She pulled open the top drawer and withdrew a neatly ironed and folded stack of linen napkins. "And I wonder what you have to gain."

"You insult me."

She turned, met his blue gaze and stifled an unconscious shiver. "I didn't mean to. It's just that...I don't see how you can make such an offer. You've made it plain that I'm a nuisance."

"Consider it something I need to do for Slade."

The immediate bond he'd developed with her son had always been a bit of a mystery to her. "You have a son of your own. Why do you have such an attachment to mine?"

He took the napkins from her hand, his fingers brushing hers. A long and knowing look passed between them. He drew his gaze away first and placed each delicately hemmed piece of linen on the left of the plates. "Maybe because I have a son of my own. Maybe because I was a boy once myself. I didn't have a ma. Nikolaus doesn't have a ma, and Slade doesn't have a pa. Not one worth a plug nickel, anyway."

She dragged her attention from his long fingers wrapped around a white napkin and searched his face. He'd said it dryly, a comment a person made to another when both agreed on a subject. How did he see her? Did he think less of her because she'd never married Miguel, or because she'd consorted with him in the first place? "Anton, I was very young..."

She'd seen him in physical pain, and the expression that now crossed his golden features was the same.

"You don't have to explain," he said. "You don't owe me anything."

"Don't I?"

He looked up sharply. "No."

"You rescued Slade from that railcar, sacrificed your room for weeks, got yourself stabbed in the shoulder over my—my—" She faltered. "Over me."

"You paid me back by nursing me through it. You've put in your share of work around the place." He laid the last napkin in place and grinned. "All of Nikolaus' dungarees and shirts are mended."

Warmth crept into her cheeks. She hadn't realized he'd noticed. "But, if we—well, if you did this thing for me—"

"Got married."

"Then I would owe you something."

He shrugged noncommittally. "Mend my shirts."

Annette appeared in the doorway with a tray.

Anton turned to leave, pausing at Rain Shadow's side. "Keep thinking," he murmured in her ear.

She sat across from him at dinner, Two Feathers and Slade flanking her. The Neubauers joined hands and lowered their heads, Rain Shadow and her family following suit. Franz prayed, thanking his God for their food, health and children, and asking Him to protect and guide them. Amens echoed around the room, and the bowls and platters circulated with enthusiasm.

The Neubauer brothers told amusing tales about one another during dinner. Slade and Nikolaus absorbed each word, listening in wide-eyed fascination to Johann's stories of his childhood, of growing up with brothers and sisters and parents. Johann knew where his parents had been born, he even had a Bible with his entire family's births and deaths recorded.

Rain Shadow met Anton's gaze. This family knew each and every ancestor, shared their stories like the Indians. Everyone at the table had memories of families... everyone, that was, except her.

A chasm opened between her breasts, an unexplainable hurt and inferiority, a gnawing, insatiable hunger that had nothing to do with the feast spread before her on the table. Rain Shadow swallowed the ache and focused on the man across from her. "Your grandfather taught you to fix clocks?"

Anton nodded. "I have a shop in town that belonged to him."

Annette pushed her chair back. "Did you fellas say you were going to wash the dishes?"

Franz took his wife's hand and pressed it to his lips. "Did you say you wanted your grandma's china entrusted to these delicate hands?" He and his brothers raised enormous palms toward her.

Annette laughed and waved her apron at them. "Oh, shoo, you bunch of conniving sluggards!"

The men stood and headed toward the parlor. Annette threaded her fingers through her husband's and leaned toward him. "My mother warned me about you."

Franz bobbed his head and kissed her quickly. "Aren't you glad she was right?"

Rain Shadow met Anton's gaze where he stood in the doorway watching her. He'd had a wife. A proper wife just like his brothers', and he'd lost her.

He had a family. He didn't need Rain Shadow.

He wanted her.

She needed him.

The following morning Jakob rode up the long drive to the barn and called out. From the barn, Rain Shadow watched Anton and Johann meet him. They spoke briefly, and Jakob galloped toward Franz and Annette's.

"What's wrong?" Rain Shadow asked Anton when he stepped through the doorway.

"Have to dig a new well on Jakob's land." He strode to the back and returned with shovels.

Instinctively sensing trouble, she watched him carry harnesses from the tack room. "What's wrong with their well?"

"Salt in it."

"Someone poured salt in their well?"

"Probably yesterday while we were all at Franz's."

Horror prickled at her scalp. "Is the stock sick?"

"Nah. They're too smart to drink it. We'll need to carry water until the new well's dug. Good thing the ground's not frozen solid yet."

"I'll help," she said quickly, knowing she was responsible for the Neubauers' misfortune.

"You have to stay with Slade." He stared at her pointedly. "We all know who did this."

She wiped her palms on her trousers. *Miguel.* And he'd been bold enough, certain enough of their whereabouts to know just when and where to cause trouble. A tremor began in her chest and radiated outward until her shoulders shook. The Neubauers! This warm, wonderful family was under siege because of her!

As soon as Miguel appeared, she should have run as fast and far as she could. If only Slade had been able to travel. Was it safe to go now? Should she bundle up her son and father and run? Anger and frustration welled within her until she could easily burst.

She wanted to scream. She wanted to hit someone or something. She needed to cry and hated herself for the weakness.

"Rain Shadow."

Anton's hand rested on her shoulder, and she realized she'd turned her back on him and stood shaking. She found her voice. "I'll stay with the boys and look after the stock. You go dig."

From behind, he roped her braid around his fist, forced her head around, shoulders and body following, until she curled into the curve of his arm. It was easy, then, to lay her forehead against the warmth of his broad chest and fold her arms around his waist. She turned her face, and his heart beat steadily beneath her cheek.

Warm. Solid. Safe.

Too easy. Too easy to let herself grow soft and comfortable. Too easy to open a small door of trust and cleave to this immovable man. He was a boulder in a raging river, but she could cling only temporarily until the current carried her downstream.

She recognized his smell—horses and leather, soap and his own musky scent. From that day on, whenever she thought of Pennsylvania, she would smell sunshine and warm growing things, hear the steady beat of his heart and see a golden man, feet firmly planted on his own soil.

Sissy Clanton was a fool. A prim and proper, pale and freckled fool.

Anton released her hair, his thumb sliding along her jaw, caressing the sensitive skin behind her ear. Rain Shadow sensed the subtle change in his body. Her thoughts, turned inward until now, flowered out until she recognized the hard length of his body along hers, noticed her breasts crushed against his jacket front.

Her nipples grew sensitive to the brush of her flannel shirt, and she remembered another day she'd turned into his arms for comfort. He'd kissed her the way she'd never dreamed anyone would kiss her, pressed his face into her shirt and opened it, exposing her to his heated blue gaze and the sunlight filtering through the window.

She would remember each moment with him as long as she lived. Memories of expectant sunshine, golden hair and lashes, vivid blue eyes. She could carry the mementos with her anywhere, keep them to cheer endless train rides, savor them on lonely nights by a fire, fold them away for the years ahead.

She stepped back, hands slowly falling from his waist, and looked up.

"One of us will stay here with you," he stated softly.

"No. The more of you who work, the sooner you'll have the well dug."

He ran his hand across his jaw. "I can't leave you alone."

"Anton. I'm a better shot than any of you," she said, and wondered belatedly if she'd wounded his male pride again.

"Better than all of us put together, probably," he said with a wry shrug that reassured her. That steel-bright blue gaze fixed on her, guarded, unfathomable. "Will you be okay?"

She nodded. She'd be okay. . . at least for the moment.

It had been dark an hour, but the men had taken lanterns. Lydia had come and helped milk earlier, and Rain Shadow had asked how to use the stove and oven. Now she cleared away the dishes from the simple meal she'd prepared for herself and the boys.

"I have to use the outhouse, Ma." Slade hopped across the kitchen, the crutch Johann had made him tucked under one arm.

"Get your jackets, both of you. This is your last trip for the night." She slipped into her coat and buckled on her holster, checking her revolver for the tenth time.

Their breath puffed out ahead of them, Slade's huffing in gusts because of his rapid hopping. "Look how big the moon is!" Nikolaus exclaimed, stopping, and Slade ran into his back. The two of them chortled and ducked into the outhouse. Rain Shadow studied the silhouette of the farmhouse in the moonlight.

She had to leave. Endangering the Neubauers, disrupting their lives was inexcusable. Slade was getting by on his crutch. There was no reason to stay any longer.

After her turn, they headed back, twigs snapping beneath their feet. A vague scent teased her nostrils, raised the hair on the back of her neck. Cigar smoke, expensive and distinctive. Had it only been her imagination?

"Stop," she whispered.

Ahead of her the boys froze obediently, straining to hear or see what she saw. She sniffed the air, listened to the brittle maple branches clicking in the brisk wind. In the distance a calf bawled.

"It's nothing. Go on." She scurried them onto the back porch. "Lock the door while I check the horses."

Crossing the dooryard, she pulled her collar over her chin and settled her flat-brimmed hat more securely on her head. Loping up the grade toward the barn, the dooryard pitched and rolled in the sway of lantern light. Ahead, a horse nickered. Intuition prickled at Rain Shadow's scalp.

In a split second, she drew and aimed dead center of the figure ahead.

Twenty feet from the corner of the barn, Miguel stood beside the animal. In the cold, pale moonlight the silver conches on his saddle glittered. He wore a hat much like hers.

Rain Shadow seethed with anger. How dare he show up here again! Why couldn't he leave her alone to get on with her life? What on earth was the morbid attraction he held for her? She drew a cleansing breath to calm herself. "What do you want?"

"You do not believe I wanted to apologize?"

"Some apology."

"The farmer made a mistake."

"*I* made the mistake, Miguel, in ever getting involved with you in the first place."

He struck a match, cupped his bare hands around it and lit a long, thin cheroot, illuminating his stark features in sharp relief. He blew the match out, and the cigar tip glowed orange in the darkness. "*Si,* I made a mistake, too. I still wish for you to hear me out."

How could she ever have fallen for his smooth line? The thought that she'd been intimate with the man at one time revolted her. "Talk."

"Put the gun away and we will talk."

"Talk, Miguel."

"You are in such a hurry, little one." He took a half step toward her, stopped by the sound of her hammer cocking. "Very well. I want you to marry me."

"You have a wife!" she blurted.

"No. I am no longer married to the *comtesse.*"

"Did you find riper pickings?"

He paused before answering. "She did."

"I don't believe you."

"It is difficult to believe she liked another man better. I regret my mistakes, and I want you now."

"Even if that were true, I wouldn't marry you."

"No?" He puffed, and the moonlight illuminated a drifting smoke ring.

"No."

"Why not?"

"I'm already married."

He was silent for a long minute. "The farmer?"

"The farmer," she agreed, hating herself for using Anton again, but helpless to stop.

He studied the end of his cheroot. "And the child?"

"The child is his."

"How can that be?"

"I met Anton after the London tour," she lied again. "He was married to another woman at the time, and was very unhappy. We fell in love. I knew it was wrong so I left. I didn't want our baby to bring scandal to Anton and his family. I learned recently that she'd died, so I came to see for myself."

"How convenient."

"You can see there's no reason for you to hang around any longer. I'm not leaving."

"Do you not have a contest in the spring?"

So, he knew about that. "I'll go to Philadelphia, but I'll return. This is my home now."

The cigar glowed eerily against the darkness, and the acrid scent assaulted her nostrils.

"Sleep with me, then. Tonight while he is gone."

Disgust shrouded her heart, shock sinking into every cell. How could she have been enamored of this contemptible ass? How could she have let him touch her? Plant his seed in her? Anger seared a red-hot blur before her eyes, and she prayed he didn't make a move until it cleared. "You're insane."

"Not at all. I want you. I will settle for making love to you one last time."

"You don't love me."

"I want you."

Rain Shadow had never shot a person in her life. She'd shot animals—foxes, squirrels, birds of all feather. She'd killed a wolf once. She imagined pulling the trigger now, seeing Miguel jerk as the bullet hit his body. She pictured him on the ground, his life's blood oozing from a neat hole.

She hated him. Despised him.

But she couldn't do it.

Leveling the barrel, she took careful aim in the bleached moonlight. A split second later, Ruiz' hat jerked into the air.

Miguel flinched and shot a glance over his shoulder in the direction his hat had sailed.

"The next bullet will be between your hateful eyes," she spat. "Get out of here, and don't come back!"

Slowly, he mounted his horse, sat the saddle tall and straight. "You frustrate me, *querida*, but never doubt I will be back." The horse turned away at his invisible command. "You have something I want," he said over his shoulder.

"Mama, are you out there?"

In horror, Rain Shadow turned and saw Slade step into the circle of lantern light. "Slade, go back to the house. Now!"

Miguel guided the stallion in a semicircle, turning back. Heart thudding, Rain Shadow shot a glance to make certain Slade was gone, and relief drained into her soul.

Miguel's horse snorted and broke into a run. She listened to the hoofbeats fade into the distance. He wasn't finished. His threat seized her in its unholy talons. She could only pray he believed the lie about her son's parentage. If he ever saw Slade up close, he would know the truth. Slade was dark like her, but his black eyes and narrow, handsome face were Miguel's. What then? What if he knew he'd fathered her child? He would use him toward his ultimate purpose. He could take him to spite her—spirit him away somewhere—and do it legally!

"Mama, is he gone?"

Her son's anxious voice brought quick tears to her throat. She swallowed. Nothing would happen to him as long as she drew breath! "He's gone. I told you to go back to the house."

"I couldn't leave you alone."

She walked to where he stood. "I should punish you for not minding me." Instead, she bent and hugged him close. "Go in with Nikky now."

He pushed away and hopped toward the house. If she left, Miguel would follow. She couldn't expose Slade to that danger.

Several silent minutes passed before she heard hoofbeats growing steadily closer from the opposite direction Miguel had gone. Anton, followed closely by Franz and Two Feathers. Relief washed over her.

With unsteady hands, she hung the lantern on the outside of the barn. She drew a deep breath and met them on the drive.

Anton took one long, assessing look at her and slid from his horse. "Ruiz?"

She nodded. "He's gone."

"I will stay with you tonight, daughter." Winded, Two Feathers slid from his mount.

"We were damned fools to let him trick us like this!" Anton swore, picked up a rock from the drive and pitched it forcefully into the darkness.

"I agree." Franz spoke from atop his horse. "But I don't think he'll be back tonight. I'm heading home."

Rain Shadow watched him gallop down the drive, ashamed of the extra work and concern she'd put the family through. Two Feathers walked his mount toward the corral.

"Anton."

Obviously irritated, he turned toward her, hand on hip. "What."

"I'll marry you." The words hung between them so long, she wondered if he'd heard her. He exhaled, a long white gust releasing some emotion she wondered at.

"Tomorrow?"

Tomorrow? "Is that possible?"

"We'll ride into town—or Pittsburgh if you'd rather."

"Either. I don't care."

"Butler is closer. We'll all go together."

"That's fine."

"There's a lawyer I've talked to about adopting him. We can fill out the papers after the ceremony."

She found her voice. "You want to adopt Slade?"

"It's a sure way to see that Ruiz has no rights. You'll say Slade's real father died, and we'll sign the papers. They'll go to Philadelphia and be returned for the final signatures within a month."

"What about . . . ?"

"What?"

She peered at him from beneath the brim of her hat. "What will happen after this ordeal is over? I mean, when Miguel is gone."

"We can have the marriage annulled."

She remembered his previous explanation, the part about not consummating the marriage. "Oh."

He slid his hat off, combed his fingers through his hair and settled the Stetson once again.

She glanced toward the house, considering the restraint and frustration involved. Feeling as she did about Anton, would it be possible to share a house without touching? Kissing? Without giving in to the feelings she had for him? Only if his self-control was much stronger than hers.

From a dark, hidden corner of her mind, worry about making Slade Anton's legal son hovered, too. She couldn't think about that right now. Protecting him came first. She would deal with other matters when the time arose.

"Tomorrow, then. Good night, Anton."

"'Night."

He watched her small figure walk to the house. Her acceptance of his help had been imperative—he'd been almost desperate for her to go along with this marriage plan. But why was he marrying another woman who didn't love him? Marrying for the sake of convenience when he knew the risk involved?

He'd been prepared to marry Sissy for convenience. This was the same difference, only better—he knew ahead of time this marriage wouldn't last! This time, knowing it was a sham—both of them knowing it was a sham—he wouldn't knock himself out to please her. He'd get rid of Ruiz, see Slade's future started off on the right foot and be done with it. Then he could think about Helena McLaury again. Somehow, the thought held even less appeal than before.

"Okay," he said out loud. *But be careful! You know what she does to you. You know how you react when you get close to her. You don't need the trouble.* "I'll be careful," he promised the moon.

Rain Shadow glanced at Anton beside her atop his bay. Her husband. Just like the couples in the wagon behind them, they were man and wife—united by the white man's Justice of the Peace, a legal document signed and folded and tucked into Anton's vest pocket.

The first of December was as good as any day for a wedding, she guessed. A few snowflakes fell as she and Anton rode home from Butler on horseback. Rain Shadow huddled inside her Hudson Bay blanket coat, a gift from Will the winter before. On the crisp air, voices lifted in song. Songs of shepherds and the Christ child, the Neubauer men's resonant voices joining their wives', Lydia's spine-tingling soprano carrying the highest notes when the others backed off.

Anton had explained the plan to his family, and they'd gone along with the theatrics as if they were real. Once the justice had pronounced them man and wife, Anton had laid his cheek alongside hers, as if some gesture was expected of him. Her temporary in-laws had embraced her as though she were really one of the family, Two Feathers merely nodding sagely.

What was Anton thinking now? Feeling?

What should a man feel on his wedding day? Anton avoided her eyes, squinting instead at the low-hanging gray sky. How had he felt after marrying Peine? Eager. Proud. Hopeful, no doubt. How different the emotions beneath the calm exterior he presented today were. Rash. Unsure. Cheated.

What should a woman feel on her wedding day? Rain Shadow imagined Annette and Lydia's joy at marrying the men they loved. There was nothing joyful about her union with Anton, and she'd been numb since she'd made the decision, going through the motions without feeling anything.

Locked in. Guilty. Lonely. Heavyheartedness descended on her, as oppressive as the storm clouds gathering overhead. She observed the boys, knowing they were the most vulnerable characters in this charade. Even though she had explained the situation to them more than once, they smiled as smugly as if they'd thought of the plan themselves and hoped they could remain brothers.

She didn't want to be another dark cloud over their heads, but she resigned herself to reminding the children constantly. As soon as the situation cleared, she and Slade would move on. They all had their own lives to lead. The

Neubauers had been kind enough to care for Slade, even to the extreme of carrying out this hoax for his protection, but she couldn't expect them to be patient and generous forever.

Once at the homestead, the women set out a meal, and Rain Shadow naturally discovered her place at Anton's side. She ate beside him, feeling like an impostor. By the time she'd helped clear and wash the dishes, the men had a fire blazing in the parlor, popcorn popped and the checkers out. Jakob played his fiddle, and even Rain Shadow was drawn into a dance around the room.

The night drew to a close, the children growing sleepy. Jakob and Franz bundled their families off into the darkness.

"We have a surprise for you," Johann announced, turning into the parlor.

Anton glanced up from the sofa where he sat finger-combing Nikky's hair. His son lay contentedly, head on Anton's thigh. "What is it?"

"You'll have to come out back with us," Anton's father said with a sly grin.

"Tonight?"

"Yep."

Immediately, Nikolaus and Slade were wide awake, eagerly bringing their parents' coats and hats and donning their own.

Rain Shadow pulled her collar over her chin and followed them. They veered east of the barn and stopped before the cabin she'd seen and thought their fathers were using.

Johann pushed the door open and carried the lantern in, the others following. Placing the light on a trestle table, he lit another lamp, revealing the interior. The immaculately clean cabin was roomy, furnished with old but sturdy tables and chairs. A stove and cabinet identified the cooking area, rocking chairs and oval braided rugs offering a place of comfort near the fireplace.

Rain Shadow studied her surroundings with surprise. "Whose home is this?"

Anton's boots rapped on the stone hearth. "This is the place my grandfather built when they first got the farm. Pa was born in there."

Rain Shadow stepped through the bedroom doorway. An enormous rope bed stood in the center of the room, a colorful quilt spread across its foot.

"Do you like it, Ma?" Slade asked, tugging at her wrist.

"Of course. It's very nice. Seems so warm and comfortable." She could picture Anton's grandmother moving about these rooms, cooking over the fire and setting meals on the table. "No wonder Grampa and Johann have spent so much time out here." She smiled.

"It's for us, Ma," Slade said enthusiastically. "Ain't it somethin'?"

She stared at her son without comprehension.

"We fixed it up for you," Johann explained. "There's more to do, but we figured you could do the rest yourself. Make it seem more like home, that way. There's dishes in the attic back at the house." His desire to please her was evident in the uncertain smile he offered. She stared into faded blue eyes. He looked endearingly like Anton, stooped only slightly with age.

She shot Two Feathers a glance, but he'd drawn a mask over his chiseled Lakota features. He stared calmly, waiting for her reaction. Everyone waited, she realized.

"I'm not sure I understand."

"We can stay here," Nikky supplied. "You'n Slade and me'n Pa. Won't it be great?" He yanked his coat and hat off excitedly. "C'mon, Slade, let's go get our beds ready! Oh, yeah." He retrieved his coat and hung it on a peg near the door.

Slade followed his example, forgetting the crutch in his enthusiasm. They ran to a ladder leading to the loft above.

"Slade, your leg!" Rain Shadow exclaimed.

"It's okay, Ma. I've been practicing. I can get up and down without no trouble." They scampered up and over the edge.

She stared after them. They'd planned for her to stay out here in this cabin with Anton?

"Without any trouble," she corrected distractedly, and slid her confused gaze toward her—husband.

As if as surprised as she, Anton gave a nearly imperceptible shrug.

Do something, she pleaded with her eyes.

I can't hurt their feelings, his baffled gaze seemed to reply.

"I know how uncomfortable you are in the house," Johann supplied. "We thought this would be the best thing. You're not out in the weather, but it's not the big house, either."

She knew he considered exposure to Miguel more dangerous than the weather, and she had been obstinate about leaving her lodge. "And you, Father?" she asked. "Will you stay here with us?"

Two Feathers glanced toward the hearth. "My bones have taken a liking to the feather bed, daughter. Winter nights are longer and colder than I remember."

She had talked him out of their lodge for safety, and she could hardly ask him to sleep in the loft with the boys or lie on the stone hearth because she didn't trust herself alone with Anton. She nodded, and gave him what she hoped was a reassuring smile.

Overhead came thumps, and muffled laughter—the sounds of brothers tussling before bed. Exactly what she'd feared all along. How long would this arrangement last? *Until Miguel lost interest.* Any length of time was unhealthy for her mental state.

Rain Shadow watched their fathers pull the solid door shut behind them. She felt as if she were about to participate in her most difficult competition ever. Everything she held dear rode on the outcome, and yet somehow, some way, losing would be winning. Her heart fluttered beneath her shirt. She steeled her wayward thoughts and her traitorous body.

She couldn't afford to leave any part of herself behind. Not her goal, not her independence, and least of all, not her heart. But this man—whose muscles in his broad back flexed and bunched as he knelt and fed logs to the fire—this husband—wouldn't have to take a thing. She feared she'd give him anything he wanted.

Chapter Twelve

"Would you like some coffee?" Anton held a cup toward her.

Rain Shadow accepted the steaming mug and perched on a bench at the trestle table. She'd finished putting some of her clothing away, and overhead the boys had finally quieted. Her gaze collided with his, and she forced herself to look at her fingers on the cup.

"I found blankets in the trunk," he said finally. "I'll make a place by the fire."

Heat rose in her cheeks. "Why don't you let me? I've slept on the ground all my life."

"All the more reason for you to be comfortable now." He took a sip, and she dared a glance. "Besides," he added. "I probably won't get much sleep, so I'll check on the animals every so often."

What would rob him of sleep? Listening for Miguel? Thinking of her? Imagining him lying in here, she knew she wouldn't sleep well, either.

The air between them seemed combustible, their unexpressed emotions crackling. Anton felt like a walnut tossed into the air; in an instant she would zero in on him and he'd shatter into a million fragments. Wooing disaster, he let his eyes meet hers. He read her desire, as pure and hot and unexpected as ever, and he wished for the thousandth time that he'd met her before his heart had turned to stone.

He'd done the right thing—the honorable thing—by marrying her and providing protection for her and Slade. But he couldn't allow anything more. Could he?

Exercising more self-discipline than he knew he possessed, Anton stood and gathered the pile of blankets. Behind him he heard her set the cups aside. A moment later she spoke from the bedroom doorway, though he hadn't heard her steps.

"Good night, then, Anton."

"G'night." He blew out the last lantern. She closed the wooden door, and blackness enveloped the room. Stripping off his boots, shirt and dungarees, he slipped beneath the covers and stacked his hands beneath his head, staring into the darkness.

Muted sounds came from the other room, and he imagined her undressing, brushing her marvelous ebony hair out until it crackled, and climbing onto the enormous rope bed. He closed his eyes and wondered what would happen if he went to her, slid into the bed beside her and pressed himself against her silken length. His body responded, and he cursed softly at the rafters. How the hell would he ever survive this?

He'd really done it. Bound her to him with a two-dollar ceremony and a certificate. Somewhere in the far recesses of his mind, he should be wondering why he'd been determined to protect her in this manner. He'd assured himself it was the only way, and that answer would have to do. For now, anyway. He had too many other concerns to lose sleep over. Finally, in the rosy-hued hours before dawn, he slept.

The first long day Anton watched Rain Shadow carry boxes from the main house and worry over just which yellowed doily or old dish should be placed where. The cabin reeked of lemon oil, wood smoke and occasionally the burnt remains of some unrecognizable thing she'd incinerated on the stove.

The second long night he watched her help the boys with their numbers and send them up to the loft. She worked by the fire for a while, then closed herself in the bedroom while he lay on his pallet near the fire thinking of Two Feathers' comfortable bones in a feather bed and denied thoughts of the woman who haunted his dreams.

This second day she'd accused him of being cranky. Out of obstinacy he'd cleaned and repaired a mantel clock and placed it beside a chipped vase she'd salvaged from the main house's attic.

The third interminable night wore his endurance to the bone, and the following morning he chopped wood until physically exhausted.

Tonight, he once again wondered at her peculiar behavior, this hellcat, who when they'd first met had scorned any and every hint of domesticity and now behaved as if the very fate of the universe depended on the arrangement of the dishes on the table. And yet something about her concern over the discarded dishes and her intense attempts at meals touched him in a place he'd planned never to leave vulnerable again. For many years, he hadn't known the comfort a woman provided. He shouldn't get used to it now.

He studied her dark head bent over her sewing and realized how much he liked having her with him, how good her cleaning and fussing made him feel. And liking this warped arrangement frightened him more than he chose to admit. Having a woman near would be easy to get used to if he didn't know how much hurt was involved.

She stabbed the needle she'd been using into the dress material and rose. She strapped the holster bearing her

Smith & Wesson revolver to her leg and caught her coat. "I'm going to check on the horses."

Anton stared sightlessly at the door. The change in her frightened him, too. Their former bickering and occasional outbursts had at least been a release, an outlet for the tension that built up between them. Oh, but she was a fighter! She wouldn't holler uncle no matter how hard her arm was twisted. That's why her acceptance of his proposal and protection bothered him.

Ruiz had backed her into a corner. Her fragile, transparent beauty was a deceptive camouflage for the self-willed spirit beneath. Lord help Ruiz if he ever left his backside unprotected! And Lord help *him,* Anton snorted to himself, if he ever succumbed to her magnetic appeal! Was that what he was really afraid of?

The wind caught the enormous wooden door, and Rain Shadow fought it closed behind her. She carried the lantern, shadows bobbing, past the wagons toward the stalls. Ahead, dark spots on the straw-littered floor caught her attention. She knelt and studied the drops.

Blood.

Several feet ahead lay a familiar small shape. Rain Shadow knew before she reached it what it was. The gray kitten lay cold and lifeless, its fur matted black with blood.

Her pulse roared in her temples, and the barn seemed silent in those seconds. *Jack!* she thought immediately, and bolted along the stalls. "Jack!"

The paint bobbed his head and whinnied attentively.

"Jack," she whispered with relief. She ran her hands across his solid neck and withers and affectionately laid her forehead against his warm shoulder. Miguel could have harmed him! He'd been right here! He knew how much she loved her son, her father, her pony...had he even known she cared for the gray kitten? What if Miguel thought she loved Anton, too!

She jerked her head up. She hadn't stopped to consider the added danger she had placed Anton in! "I should have gone," she whispered.

Wood creaked and slammed as though the wind had caught the barn door again. Rain Shadow tensed.

"Well, for—" Anton's muffled curse echoed down the corridor. She heard his boots strike the floor and pause at the spot where the kitten lay. "Rain Shadow?"

"Back here."

He appeared before the stall, a rifle tucked under one arm. Their gazes locked, a muscle in his jaw ticking. "Animals all right?"

At the reminder that she'd checked only her own horse, shame flooded her. She drew her revolver, and together they searched the stalls, grain bins and hayloft.

"That son of a miserable—" Anton knelt and wrapped the dead animal in a burlap feed bag. Shovel in one hand, bag and rifle in the other, he strode from the barn. When he returned she stood waiting.

He blew out the lantern. "We don't carry this across the yard anymore. He could pick us off like your blasted bean cans. Tomorrow we're getting a couple of dogs."

"Why, so he can slit their throats, too?" She stopped behind him.

In the pitch black, she sensed him turn to face her and knew a furious tension coiled within his body. "No, so they can warn us he's out there. And if it takes a dog or two, that's better than the stock or one of us."

He was right, but was it too late for any of this? What was happening? "This was a mistake. I never should have stayed here. All I did was put you and your family in greater danger! I'm sorry, Anton. I'm so sorry. It was selfish of me to stay. I have to go."

She groped for the wooden door handle, but found his arm. Pushing him aside, she wrenched open the door. He stopped her with a strong hand on her wrist. "Rain Shadow—"

She broke free and ran. Halfway to the cabin, he caught her around the waist, the momentum knocking them both to the ground. Rain Shadow lay beneath him, her cheek pressed against the frozen grass, his breath harsh against her temple. His rifle bit into the small of her back, but she lay immobile.

Slowly, he lifted his weight and rolled her over to face him, holding one wrist in a loose grip. "Think," he rasped. "Where would you go?"

"Anywhere, it doesn't matter. I'll hide Slade somewhere."

"Slade tells me you want him to go to school. How can you hide him in school?"

"We can use different names."

"And your contest?"

She rolled her eyes upward, avoiding his face, feeling hysteria well, knowing her behavior and words had grown irrational. "It doesn't matter anymore."

"It doesn't matter?"

"No." A chill racked her body, and she shook beneath him.

"Are you better than Annie Oakley?"

"Yes," she hissed.

"Then prove it."

She couldn't read his expression. "What the hell do you care?"

She sensed the change in his body, sensed she'd gone too far, and she hated hurting him, hated angering him. *I'm sorry*. Without considering, she yanked her hand from his grasp, the other from beneath his chest, and framed his cold face. Raising her head, she kissed him, their icy noses bumping before he angled his head and returned her desperate kiss. With the frigid ground along her spine and the chill wind whipping their hair in a reckless tangle, she lost herself in the glorious heat of his seeking tongue.

Anton's breath became labored. His hand moved inside her coat and covered her breast through her clothing. Rain Shadow almost groaned with frustration. How good he made her feel! How much she needed these feelings! But the bitter wind, their layers of clothing were intolerable.

She pulled her mouth from his, breathed against his chin. "Let's go inside. Please."

Anton helped her off the ground, picked up his rifle and stepped back. "I left the barn door open."

She nodded and ran to the cabin.

He watched her go, his heart sick with a long-buried memory. *Peine.* Peine had goaded him into anger deliberately. He couldn't remember how many times, if ever, he'd made love to her without a fight, without anger as a prelude to the act. He'd made their children in anger, no doubt. He knew it was something in Peine's character, a flaw, that she hated him so. She'd angered him to the point of taking her roughly. Maybe his anger helped her endure it, as though she had no choice.

He didn't know. He just knew it made him sick. Was he capable of anything else? Was he lusting after Rain Shadow because she made him angry? The thought turned his stomach. He hadn't looked twice at Sissy; hadn't been able to imagine touching her. Rain Shadow made him think and feel too much when he wanted to feel nothing and think less.

He secured the wooden door and ran to the cabin. She waited in the rocker near the fire, her shiny hair an ebony mass of tangles. Anton hung his coat and warmed his hands over the flames she'd stoked, feeling her gaze on his back. Lord help him, he could smell her from here. Her. No perfume or talc masking a scent more erotic than anything bottled in France. As always his response screamed through his veins, accentuated his senses and hammered into his belly. Finally, he turned to her.

She swallowed.

He wanted to kneel before her and remove her ridiculous trousers, peel her shirt away...what did she wear underneath? The erotic fantasy seared decadent images in his mind until his body grew taut.

She shivered.

"Cold?" At her nod, he knelt on the braided rug at her feet and reached for her boot. She extended her leg, and he pulled off her boot, then her woolen sock. She curled her toes into the rug while he bared the other foot. Holding her ankle, he massaged her cold toes and polished the sole of her foot with his thumb until warmth returned. He treated the other foot the same, finally spreading his palm from heel to toe, comparing the length of her foot to his hand. His fingers extended well over the end of her toes.

She smiled.

He took her hands, rubbed them vigorously between his and slanted his head toward her face. Firelight flickered over her features, lashes drooping over smoldering violet eyes. He read the desire in her eyes, her open lips, the traitorous breath that escaped her flared nostrils. Lord, he wanted her. Satisfaction impaired his judgment; *he wasn't angry*. His body throbbed with ungratified longing.

Her gaze shifted to the loft above.

He should have used that tiny hesitation to collect his wits and remember the danger in displaying the least vulnerability, but he discovered his heart wasn't as hard as the incautious part of him that strained against his denims. How could he resist her when she looked at him as if he was the only pool of water in the middle of a desert? "They're asleep," he assured her.

It was so like her to reach for him, to take what she wanted. No shrinking violet, Rain Shadow was ardent rather than romantic, one of the many unusual things that drew him to her, much as he resisted. She placed her fingers over his lips, and he kissed them. She ran her index finger across his lower lip, and he dropped his gaze to the pulse at her throat, beheld the rise and fall of her breasts beneath her shirt.

Her hands fell to his shoulders. Anton rose to his knees to kiss her. She met his lips and plucked a series of moist kisses across his mouth. He returned the caress, sliding his nose into the soft skin behind her ear, running his teeth along the column of her throat. He opened his mouth wide and sucked at her flesh.

The rocker creaked as she slid forward and found his shirt buttons. Her fingers worked them loose and slid inside.

She traced his collarbone, his shoulders, her cool fingertips sliding over his heated skin. Her touch made him feel like a man again, a prideful, ego-boosting sensation he hadn't experienced for a long, long time. She ran her palms across his chest, his muscles reflexively tensing. No one had ever touched him like this. In awe of the pleasure she took in him, his flesh, his kiss, he forgot to breathe.

His hungry expression kindled Rain Shadow's appetite. She could barely think when she touched him, less when he touched her; she could only feel. And right now she felt as if a fire had ignited deep inside her and spread beneath her skin. He was a beautiful, golden man, and she needed him to soothe the flame his eyes, lips and hands fueled. She should have felt clumsy and inexperienced, but stroking her palms down his chest to his hard, flat belly, his reaction gave her a power that excited her beyond measure.

He inhaled so sharply, air whistled through his teeth. He clamped his fingers over her wrists and wrapped her arms around his waist, covering her mouth in an unrestrained melding of lips and tongues and teeth.

Rain Shadow dug her fingers into his back, eagerly returning his kiss, silently cursing the barrier of their clothing between them.

"Anton," she whispered against his lips.

He pulled back, holding her so he could look at her.

She threaded her fingers into his hair.

He loosened her grip and held her hands between them, regret in his eyes. "I can't do this just to prove something to myself."

She tried to focus on his words.

"It's not fair to you."

"Anton, I'm not sure what you're saying."

He released her, and immediately coldness and emptiness enveloped her. Sitting on the floor, he scrubbed a hand across his face, hung his head and bracketed his temples with thumb and fingers. She stared at him in confusion.

As if sorting his words carefully, he dropped his hand, wrist draped across his knee, and met her gaze. "I'm not a gentleman."

She would have laughed had her body not been weeping for his. She made a pretense of straightening her clothing. "You'll have to understand if that doesn't come as a revelation to me."

"Listen." He stood and paced the small room, coming to stand behind her chair. The clock on the mantel ticked away interminable minutes. Wind whistled at the crack beneath the door. "You scare me," he whispered.

Her heart tumbled drunkenly. She curled her toes into the rug. "Why?"

"You want everything just as much, just as hard and fast as I do."

She only knew she wanted *him*. No doubt she'd breached some unspoken rule of propriety. Perhaps wives didn't want everything as hard and fast as their husbands. Humiliation burned her cheeks. "How unladylike of me."

"No, Rain Shadow." He knelt beside her chair.

She forced herself to meet his earnest gaze.

"No," he whispered. "I was proving something to myself."

"That you could have me if you wanted?"

"No!" He took her hand and rubbed his thumb across the back. "Please, don't think that."

"What am I supposed to think?" She watched his thumb stroke back and forth and wanted to draw it to her mouth, wanted to pull all of him against her, inside her.

He laid her hand in her lap. "Just think about what you really want. Think about it tomorrow when we're not together, and you can see more clearly."

When you're not near, and my judgment isn't influenced by my traitorous body, you mean. "All right."

"Go to bed, now."

She rose obediently, gathering her boots and socks. The clock chimed, punctuating her good-night.

"Good night, Rain Shadow. Sleep well."

Rain Shadow almost laughed. Any sleep at all would be a miracle.

"Do I hafta finish these numbers, Ma? You know I can do 'em." Slade twirled a tooth-scarred pencil between his fingers and served her his best martyred-little-boy expression.

Rain Shadow sliced a slab of bacon. "Your mind needs to be as healthy as your body."

"I know, Ma. But you know how sometimes your...seat hurts after you practice too much? Or your arms? That's how my head feels today."

Rain Shadow met Anton's amused gaze. Perched in the rocker, Nikolaus at his feet in a pile of wood shavings, Anton whittled a length of birch.

"All right," she conceded.

Slade grinned.

"Ain't it about time for me and Slade to go to Aunt Annette's?" Nikolaus asked.

Anton glanced at the mantel clock. "Yep, it is. Wrap up warm. I'll walk with you."

"I have to get my bag." Nikolaus bounded for the ladder. "C'mon, Slade. Get your clothes ready."

Rain Shadow glanced from one boy to the other. "What do you mean?"

Nikolaus paused on the bottom rung. "I always spend the night when we pull taffy. Slade'll stay, too, won't he?"

Unsettled, she laid the knife down and wiped her hands on a clean flour sack. The thought of Slade not being here with her didn't rest easily on her conscience. Too many troubling things had happened recently. "I—I don't know...."

She cast Anton a nervous glance.

"He's as safe with my brother as he is with me," Anton assured her softly.

Three sets of eyes awaited her decision. Time stopped. Anton had brought several dogs home a few days earlier, and there hadn't been an incident since. If Anton didn't have a concern over the boys staying at Annette and Franz's, she guessed it would be safe. He'd been right the other day when she'd panicked; she couldn't hide her son away forever. Besides, how could she let Nikky go without him? "Use the outhouse on the way, and don't go out again until morning."

"Aw-right!" Nikolaus bounded up the ladder.

Slade gave her a quick hug. "Thanks."

Anton stood and brushed shavings from his lap. "I'll clean this up later."

She turned to the dinner she'd started. "They'll eat there?"

He nodded and grabbed his coat.

"You don't have to hurry. Our meal will take a while longer."

Their sons returned, laden with the worn saddlebags they played with full to bursting. Slade hugged her soundly, and she kissed his forehead.

Nikolaus stood timidly between her and the door, a half wistful expression on his cherubic features.

"'Bye, Nikky," she said with a smile.

"'Bye, Rain Shadow." He flipped his mittened hand in an awkward wave.

She'd watched the touches between her son and Anton, Anton's enormous hand guiding Slade's narrow one over a wooden horse they shaped, the three enthusiastically wrestling on the floor, the man affectionately ruffling her boy's hair.

Did Nikky crave a motherly touch as much as Slade needed a fatherly one? Rain Shadow feared she would embarrass him, or worse yet—feared that she'd misconstrued his hesitation. How could she have? He was a little boy without a mother.

"Wait." She searched the hooks near the door until she found a woolen cap. Kneeling, she pulled it over his golden curls and flattened it around his ears. "Can't have you catching cold."

Face-to-face, he smiled disarmingly, his sky-blue eyes and freckle-dusted cheeks an angelic vision. His mother must have been beautiful—was beautiful, she corrected herself, recalling the daguerreotype in Anton's room. "Have fun," she said, and dotted his nose with her index finger.

Impulsively, he flung his arms around her neck and hugged her soundly. She wrapped her arms around his back and returned the embrace, her eyes flooding with tears.

How had this happened? When had she started to love Anton's son? Nikolaus released her, turned to his father, and the three left, a gust of winter wind swirling about her ankles.

Thank goodness Nikolaus had Annette, and he obviously held a special place in her heart. Rain Shadow couldn't let this be her concern; she wouldn't be here long enough to give Nikky the attention he needed; Annette would.

Staring at the closed wooden door, recognition seeped into her pores. Anton would return shortly. And they would be alone together. The memory of their kisses a few nights earlier brought a flush to her cheeks.

Think about it ... think about what you really want ...

What did she really want? Before the train had derailed and she'd discovered her son in Anton's dimly lit bedroom, she'd been certain she wanted to be the best sharpshooter known to mankind. Certain she didn't want to be dependent on a man for anything. Those certainties had grown hazy and confusing beneath Anton's somber blue gaze. Her resolve vanished within the heated embrace of his muscled arms. What had he done to her?

What was she doing living in this cabin with him, mending his shirts and cooking his meals? His meals! She spun toward the table, praying she'd have an edible one ready. A batch of biscuits wouldn't take long. The stove took a knack she couldn't seem to master. She could outshoot and outride any worthy opponent, accurately throw a knife at a target from twenty-five feet, catch enough game or fish to survive ten winters, but she had yet to prepare a meal without charring something.

In her haste, she spilled milk down the front of her dress. Aggravated, she gathered skillets and ingredients, and cooked over the fireplace, a tried and true method. The bacon, turned often on the trivet, browned evenly. The biscuits, just the right distance from the fire, were golden brown. Rain Shadow opened one of the jars of green beans Lydia had given her, and peaches, too.

Glancing down at her soiled dress and apron, she washed her face and hands, dashed into the bedroom and peeled the wet clothing off. Her underthings were damp, as well, so she hung them over the back of a chair, brushed her hair out quickly and attempted to pin it to her head the way Annette and Lydia did.

"Smells good!" Anton's voice boomed from the other room.

"It's ready. Just a minute!" She reached into her trunk and drew out the first dress she touched, ivory doeskin. She really should wear one of her new ones, but they took so long to adjust and button, and all those underclothes were required. She'd actually fixed a decent meal, she couldn't let it scorch now. She slipped the soft leather dress over her head.

Anton looked up from the wood shavings he'd swept into a tidy pile. His intense blue eyes riveted on her, radiating approval.

Rain Shadow. Undeniably, irresistibly beautiful. Exotic. Try as he did to stick to his idealistic thoughts and plans, her unconventional appearance, habits and spunk entranced him. He watched her grab a flour sack and remove the skillet from the fire. Her pale dress clung to every perfect curve, displayed her smooth, slender calves and ankles. She looked lovely in her new cotton dresses, lovelier than every woman he knew, but this...this was the manner of dress that ignited his blood, drummed it through his veins in a tortuous blaze he was hard-pressed to squelch.

Studying her, he realized her hair wasn't Indianlike at all. The ever-present braid upheld the illusion of straight black hair, but gathered in a loose knot, tendrils curled becomingly at her neck and cheeks. The fire's glow cast alluring highlights in it. A few pins removed, and the tresses would fall around her like a silken curtain.

He remembered how she'd responded to him the other night, how close he'd been to giving in to his desire. She wouldn't have stopped him. He knew it. Knew with an assuredness he'd never known before. Knew if he gave in now, it would all be over.

And they were completely alone....

Chapter Thirteen

Snowflakes swirled on the frozen ground beneath Miguel's horse's hooves. Clouds played cat and mouse with the moon. He eyed the cabin murderously. The wind caught at the brim of his hat. He unrolled a blanket from behind his saddle and draped it across his head and shoulders.

He should have taken the necklace by force when he found her. Instead he had wheedled and cajoled. After all his watchful, careful plots and plans, she had humiliated him. If she had stepped into the night without her holster he could have had the locket. The *puta!*

He should have shot her. He should have shot Neubauer. They had made a fool of him! Miguel de Ruiz, descendant of one of the most prominent families in Argentina! She had told him the child was Neubauer's. If not for the conversation he had overheard in the saloon, Miguel might never have known. Resentment flared anew at the memory.

"D'juh hear the oldest Neubauer son went and got hisself hitched again?"

A bleary-eyed farmer had leaned into his beer and peered at his neighbor. "Thought that Clanton girl was being courted by that Beker fella from Accord."

"Weren't her."

The other's brows shot up. "No? Who then? McLaury's youngest?"

"Nope. Done married hisseff that Indian princess from the Wild West Show."

"She's a looker."

"Got herself a kid, too. Nice looking boy. 'Bout a year older'n his own boy... must be 'bout seven. Black hair and eyes. 'Bout as different from Nikolaus as night and day, but I seen Anton with him, and he treats the boy just like his own."

"Any wife's gotta be better than that city woman he had afore."

Ruiz had seethed anew, the remainder of the conversation going unheard. Seven. The boy was seven. A little more than seven years ago he had met her on board the *Nebraska* and had taken her.

She had been a virgin. Now she was a liar.

He had a son.

A son he could take back to his country and present to his father. An accomplishment. His father would welcome Miguel with open arms if he knew he had a grandson. His three brothers had each taken their inheritance and carved their fortune in various investments—mining, manufacturing, shipping. Was it his fault his funds had dwindled before he had time to choose a worthy investment?

A little more than seven years ago when his father had shunned him, only one of his brothers had been married, and his wife had borne him two daughters. Miguel pulled the blanket tighter around his hunched shoulders and absorbed the significance of that fact.

He had a son. Even if his brothers had had sons since, his was the first. All along he had had a son. All along she had withheld the information. Lied when confronted.

She would be sorry. Sorry she had shunned him as his father had. Sorry she had kept his son from him. He would see to it.

Neubauer had accompanied the children to the other house, then returned. He and Rain Shadow were occupied for the evening. All Miguel need do was bide his time. A little longer. An opportunity would present itself.

He gazed into the night winter sky. Perhaps in the morning. If the weather cooperated, the snow would cover his tracks. He would be home in a matter of weeks. He imagined presenting the child to his father. Family was everything in his culture. No doubt his father pined for a way to make peace. No doubt he would welcome his son and grandson home. Home with its many comforts—a warm fire, a bottle of port, servants to attend his every need. Home . . . with his son.

They were alone in the snug cabin, its sturdy log walls and snapping fire cocooning them from the winter cold and wind. Apprehension quavered in the pit of Rain Shadow's belly, sending signals to every limb. She willed herself not to tremble.

Her eyes met his, something dark and absorbing drawing her into the heat of his unconscious seduction. On the tabletop between them were the vestiges of his culture, material things proclaiming his family ties, his heritage. Delicate blue-scrolled china plates, cups and saucers. A reed-slim vase where she'd placed a single dried flower. Did Anton find her artless efforts lacking? She'd tried so hard to prepare a suitable meal, serve it in the manner he was accustomed to. The disquieting look in his eyes gave no indication of how he liked the food.

She was reminded of the calm before a storm, those minutes of heavy, oppressive stillness before wind gusted and rain poured from the skies in torrents. A volatile undercurrent passed between them.

Her exotic violet eyes drew him, and unblinking, he studied the twin ebony wings of her brows, her slightly parted, seductive lips. He remembered the satiny feel of them beneath his, the hungry way she responded to his mouth with hers. He was light-headed, as if he'd had too many beers, the way she always made him feel, the way he didn't want to feel about her—about any woman.

Under his gaze, her breathing changed tempo. Her breasts rose and fell beneath the quill work on her dress, diminishing his resolve to stay clear of this woman whose soft voice and strong body sent a surge of blood to that part of him that wouldn't listen to reason.

He wanted to climb across the table and pull her against him, crush her lips beneath his and taste the nectar of her mouth. Anton imagined sliding his hands beneath the dress, up her silken thighs. He envisioned gripping her rounded buttocks and sitting her before him on the table, burying himself in her exquisite scents and softness. His entire body tightened with desire at the image.

I have to have her.

The thought was a mistake.

Wasn't it? She was willing. She'd made that plenty obvious the other night. All he had to do was close the four short feet between them, touch her hair and skin the way he yearned to, and the torture would end. Was he denying himself for nothing? Was he so noble? No, he answered himself. He didn't love her.

All the better, his mind argued. *You don't love her, so she can't hurt you.* His blood pumped hot and thick, erotic images stealing his breath and his sanity. His fingertips tingled as though her silken skin was beneath them now. It had been a long, long time since he'd been with a willing woman.

"Is there anything wrong?" Her full lips parted. "Is there something else you want?" Her eloquent eyes were uncertain, waiting for reassurance. "Anton?"

The air was suffocating, the silence deafening, like that dead still before the storm.

"You." His reply split the quiet like a lightning bolt. "I want you."

Rain Shadow caught her breath and resisted pressing her palms to her racing heart. How much had that admission cost him? Though he obviously had no appetite for the food on his plate, his eyes devoured her. A tremor began in her arms and legs and whipped through her body. The famished look in his eyes and the taut lines around his mouth were almost frightening. Frightening because of his enormous appetites, his extreme emotions and actions. Frightening because of the consuming desire she recognized...and reciprocated.

Alarming, though arousing.

Startling, yet dizzily exciting.

Exciting in a way that melted every last defense into a liquid pool of fire. She opened her mouth and flicked her tongue across her lips.

His nostrils flared.

Her heart thundered. "So, come get me."

The tumultuous storm broke in the depths of his untamed eyes. He stood, the chair clattering to the floor behind him. Rain Shadow's heart thundered a warning in her breast. She rose and met his mouth with hers. He made a noise deep in his throat, a sound of torture and surrender. His kiss was long and hard, stealing her breath and her common sense. His long, sinewed arms wrapped around her and held her possessively against him.

Anton ran eager fingers through her hair, and pins scattered across the tabletop and floor. Released, the raven

tresses spread around her shoulders. He pulled his mouth
from hers and buried his face in her hair, nudged his nose
along her neck and nipped at the tender cord beneath her
ear, assailing her with exquisite tremors.

He inhaled deeply. "Ah, you smell good."

Instinctively, she raised her arms and wrapped them
around his shoulders. The movement grazed her sensitive
breasts against his chest. Mouth at her ear, his fingers found
the thin leather tie behind her neck and loosened it. He
peeled the soft garment forward, coaxing her arms from his
neck. The dress caught on her forearms, baring her upper
body to him.

Alive and trembling, she watched him, read his approval
behind eyes of blue fire. He kissed her again with his lips
and his tongue, then pulled back. Sliding his palms along
her sides, he reached both thumbs inward and grazed her
nipples. Rain Shadow felt them harden and saw the effect
of her immediate response on his enraptured face. Her
body's answer invited his palms to cup her, to test her weight
and shape. She was aware of each rough callus at the base
of his fingers, trembled at the glorious texture of his palms
against her tender skin. Boldly, she watched his tanned
hands dwarf her breasts. The sight spiraled erotic pleasure
and turned it into an overwhelming ache. He turned his
wrists and kneaded her gently.

One hand trailed upward, and he raised her chin with a
knuckle, forcing her to look up. She met his greedy lips and
yanked her restless arms from the confines of her dress,
framing his face with both hands. Impatiently, she pressed
herself into his hand, and he wrapped his other arm around
her, drawing her against him. The kiss grew demanding.
Tormenting.

Mouth slanted over hers, he slid both hands to her waist
and gathered her dress until he could slip his hands be-

neath. His fingers glided over her hips, paused in consideration at the soft leather thong she wore and grasped her buttocks firmly.

She had to touch him. Had to press closer. Had to feel more of him. All of him. She left his mouth, leaned back enough to unbutton his shirt and spread it open. At the first touch of her fingers against his skin, he gritted his teeth and groaned. Impatiently, he jerked one arm at a time from the sleeves and flung the garment behind him.

Without warning, he reached behind her and swept the table with one clean swing of his forearm. China clattered and flew. A cup and saucer smashed against the floorboards. In the next instant he lifted her, and she found herself sitting atop the table. Disconcerted, she stared at the destruction. "Oh, Anton! The dishes!"

He flicked the sugar bowl and settled her more comfortably. "To hell with the dishes."

"But—they're special."

Palms rough and warm on her hipbones, he spoke against her parted lips. "We'll buy more."

His mouth stilled further conversation. His tongue, making intimate love, searched every crevice and discovered each nuance that drew a feverish response from her. It was natural to twine her arms and legs around him and feel him pressed intimately against her—intimate yet immensely unsatisfying. Beneath her palms, his shoulders were sinewy and strong. She explored his corded neck, hard biceps and the broad expanse of his back.

His hands devoured her hips, the indentation at her waist, kneaded and flattened her breasts. He spread suckling kisses along her collarbone. Her whole being hummed with feelings, all vibrant fire and crystal-edged responses. He'd unleashed a howling storm.

Rain Shadow threaded her fingers in his sandy hair and anticipated his next kisses. Her heart pulsed erratically beneath the surface of her skin. Every screaming nerve ending poised in expectation. Anton dipped his head and took the hardened core of one breast into his mouth. She dropped her head back and shuddered. Her body responded like a spring thaw, melting and flooding in uncontrollable torrents.

He wet her breast completely before turning his attention to the other. Rain Shadow opened her eyes and watched his tongue circle her nipple, lave it flat, then back to a bud and finally pull her inside his mouth. She hadn't known, hadn't realized anything could feel like this. A powerless sensation crept into her limbs, saturated her senses as his strong hands and masculine scent filled her world until there was nothing else. No one. Only him. *Anton.*

"Anton...." She couldn't raise her voice above a hoarse whisper.

He covered her damp breasts with his enormous palms and gazed into her eyes. "I know."

Blue eyes clouded with passion, he released her breasts and slid his fingers to the soft leather thong at her hip.

Rain Shadow ended his torment and exposed the slender strip tying it in place. He tugged the tie free, his strong fingers trembling ever so slightly. Her undergarment lay like a forgotten scrap on the table beneath her. Both moved their hands to the waistband of his denims. Anton was quicker. He unbuttoned, but she shoved them down his thighs, glad he'd removed his wet boots at the door so he had only to kick free of the restricting trousers.

He guided himself to her, pausing not to consider but in consideration, and kissed her waiting mouth. She wrapped her arms around his shoulders, and he offered himself slowly. Maddeningly slow. So slow she wrapped her legs around his hips and drew him into her completely. Any discomfort was forgotten in a few wondrous and swift strokes.

"Ah, Rain—Shadow...." Moisture glowed on his golden skin. She clung to him, riding the searing wave of mounting sensation.

Unleashed senses came into acute focus. Anton was aware of her fingers gripping his shoulders, but so intense was the frenzied pleasure of burying himself deep within her that he ignored the pain. He was aware of his choppy breath, the heightened scent of her aroused body, the strength of her thighs gripping his hips and the captivating sight of her arched throat.

Head thrown back in abandonment, her midnight-black hair caressed the backs of his fingers on her hips. Her tongue slid across her swollen lips in an unconscious gesture, and her closed eyelids trembled. Peine, who would never have allowed herself such an undignified position in the first place, would have kept her eyes closed against the sight of him and the unpleasantness of the deed he performed.

He pulled back to watch. Her body fascinated him. Astounded him. Aroused him more than he'd known was humanly possible. Her dark skin glowed with passion, a sight he gloried in. Peine had ashamedly tried to keep her pale, powdered body from him. Rain Shadow was physically strong, as he'd known, but sleek, lithe and feminine, passion endowing her limbs with an energy equal to his. Her heightened pulse beat visibly at the base of her throat, the gold locket skittering jerkily against her skin. Damp tendrils of hair spiraled at her neck and temples. Her expressions were glorious, unaffected, and her high, honeyed breasts tight and hard....

Her honest reaction was amazing. Her resplendent an-
swers to his kiss, his hands, the thrust of his unrelenting
body were more than he'd ever hoped for.

"You're beautiful," he said, and watched her eyelids
flicker open.

She pulled him close and pressed her lips against his collarbone, darted her tongue along his throat, licked at the
tangle of scars on his shoulder. Anton ground his teeth,
praying for endurance. Something escaped her lips, not a
gasp, not a hiccup, but a sound that enervated and excited
at the same time. She bit his chin hard enough to hurt.

He recognized the sudden added tension in her limbs,
grasped her buttocks accordingly and caught the tiny gasps
escaping her lips with his own. In startled wonderment, he
felt her convulse gently around him.

Her response was too precious. Too good to be happening to him. And totally unexpected.

Rain Shadow was filled, body, soul and senses. Anton
grasped her bare hips, and she returned the possessive embrace. He was splendid, golden and beautiful, his eyes
darkened to a deep, sultry blue, the muscles of his arms and
shoulders flexing in smooth rhythm to his accelerated
thrusts. With a throaty, rasping cry, he shuddered against
her.

His hands slipped over her satin-slick skin, long fingers
caressing her spine. Much too quickly, the waves subsided.

Inevitable. From the first time their eyes met this had been
inevitable. She couldn't have stopped it any more than she
could have stopped a hurricane. Wouldn't have wanted to.

"Rain Shadow...."

She lifted her gaze from the jagged pulse at his throat,
past the teeth marks on his chin to his heart-reaching eyes.

"You're so beautiful," he whispered.

"So are you."

"Perfect."

She smiled.

Concern flicked across his heat-flushed face. "Did it—did I—hurt you?"

"Not so I noticed."

He pressed a kiss against her damp forehead.

She flexed her fingers, suddenly realizing how hard she'd gripped his shoulders. "Did I hurt you?"

"Yeah."

He laughed first, and she joined him.

He dropped his gaze to her innocently seductive breasts and the locket hanging between them, and wondered for the first time if the hard surface of the table was uncomfortable. "Sorry. The table wasn't comfortable for you, was it?"

"Just the..."

"The what?"

She squirmed ever so slightly, and he felt himself still thick and swollen inside her.

"The sugar."

Without surrendering their precious link, Anton raised her with one arm and brushed the other palm over the grains on her satin-smooth buttocks, his vow to resist her forgotten...forgetting who she was and wasn't...who he was and the mistakes he'd made before. Still wrapped around him, her breath caught in her throat, she made a tiny sound he knew he'd remember forever, an intimate sound of surprise and pleasure that devastated his senses.

With the slightest urge of his arms, she tightened her arms and legs around him, and he held her against him, her hair sliding cool and silken against his skin. Better than he'd imagined. How he wanted this woman. "Are you too sore?"

She tossed her head in denial.

He crossed the room and carried her into the darkened bedroom, knelt on the bed and fell forward heavily, burying her beneath him.

In the softness of the bed, Rain Shadow stretched out with a sigh and gloried in his strength and weight, hoping he would take his time. She felt a sense of security and belonging in his arms that she'd never known. She wound her fingers through his golden hair, pressed her nose against his damp neck and inhaled as if to draw all of him inside her lungs. She tasted his skin, a salty, earthy taste, nourishment that could easily feed her hungry soul indefinitely. He moved inside her, slick-hard and simmering with control, and her renewed enjoyment surprised her.

Anton sought her mouth in the darkness, touched his warm, damp lips to hers gently, more gently than he'd ever kissed her before. She framed his face with her hands, impressing this moment, these exquisite feelings, scents and tastes into memories to carry with her for an eternity.

Anton turned his head and bit her thumb gently. Almost lazily, he drew one of her knees up his side and caressed the sole of her foot, her ankle, the back of her sensitive thigh, her hip and the base of her spine. Intuitively his fingers returned to her thigh and drew slow figure eights from behind her knee to her hip, matching her increased movement and burying himself exquisitely slow and deep. "Does that feel good?"

She groaned against his jaw, sought his mouth.

"Tell me."

"Yes," she assured him. "Don't stop." Soon she would have to leave. Leave his arms, his home, leave the only small measure of security she'd ever known. But for now, for this minute, this hour, this night, he was hers. She ran her hands over his strong shoulders, his hard biceps, down the smooth plane of his back and dug her fingers into his hips, holding him as close as possible for two people to be.

"Kiss me now," he groaned.

Gladly, she kissed him back, shaking with the passion he evoked. She'd never felt so cherished. It was probably just a foolish fantasy because of the way he made her feel and the way she felt about him. The emotion she experienced compared to no other. What was this all-consuming need she had for him, for his approval, his attention, his body? She loved her child. She loved Two Feathers. But this was different. Wasn't it?

He buried his face in her hair.

She wanted him. She needed him. Tears clogged the back of her throat. "I love you," she whispered into his ear.

Anton felt her tremors, felt her breath against his bad ear. Needing to hear her pleasured sighs, he lent his other ear to her mouth and petted her, gentling her spirit at the same time he satiated her body. She writhed against him in a final, beautiful burst of pleasure, and he shuddered into her, his climax abating in lethargic waves.

He rolled beside her, tugged her alongside his length, and she cuddled him naturally, trustingly. Rational thought returned slowly. Reluctantly, Anton opened his eyes and stared at the ceiling. "Rain Shadow?"

"Yes." Her voice was a soft whisper against his chest.

They had no future, had made no promises. She had plans that didn't include him. Soon she'd be the reigning princess of the Wild West Show, international fame and glory a far cry from farm life in rural Pennsylvania. He'd forgotten to be careful, forgotten he was a man who had nothing to give—a man unworthy to accept what she gave. "I had no right to do that."

She was silent for a moment. "I am your wife."

"Yes." *No.* A wife didn't respond like that. A wife didn't turn to surging heat and hot-burning responses in his arms. Peine never had. And he was hard-pressed to imagine Lydia or Annette wrapped around her husband, head flung back in sensual abandonment. She'd run her hands across his body, heedless of his imperfections, and he'd soared to heights never before explored. Had she known how her touch inflamed him? Or had she cared?

His wife.

He closed his eyes...smelled her on his skin, felt her warm and alive along his side. Nothing that good could happen to him; he had no place getting his hopes raised. He had to remain realistic. She was grateful for his protection. He'd wanted her since he'd first seen her.

Now he'd have her out of his system. Completely and totally, he assured himself, and fell asleep with her head tucked under his chin, her satin-soft leg entwined with his. That was what he wanted, wasn't it?

The glowing barn undulated, one moment graphically clear, the next blurred by shimmering orange waves of heat and...tears. Anton watched keenly. Heat warmed his face while a cool breeze flirted with his back.

The sound of a woman's voice prickled his scalp, sent shudders along his spine and tore the breath from his lungs. The eerie singsong chant coaxed him toward the jagged opening in the side of the barn.

His leaden feet moved awkwardly but steadily, carrying him closer to the shimmering heat. Every self-preserving instinct screamed to stay back, stay clear of the devouring flames. Still the lilting voice drew him ever forward. At the opening in the splintered wood, he stared into the barn, helpless to tear his eyes from the raven-haired woman silhouetted before the shimmering yellow and orange inferno.

She called to him without saying a word.

"It's too hot," he said. She ignored his protest and beckoned him forward. Amazingly, the opening widened to permit him passage. He stepped through the portal. He'd never been in the fire before. It wasn't as painful as he thought it would be. Maybe he was dead.

The woman's bare golden body glowed with perspiration. Claws and shells hung from a thong at her neck, and she chanted, her graceful limbs swaying in a hypnotic rhythm. She smiled at him, the smile of one as wise and as old as the sun and the sky. Reaching out a long, slim arm, she touched his shoulder. Searing pain tore through his flesh.

"Come," she spoke at last. She stepped backward, scant inches from the crackling inferno.

No. No. His mind raged in defense, but his tongue refused the words. His traitorous feet drew him forward. Heat blasted his skin. Racking pain pushed his mind toward the edge of sanity.

"Don't be afraid," she crooned, taking his hand and drawing it to her glowing flesh.

His hand shriveled. Blisters erupted on his face. His skin stretched and peeled. Still he followed her, drawn into the core of the fire. Destruction hissed blue jets of soul-scorching flame in every direction.

"We're together now," she sang tonelessly. Smoke wreathed her head. Her skin turned deathly white, her hair as orange as the glowing embers. Glittering green eyes held him spellbound. Lying eyes. Eyes Anton recognized with horror.

Peine!

She'd dragged him into hell! Again!

Anton bolted upright. The coverlet lay twisted around one ankle, trailing onto the floor. On the night table his pocket watch ticked in the silence of the dark room.

Tick. Tick. Tick.

From beside him, small, strong hands rubbed his perspiring shoulder. "The dream again?"

Rain Shadow.

In the silent, dark room, the silken length of her thigh against his hip and her comforting hand assured him of reality. Night was dark. The bed was soft. Air felt good in his lungs. The earth still existed. Everything was as it should be. Slowly, his heart returned to a normal cadence, and he flopped back on the pillows.

Rain Shadow gathered the fallen covers and pulled them over them both, tucking herself along his length. He angled his chin to fit her head in the hollow of his neck and stroked her hair.

"You loved her very much, didn't you?"

The question caught him by surprise. His hand stilled. He stared into the darkness overhead. Had he called out Peine's name while he dreamed? "I'm not any smarter than I look."

"She was beautiful."

"How do you know?"

"I've seen your wedding portrait."

His fingers moved over her hair again. "I keep it for Nikolaus."

The wind whistled at the shuttered windows. "Do you think they're all right?"

He took her hand from his chest and kissed her fingers. "The boys are just fine. Go back to sleep. I'm sorry I woke you."

"I wasn't asleep." Her breath tickled the hair on his chest. He sensed her slight smile. "I've never slept with a man before. I wanted to remember all of it. Make it last, sort of."

Anton couldn't believe she felt that way about him, but everything about her smacked of honesty and naiveté. He swallowed a hot-burning sadness and regretted with all his heart that she wouldn't be the woman he made the rest of his life with. She had other plans.

She'd wanted it all just as badly as he had—that had been half the thrill—but he couldn't help believing she'd regret what they'd done after she had time to think. He couldn't bear to see disgust cloud her eyes when she came to her senses. He'd allowed a few of his fences to fall, but they could be mended again. And the safest way was to start building them before she had a chance to knock down any more.

Anton closed his eyes and prayed for the strength.

Thin winter light cast a gray pall over the bed. Rain Shadow woke to the creak of the bed ropes. The bed dipped, and she rolled her head. Anton sat with his broad back to her, pulling on his denims. He stood and pulled them up his thighs, his firm buttocks a vivid reminder of the night before.

"Good morning," she said, sleepily.

He faced her, reaching for his shirt. His expression was almost one of embarrassment.

She frowned. "Anton, are you sorry?"

The shirt dangled from his fingertips. He shrugged noncommittally, but his gaze traveled to her. "I thought I'd give you a chance to get up alone."

She raised on her elbows, and the sheet slipped lower. "Should I be—embarrassed?"

His blue eyes widened at her frank question. "My wife—" he began.

Something in her chest shifted and ached at the mention of the woman he loved, but shamelessly, Rain Shadow wanted to hear it. "What?"

"She didn't like to see me without my shirt. And we always—" he ran a hand over the stubble on his cheek "—made love in the dark."

Silence stretched between them. Rain Shadow wondered at a relationship where lovers were inhibited about their bodies. She realized her upbringing had given her a different outlook, but was that the way a man expected a woman to behave? "And you prefer it that way?" she asked at last.

He perched on the bed's edge. "Don't you?"

"I don't know. The few times Miguel and I—" She broke off, searching for an appropriate word, but didn't know one. "Well, it was in secret and over quickly. I don't know how men and women behave, but..."

This time he prodded her. "Go on."

"Do you like looking at me?"

Blue fire ignited in his gaze. "More than you know."

"That's how I feel about you, too. I know I'm not a lady, Anton. I could never be the woman your wife was. I'm not sophisticated, and I don't know what's proper or what men like. I only know you make me happy, and if—"

"Whoa!" He studied her with surprise. "You're not disgusted?"

She returned his stare. "With what?"

His lips moved before he spoke. "With me. With the way we..."

Something vulnerable wavered behind his half-veiled eyes, and she knew what she said next would be important. How could he think she was disgusted? "Anton, what we shared last night was beautiful."

Shirt forgotten on the bed, he leaned over her, threaded his fingers through her hair and spread it away from her face. "You're beautiful."

She smiled.

"You have the wrong idea. You're a hundred times the woman Peine was. With her there was no peace, no satisfaction. She never gave me anything, wasn't satisfied with me..." He stared at the pillow next to her head as if deep in thought. "She was never satisfied with herself. She found no joy in anything." His gaze came back to hers. "You gave me more last night than she did in four years of marriage. You're happy with so little, Rain Shadow."

Something raw and painful twisted in her breast. *So little.* This short, bittersweet time together, the physical release she'd been for him. She'd told him she loved him, and he'd responded with his body, not his heart, as if the admission meant nothing to him—as if he hadn't even heard it. His beautiful wife had been a disappointment. Peine had dissatisfied him. But he'd loved her.

Rain Shadow thought of him desperately making love to a woman who didn't return his passion, and her aching heart surrendered more completely. *Was* she happy with so little?

No. But he'd never know. She was a physical outlet. Someone to slake his passion until a proper woman came along. She could give him that. Wanted to give him that. It fleetingly occurred to her that she should get up and dress before the boys came back, but he pulled the sheet away from her breasts, and her hands automatically came up to his chest. There was time.

She understood. In some bruised corner of her own heart, she understood. Miguel had never given her anything, either, except heartache and, unknowingly, Slade. And even though he didn't return her love, Anton offered more than she'd ever had before.

However temporary, she meant to have it.

Chapter Fourteen

Falling snowflakes glistened in the morning sunlight when Anton opened the cabin door. Rain Shadow tipped her face heavenward, blinked away the flakes and smiled.

"Suppose we missed breakfast?" Anton asked from beside her.

"Don't flatter yourself. It's still plenty early."

He laughed and challenged her to a race. She was more agile, but his long legs kept him ahead of her. She considered faking a twisted ankle, but he slowed and pointed toward Franz and Annette's.

Franz ran toward them, coatless, his shirttails flapping in the bitter wind.

"What the—" Anton watched his brother race closer. He broke into a run, Rain Shadow at his heels, and met Franz on a slope.

Slow dread paralyzed Rain Shadow's lungs and heart. She held her breath, waiting for Franz's words, hoping against hope that the stricken look on his face had nothing to do with Slade.

"The boys," Franz panted, and her heart turned over slow and sluggish. "They're gone."

"What do you mean they're gone?" Anton asked, impatiently.

Her brain seemed to take minutes to absorb Franz's words. *Slade. Her precious son.*

"Pa must've taken them to the outhouse before anyone else was awake. They didn't come to breakfast, so I went to check. I found Pa on the ground with his head busted, and the boys were nowhere in sight."

Nikky! Not, Nikky, too! Rain Shadow fought the numbing panic that fogged her reactions. How long had they been gone?

"Why didn't the dogs bark?" Anton asked, disgust lacing his voice.

Franz surveyed the landscape. "Ruiz must've done something to the dogs. I haven't seen neither hide nor hair of 'em since last night."

Anton swore and ran on.

Rain Shadow followed.

Two Feathers knelt over Johann. He turned his head at their approach, the color drained from his stoic features. Jakob's father lay motionless, bright crimson blood dripping from a gash on his temple onto the frozen ground.

"Let's get him in the house," Anton barked.

"Annette sent Jakob for Doc," Franz supplied.

Johann, oh, Johann, Rain Shadow's heart cried. Instinctively, she searched the ground for footprints. Evidence of narrow boots led from the trampled area where Johann lay to a spot behind the barn where a horse had been staked.

"The tracks point west," she said to Two Feathers, who watched the brothers carry their father into the house.

"I should have heard something." Self-blame rose in his voice.

"It's not your fault, Father. There's nothing you could have done."

"I would have killed him and kept him from the spirit world. His heart is black. He has caused you pain since we crossed the Great Waters." Her father kept his stoic profile in her vision, as if he couldn't allow himself to face her. "Now my grandson."

Rain Shadow took his forearm. "Slade will be all right, I promise. I'll bring him back."

Two Feathers met her eyes, and his filled with tears. "Take great care, my child."

Cold unnoticed, they stared at one another, snowflakes swirling between them. She hugged him fiercely, turned and ran. More calm and collected than she had any right to be, she reasoned each step, first taking canteens and saddle-bags from her lodge. In the cabin, she changed into her leather pants and shirt and was packing food and ammunition when Anton threw open the door.

She stared into his haunted blue eyes. *Your son, Anton. Your father. I'm so sorry. This is all my fault.*

"We'll find them," was all he said. He stripped, pulled on long underwear and warm clothing and nodded to her bags. "Everything we need?"

Their partnership went unspoken. The fact that he'd never considered her staying behind didn't go unnoticed. Somehow, since the day he'd told her to make herself useful, she'd won his respect. And just in time. The stakes were way too high to waste energy in disagreement.

The tracks led west, then veered off in a northwesterly direction.

"Got any idea where he's headed?" she asked Anton around noon.

He shook his head. He'd been silent most of the morning. Was he blaming her? His precious son had been involved, thanks to her. His father lay unconscious at the farm. Tears clogged her throat. How badly was he hurt? What if he died?

No. She couldn't think like that. If she allowed herself one second to consider that possibility, it would only lead to the same thoughts about Nikky and Slade.

Gray clouds obliterated the sun, and the landscape manifested itself desolate, more dreary as the afternoon wore on. Finally, they stopped to build a fire and eat a meager meal. Rain Shadow wondered if Miguel had fed the boys. By now they would be cold, hungry and mighty uncomfortable riding three atop one horse.

The snow began falling in earnest about the same time they stamped out their fire. The tracks—their only guide— would soon be obliterated. Rain Shadow avoided Anton's eyes. She couldn't bear the stark fear she read in their joyless blue depths and dreaded watching that fear turn to accusation and resentment.

Night fell, and Rain Shadow constructed a low sleeping tent made of hides. Anton built a fire, and they ate biscuits and bacon. Inside the tent, they removed their clothing and crawled into the blankets together, relying on their combined body heat to warm them through the night.

Rain Shadow lay with Anton's solid form along the length of her body, her spine curved against him. He curled himself around her protectively, but made no move to touch her intimately. He hadn't spoken much their entire ride, and only when necessary while setting up camp. The inch or more of snow blanketing the earth insulated them from even the slightest noise. The only sounds she heard were his heartbeat against her back, his pocket watch in their pile of clothing and the damning voices in her head.

Every fear of Miguel she'd ever experienced had sharply focused into reality. He'd done everything she'd anticipated plus a whole lot more. Why had he come looking for her after all this time? Traveling with the Wild West Show was far from inconspicuous. Should she have left it years ago? Had she been so obsessed with finding her family that she'd ignored a basic step in her son's protection?

But how could she have known? Miguel hadn't wanted her! He'd made that plain enough. Why should she have anticipated he'd come looking for her? *Tunkasila Wankan Tanka…Grandfather Great Spirit, Tative Topa, God of the Four Winds, return my son to me safely. Return Anton's son without harm, and restore Johann…don't let him die. Help me, I pray to You, don't let any of them die….* She ached with the terrifying thought.

Age-old remorse and guilt flooded back cold and hard. All of this stemmed from her one mistake, the reverberations continuing like a stone hurled into smooth water, the circles ever widening, touching more and more lives. And the truth sat at the bottom of the pond like that rock—cold and hard and unchanging: she'd brought this upon them.

Unci Maka, Grandmother Earth, help me. I promise to leave and let them resume their lives the way they were before. Anton had been looking for a wife—a proper, domestic mother for Nikky—and look what Rain Shadow's intrusion had done. In retrospect, Sissy Clanton's face came to her from the night Miguel had stabbed Anton: pale, assessing. Sissy probably wouldn't have turned down Anton's proposal had she not seen the way he took Rain Shadow's hand, had she not been witness to the spectacle of him lying on the ground bleeding, Rain Shadow hovering over him with concern.

He could be married to Sissy now. Or at least planning a wedding. *I'm sorry.* He still had a chance with one of the other young women.

Anton's hand cupped her cheek, and he turned her face toward his. She didn't know she'd been crying until he wiped the tears from her face with gentle fingers. He kissed her, and she clung to him, choking back a sob.

Their kiss held an edge of desperation. Long ago she'd learned she couldn't change the past, so she'd placed all her hopes and dreams on the future. At this moment the future looked bleak—perhaps unbearable. All she had was right now, right this minute, tonight in Anton's arms. She returned kiss for kiss, touch for touch, taking wanton comfort in the heat of his desire. He prolonged the mindlessness she sought, drawing each physical response to a height and breadth and depth that left room for nothing else.

I love you. She sobbed against his neck when the release came, cried his name and shook with the force of her chaotic emotions.

"We'll find them," he said against her hair. "If it's the last thing I do, we'll find them."

By morning it had stopped snowing.

"We find new tracks, and we've got him," Anton said, helping her pack their gear. He led their horses from cover against a bluff, and they mounted.

"Do you think we've been heading in the right direction?"

He settled his Stetson over his forehead before answering. "Y'know, I've been wondering if there is a right direction. What if he meant to circle back toward the farm? I lay awake trying to figure out his reasoning. What will he do with them?"

Rain Shadow squinted against the morning sun glaring off the pristine snow and settled her wide-brimmed hat. "I lay awake trying *not* to think about his reasoning. I guess what he'll do with them depends on his purpose."

"Think it's you or Slade?"

Without an answer, she shrugged and pulled on her snug leather gloves.

"Seems he's headed northwest. Why don't we ride a line from southwest to northeast and see if we can't cross his tracks somewhere?"

His plan sounded logical to Rain Shadow, so they rode steadily.

The morning was still early. She stopped Jack with a soft word and tilted her head.

Anton reined the General around to face her. The animal shook his massive head, and his snaffle ring clinked in the stillness.

"I smell a fire," she said.

Anton raised his face and tested the air. Off to the left stood a copse. "They could be anywhere in there," he said softly.

"Why don't we split up and skirt the outside on foot?" she suggested. "If they're in there, one of us should spot them. We'll meet back here and decide what to do."

Wariness edged his handsome features. Fatigue etched lines under his eyes, and his nose was red from the cold. Finally, he nodded his agreement.

"Anton," she whispered. "Move slowly. Stop often to listen and sniff the air. What you don't hear is as important as what you hear."

He hobbled the General and moved away from her.

Rain Shadow drew a deep breath, untied her holster thong and slipped silently into the trees, following the outer edge of the forest, the cold forgotten. Time had no place or meaning here. Tree trunks stood in stark contrast to the harsh white above and below. Above, the canopy of branches hung low with snow and ice. Below, every twig her boots snapped sounded like gunfire to her ears. She kept her eye on the position of the sun through the filtering branches, calculating how far she'd come.

The scent of smoke drifted to her again, and she paused to listen. Nothing. Not even the sound of birds or small animals. Her scalp tingled.

"I do not suppose you came alone."

The thickly accented voice stopped her dead. She turned her head slowly, her heart thundering in her chest. "I'm alone."

"You think me a fool, *querida*."

She scanned the frozen woods, her hand moving toward her holster.

"I would not do that if I were you. Throw the gun toward my voice."

With deliberate slowness, she drew her revolver from its holster, turned the butt away from her and tossed it toward the pine trees.

"Now your knife."

Damn! Bending, she slid her knife from her boot and aimed it at a trunk, wishing it was his heart. The knife lodged with a solid whack.

As if sensing her hatred, his insolent laughter punctured the stillness. A movement caught her eye. He rose from the ground where he'd blended like an animal in its natural surroundings, shook the snow from his clothing and hat and gestured at her with his rifle. "This way, my lovely. My son has an unrealistic opinion of his *madre*." Miguel picked up her gun and tucked it in his belt. "He thought she would shoot her way into my camp and rescue him."

Rain Shadow had no choice but to walk to him. He nudged her forward with the gun barrel.

She smelled the fire before she saw it. A few scant feet from the fire, huddled beneath a blanket with their backs against a tree, sat two small forms, woolen hats pulled low.

"Mama!"

"Rain Shadow!"

Ignoring Miguel's warning, she ran to them. She pulled their heads against her coat front and hugged them tightly. She peeled off her gloves and wiped the tears from their cheeks. "Don't cry any more. I'm here."

Pulling back the blanket, she discovered their bound hands. A rope at their waists secured them to the tree. Both children were cold and frightened. Rage filled her soul. She stared into her son's eyes.

"Move away from them," Ruiz said from behind her.

"They're cold!" she accused him. "Untie them and let them sit by the fire."

"I said move away!" Ruiz poked her shoulder sharply with the rifle barrel. She caught her balance and covered the boys' hands, pulled the blanket to their chins and backed away. Brazenly, she turned to face the man who threatened everything she held dear. "What do you want?"

Quick as lightning, he grabbed her coat front in a fist and hauled her face up to his. "Why did you keep him from me?"

Rain Shadow stared into obsidian eyes so like her son's. "Why do you think, Miguel?"

He shook her, and her teeth rattled. "I had a right to know! I had a son all this time, and I should have known!" A thin blue vein stood out in the center of his forehead.

"You used me, Miguel!" she shouted, and hated the way her voice cracked. "I was sixteen years old, and you let me believe we would get married in London! No sooner did the ship dock, and you married another woman! What do you think that did to me? What kind of person would do that?"

Rain Shadow drew a ragged breath and held him with her furious gaze. "I swore I'd make something of my life and my son's life, that I wouldn't let your cruelty ruin our future. And I've done that. I'm proud of myself, and I'm proud of my son!''

The look in his eyes changed. Her words had disturbed him. His grip on her collar loosened. ''I could have been proud of him, too.''

''How could I think a man who would lie to seduce me and then marry another woman would be a decent father?''

Abruptly, Ruiz released her and shoved her toward the fire. ''Sit.''

Trembling, but grateful he hadn't made a move to tie her, she squatted next to the warmth.

Miguel came to stand beside her. He stroked her cheek with his gloved fingers, trailed them across her lips, down her chin and tipped her face toward him. He leaned forward, his dark face inches from hers. ''You are so beautiful,'' he whispered.

Rain Shadow's pulse hammered. Disgust backed up into her throat. ''Not as beautiful as a franc, though, am I?''

He smiled unpleasantly. ''Each has its own merit. You would be wise to remember that.'' His smile flickered, but he managed to retain it. Releasing her chin, he sat across the fire from her. The rifle, slung almost casually over his thigh, pointed at the children.

''I want my son.'' His eyes narrowed in challenge.

Her heart leapt in her breast. Fear eddied into every pore, diluting her courage. He wanted Slade! ''You didn't even know you had a son.''

''I need to punish you for that.''

Keeping her tone conversational, she asked, ''What would you do with a child?''

''I will take him home to my father.''

Home? South America? ''Why?''

Miguel poured a cup of coffee from the dented pot over the fire and offered it to her. She refused. "Restitution," he replied, sitting back with the steaming cup.

Confused, she stared at his narrow black features and detested her helplessness. What did he owe his father that an illegitimate son would repay?

"When you came to Pennsylvania, you didn't know Slade existed. What did you come for?" The question she'd wondered all along tumbled from her lips.

He appeared to consider answering. "I wanted the necklace."

She frowned. "What necklace?"

"The locket you wear."

Rain Shadow's hand grasped her coat front instinctively. "My locket?" She frowned. "I don't understand."

He gave her a sharkish grin. "That particular stone is worth much—its quality and cut are unequaled."

His explanation rang false, but his reasons didn't matter. She unbuttoned the top of her coat and reached behind her neck. Fingers numb, she fumbled with the clasp. Without a moment's hesitation, she unfastened the chain and dangled the locket before him. "Here, then. Take it, and let us go."

Miguel de Ruiz stared. The glittering gold filigree winked in the sunlight, the amethyst stone catching the fire's glow. All he had had to do was ask. The locket was his for the taking. He took the necklace from her and weighed it in his palm, the gold still warm from her skin. Avarato would pay dearly for this treasure.

What of Rain Shadow? Could he get her to play along? Would she pose as the Avaratos' granddaughter? Of course she would...for the right price. He looked from her storm-filled eyes to the *ninos* cowering against the tree and smiled. Everyone had his price.

Chapter Fifteen

Rain Shadow met Ruiz' gaze and subdued a shudder.

"I will let you go when the time is right," he replied. "First I have a little acting role for you."

"What do you mean?"

"Do not be so impatient. You will find out in due time. Trust me."

She'd trusted him once—with her innocence—and look where it had landed her. She watched him tuck her locket inside his heavy wool coat. Leveling the rifle on her midsection, he stood, moved to Nikolaus and untied his bindings.

Blue lips quivering, Nikolaus released a shuddering frosty breath and turned enormous liquid-blue eyes toward her as though entreating her to do something. Helplessly, her heart aching, she gave him a reassuring nod and smiled.

"Why did you take him?" she asked across the few feet separating them.

"Look at them, *querida.*" His breath puffed out in white gusts. "In hats and coats I could not tell the difference. It was not such a bad move, however. I have the farmer's undivided attention, too, do I not?"

"Let Nikky go now. You have the one you want." Oblivious to the cold, she tried to reason with him.

He gave her a considering once-over. "I have worried which would be to my benefit. Set Neubauer's *nino* free and have you tell the plowboy you want to go with me? Your disloyalty might discourage him. However, while the *nino* is in my possession, I have more bargaining power. Do you not agree?"

Slade glowered at Ruiz with hatred. Rain Shadow felt its chill more clearly than the frigid air on her face. Something tender tore inside her at her child's lost innocence. Ruiz untied him. Immediately, Slade jumped to his feet and kicked his captor's shin, then swung a mittened fist in the air.

Like batting away a bee, Ruiz backhanded the boy. Slade sprawled at the base of the tree, his hat landing beside him in the snow.

"Stop!" Rain Shadow ran forward.

Ruiz swung the rifle barrel toward Slade and challenged her with a smug glare.

She stopped in her tracks.

Nikolaus sobbed.

"He rides with me," Ruiz commanded. "*That* one—" his thin black mustache curled in a sneer "—rides with you. I cannot bear his whining. First we go for your horse. Where is it?"

She swallowed hard, controlling her anger and fear. Slade picked himself up off the ground, brushed snow from his clothing and tugged his hat down over his unruly black hair. Blood trickled from the corner of his lower lip. The look he shot her conveyed embarrassed assurance.

Rain Shadow's mind reeled, and she fought to subdue the panic that rose in her chest. How long ago had she and Anton separated? She couldn't lead Ruiz directly to where Anton undoubtedly waited with the horses! Turning her head, she signaled Jack with a whistle, waited several seconds and whistled again. Within a minute the paint trotted to her side and nodded, his ice-encrusted mane bobbing with the motion.

Rain Shadow scrubbed his forehead with her gloved knuckles, wishing with all her heart it was Slade she could touch. She swallowed hard. "Good boy, Jack."

She adjusted her bedroll and saddlebags and, assuring the horse with soft words, lifted Nikolaus onto his back before mounting behind him.

Slade used the stirrups on the black stallion to climb up behind Ruiz. Their captor led them forward, the horses' breath hanging in gusts on the raw air.

Rain Shadow opened her coat and pulled Nikolaus against her body, needing the warm comfort as much as Anton's son did.

"I—wa-want—my Pa." Nikolaus no longer cried, but his voice shuddered from his recent outbursts.

"I know you do, darling." She squeezed him tight. "You'll be back with him real soon, I promise."

They left the shelter of the trees, and she prayed her promise wasn't false. Before they'd traveled far, the exhausted child slept. Rain Shadow watched Slade ahead of her, clinging to the back of the man he so obviously hated. She closed her eyes momentarily and wanted to cry herself.

Where was Ruiz taking them?

And where was Anton?

Where the hell was Rain Shadow?

She'd been gone way too long, and standing here waiting, it was colder than the north side of a gravestone at the North Pole. He stamped his benumbed feet and cursed under his breath. Beside him, Jack's ears pricked forward. Anton peered into the snow-still forest. The General nickered behind him. Dismayed, he turned to watch Jack gallop into the trees. What the...?

It only took a heartbeat to wonder what he should do. Jack obviously knew something he didn't, so Anton mounted and rode the way Rain Shadow's pony had gone. Minutes later, he studied the white-blanketed ground ahead of him, leading the General along Jack's clear prints in the snow. They led him to a clearing. The snow was trampled, and a camp fire had been doused.

Anton studied the signs while mocking himself. He was a farmer, confound it! What was he doing pretending to be an Indian scout?

You're trying to find your son, a voice in his head replied. *Your son and the woman you—*

He identified the spot where Ruiz' horse had been staked. The boys had packed a patch of snow down around a tree. He stared hard at a few crimson drops of blood on the stark white snow.

Rain Shadow's boot prints had been trampled by the horses. *She's with them.* Good. She was there to see after Nikolaus and Slade. But now all three of them were in that madman's clutches.

Even Anton could tell the droppings were fresh—he could catch up if he wanted to, if he deemed it the best solution. He decided to stay a discreet distance behind and take stock of the situation.

At noon the sun warmed him, and gratefully Anton unbuttoned his coat and removed his gloves. He ate a biscuit from the saddlebag and continued to follow the tracks. Where was Ruiz taking them?

What could he do? *Think!* he mentally shouted at himself. What could he do? He couldn't just ride up behind them waving his gun! Ruiz could use any of the three to cover himself.

Anton squinted across the expanse of glaring white landscape. The tracks led down an embankment and into another winter-bound stand of timber and brush.

Get ahead of them! Providing he could stay on their course, he could ride ahead and meet Ruiz head-on. That was it!

Anton urged the General on a passage parallel to Ruiz' and increased his pace. The route was difficult, but he ignored the limbs and branches that tore at his coat and he occasionally grabbed his hat to keep from having it torn from his head.

Almost an hour later, Anton hobbled the General and traveled the last distance on foot, praying he'd guessed the direction correctly. He chose a spot in a small stand of conifers and hunkered down behind a fallen log. Snow drifted before him like a silver blanket in the afternoon sun. He checked his rifle. He removed his gloves and blew on his fingers. He squinted into the distance, drew a breath and implored God's providence on sending Ruiz this way even if he was waiting in the wrong spot.

Cheeks and nose numb, he scanned the woods before him. A queasy feeling settled in his chest and stomach, and he forced down his panic.

An interminable time passed before he became aware of something. Rain Shadow's words came to him, the last words she'd spoken before they'd parted: *Listen and sniff the air,* she'd whispered. *What you don't hear is as important as what you hear.*

There wasn't a sound in the woods except his own breathing.

His heart thudded in his good ear. He strained to listen, cocking his head and slipping off his gloves. Dark forms appeared between the trees fifty yards away. Two horses and riders single file. Anton squinted down his rifle barrel. Ruiz rode closer, and Rain Shadow followed with one of the boys draped in front of her. Her much smaller mount placed her beneath and to the left of Anton's sights, to his advantage.

Anton held his breath and tensed his finger on the trigger. A little closer. *A little closer.* Patience now.

Where was the other boy?

Anton's concentration wavered as he recognized Nikolaus' coat and hat on the child in her arms. Where was Slade? Behind Rain Shadow? Behind Ruiz? His heart lurched—behind them somewhere on the trail?

Anton sent a prayer heavenward and made a hasty calculation of the space Slade would fill if he were behind Ruiz. He held his breath—*this should have been you. Rain Shadow, you're the crack shot*—and slowly squeezed the trigger.

Ruiz jerked sideways, half hanging from his saddle. The black stallion reared, tumbling Slade to the forest floor, where he recovered quickly and sprang to his feet. Ruiz twisted and yanked his foot from the stirrup, falling to the ground and rolling away from the animal's hooves. He staggered to his knees and aimed his rifle at Slade, one arm hanging at his side.

Anton peered over the log. His muttered curses turned the air blue.

"Stay mounted and do not move!" Ruiz shouted at Rain Shadow.

She obeyed. Nikolaus' wail pierced the silent woods. Rain Shadow bent her face to his and touched his cheek with her gloved hand.

"Show yourself, Neubauer!" Ruiz scanned the area where Anton hid. "Show yourself if you care for any of these troublemakers!" He jerked his head at Rain Shadow. "Throw his *nino* down by the other one!"

Anton revealed himself. "I'm here, Ruiz. Take on somebody your own size."

Ruiz laughed. "You are a predictable fool. Throw your rifle down."

Anton complied.

"The gun under your coat, too."

Anton unbuttoned his coat, yanked out the revolver and sent it sailing into a snowdrift.

"Now, move over here." Ruiz kept his eyes on Anton, the rifle aimed at Slade. "It seems our party has grown too large. Someone will have to stay behind."

"Papa!" Nikolaus shrieked, and twisted from Jack's back. Rain Shadow caught his sleeve and held him fast, his feet kicking the ground and sending clumps of snow into the air. "Let me go!" he howled. "I want my pa!"

Anton forced himself to watch Ruiz. The *vaquero* sneered at Nikolaus in disgust. A tiny movement caught Anton's attention, and he sneaked a glance at Slade.

Slade met his gaze deliberately, slid his glove off and edged his hand into the top of his boot.

Nikolaus' tantrum still held Ruiz' attention.

Unobtrusively, Slade slid a knife into his palm and hid it in his sleeve.

No. Anton shot him a guarded look. *Don't try it.* He stepped closer to Ruiz and noticed the bright red stain spreading outward from the hole in his sleeve.

Slade, too, inched toward the wounded man.

"Come back up with me, now, Nikky. You're safe up here." Rain Shadow had Anton's son halfway slung over her lap.

"Let them, go, Ruiz," Anton suggested mildly. "Take this thing up with me."

"I do not want you," he snarled. "You are of no use. You or your squalling brat."

Anton recognized the peculiar edge to Ruiz' thickly accented voice. His scalp tingled. The man wasn't sane. Ruiz had a fanatical tone, an obsessive look in his eye Anton recognized. Peine had had the same look, the same tone the day she'd set fire to the barn and tried to burn Lydia to death. For whatever it was worth, Anton tried to reason with him. "What do you want with them?"

"Slade is my son!"

"Real proud of that fact, are you?"

"They are my future. My fortune."

"What about their futures?"

"*Mi padre* will see that they are taken care of. Family is everything to him. All family but myself, that is. I am the—how do you call it?—black sheep of the family. He disinherited me years ago. He did not appreciate my worth. *I*, however, have the firstborn grandson." Ruiz jerked the rifle. "The little bastard is my ticket back into grace."

Anton gritted his teeth and bit back a growl.

"Anton!" Slade shouted.

Before Anton knew what was happening, metal flashed in the sunlight, and Slade lunged toward him.

Anton's first thought was to disarm Ruiz. He burst forward and kicked the rifle. It fired harmlessly into the sky.

"Anton!" Slade shouted again.

Anton reached for the knife Slade held toward him.

"No!" Ruiz, too, leapt toward the knife, his shout surprising Slade into hanging onto the handle.

Anton tackled Ruiz from the side, knocking him forward. They fell in a pile on the frozen ground, a tangle of boots and legs and thick coats. A sickening gurgle sounded from beneath Anton. He raised his head from Ruiz' back and focused on Slade.

Horror turned the boy's face ashen. Slade jerked his hand back and gaped at the blood covering his palm and seeping between his fingers.

"You all right?" Anton asked him.

Rain Shadow appeared and pulled Slade away.

"Is he all right?"

"He's fine, Anton." Mouth set in a grim line, she nodded her head toward the man beneath her husband. "It's him."

Realizing Ruiz hadn't moved, Anton pulled himself up and knelt at Ruiz' other side. He lay, eyes glazed, Slade's knife protruding from his neck. Blood bubbled from Miguel's lips, trickled across his stubbled cheek and was absorbed by the hard-packed snow.

Dead. Anton absorbed the fact. Against their will, they'd all played a hideous part in this final scene. Miguel de Ruiz had been a fool. All those years ago he could have had Rain Shadow's love, could have been her husband, could have been a father to Slade, but he'd thrown it all away. For what? What could have been more satisfying than an honest woman's love and trust? Apparently, Ruiz had alienated his father and family, as well. The *vaquero* had dealt pain to so many.

Anton stood, slid his gaze to Slade, and his chest ached for the boy. That he'd had to learn about the dark aspects of life in this manner—worse, that he'd had to witness cruelty and greed in his own father—saddened Anton beyond measure. At least Nikolaus had been a baby when his mother had died attempting to kill Lydia. Nikolaus would never have those memories to haunt him. But Slade....

Rain Shadow embraced her son. Sobbing, Nikolaus ran into Anton's side with an impact that nearly sent him sprawling. Anton lifted his son and hugged him against his chest, tears prickling at the backs of his eyes. "It's all right, son. It's over now, and you're fine."

Over Nikolaus' shoulder, he met Rain Shadow's shimmering gaze. He reached her in a second, pulling her and Slade into his embrace. The four of them hugged one another in consolation, comfort and love.

Thank you, Lord, Anton breathed, but his relief was marred by the disturbing remembrance of his father. *Lord, let Pa be all right.*

Chapter Sixteen

"Pa! Pa, wait up!" Nikolaus raced beside his father, stumbling against his thigh and panting. "You made me run my breath off!"

"I did, huh?" Anton steadied his son and resumed his walk. "D'juh get your chores done?"

"Yep." Nikolaus plucked a stick from the ground and flung it in typical little-boy fashion. "There's new kittens in the barn."

"Uh-huh."

Nikolaus studied his father's preoccupied expression and fell into step at his side, futilely attempting to match his much longer strides. Beneath their boots, the meadow grass squished, sodden from the early spring thaw. "You miss them, too, don't you?"

"What?"

Nikolaus gave an exasperated huff. "Pa, you don't pay me no mind when I talk."

Anton halted his step and faced his son, those last words sinking in. Hang it, what was he doing?

He'd been in a constant state of denial for the past two months since—a shadow passed over his heart—ever since she'd left. Eyes as blue as the soon-to-be clematis by the back porch stared at him. He reached out and ran a hand through Nikolaus' wind-ruffled hair, slid his palm to the baby-soft cheek. He loved this boy more than life itself, yet he'd been so absorbed in avoiding his own inner turmoil that he'd ignored him. He'd neglected his most precious gift from God. With an unbearable ache weighting his heart, he fell to his knees on the spongy sod and pulled his son against his chest.

"I'm sorry, Nikolaus." Anton kissed his ear and laid his cheek against his silken hair. "I'm sorry."

Sturdy little arms wrapped forgivingly around Anton's neck. "It's okay." Father and child remained that way for several emotion-filled minutes. "I know you're lonesome, Pa. Me, too. I wish they never had to go back to the show. I wish they could have stayed here and been our family like before."

The thick ache in Anton's chest stretched thin and hung slack like pulled taffy. What had he been thinking of to allow his son to become attached to Slade? From the beginning, he'd known what an enormous mistake that friendship would be. She'd never meant to stay. Never intended for their farm to be anything more than a place for Slade to recover. Hadn't wanted to stay in the first place. It had all been his doing.

He'd brought Slade home. He'd convinced her of the wisdom of leaving him here. He'd coaxed her to dances, dared her to make herself useful and eventually talked her into marrying him. *Marrying him!*

He still couldn't erase the memory of her face the night he'd made his final blunder, the night she'd told him of her plans to leave....

"There's no reason to stay. Slade and I are safe now. Your father is getting around as good as new after his bump on the head. The longer we allow this to go on, the more difficult it will be for the boys to say goodbye."

The boys, it had been. The boys, it had always been. Not a word about her—about them. A horse might as well have kicked him in the chest. "What about Christmas?" he'd blurted.

She paused in folding a shirt and stared at him.

He glanced up from the tiny watch parts on the tabletop. It was getting harder and harder to tell himself not to care.

"Christmas?" she asked.

Abruptly, he returned his attention to the timepiece. He had his pride, after all. "We all assumed you and Slade would be with us for the holidays. The boys have been working on their gifts. You can wait until after, can't you?"

Silence.

From the corner of his eye he saw her rest one slender hand on the scarred table. He remembered what the two of them had done on this table and felt himself stir. He hadn't touched her since the night they'd lain on the cold winter ground and taken comfort in one another's arms.

Apparently, she remembered, too, because her next word had a throaty quality. "Anton."

He looked up.

She was beautiful. Eyes as dark and all-consuming as a moonless midnight, hair soft and fragrant and curling ever so gently around her perfect face. Her glistening lips quivered just enough to arrest his attention. Lord, they were kissable lips, lips that made a man imagine all kinds of erotic things. His thoughts shocked him, and self-directed anger knotted his stomach.

What the devil was he thinking about her looks for? He'd taken that path once before, and he wasn't about to set off on another hell ride into lunacy over a good-looking woman. Okay, so she set his blood on fire and thrummed every last lick of good sense from his brain into his—

He tugged his gaze from her face and stared at her hand on the table. He'd planned on assuaging his lust and having it over once and for all. Satisfy this mindless craving and have it behind him, hadn't that been the plan? Why should he let her departure bother him so? Why couldn't he just say goodbye?

"I haven't known quite how to ask you this." She set aside a small pile of clean clothing and perched on the chair to his left. He had to face her or miss her words. "What will happen now that that—that the terms of our—arrangement—are changed?"

Her flawless honey-hued skin darkened in a deep blush.

"What do you mean?" Anton asked, deliberately forcing her to say the words.

"Will you still have our marriage annulled?" Her skin flamed, but she faced him determinedly.

Slowly, Anton removed his spectacles. "That arrangement was broken, wasn't it?" he asked, hating himself.

"Couldn't you . . ." Her voice trailed off.

Why was he making this more difficult for her? He stared back. "Lie?"

Her gaze skittered away, but he waited, forcing its return. "What other choice do we have?"

"We could go to the lawyer. That'd be expensive and take a lot of time." He placed his spectacles on the table. Maybe if he just bought a little more time. . . . "Or we could stay married."

Her expression was one of pure bafflement. "Why?"

"Have you considered the possibility that you might be pregnant?"

Her lips parted, but no words came out. The high color in her face only minutes before drained. "I did think of that, Anton. I'm raising one child by myself. I could care for another just as well." Her chin lifted defiantly. "It's not what

I'd want, of course, but it probably isn't going to happen anyway."

"How long until we know for sure?" he asked.

"Two weeks, I'd say." He could tell she wanted to say more, but she held his gaze silently.

There. Two weeks. Two weeks, and she'd have no reason to stay. Some sick gut reaction spoke through him. "There's another matter." He leaned back in his chair. "Those papers you signed when you married me made Slade my son—legally. I don't take that lightly."

Her face paled even more. "You wouldn't." She stood, angrily. "You wouldn't try to take my son from me."

Anton's heart pounded like man possessed. *Don't hurt her, you idiot.* "Of course not. Sit down." He waited until she obeyed. "I married you to protect Slade because I care about him."

"You don't have to tell me why you married me."

"Will you listen? The arrangement was made for Slade. I cared about him enough to take that responsibility. I still care about him. I want to—to see him—to be a part of his life." *Was that it? Was that all?*

A deep sadness welled within the depths of her lovely eyes. "Anton, how can that be?"

"He could stay here as long as he wants."

"No. He goes with me."

"Then bring him back."

"When? How?"

"Anytime. Between shows. Next winter again. You know how much he likes it here."

"You wouldn't do anything to take him from me, would you?" Her voice held a hurt he'd never heard before, knew he never wanted to hear again and loathed himself for putting there.

"I'm cantankerous, darlin', but I'm not cruel." Neither missed the endearment. "Stay for Christmas. And then come back. We'll talk then about what to do." Why couldn't he just let her go? He'd held Peine when she didn't want to be with him. He couldn't make the same mistake again. It was unfair of him. He'd manipulated Rain Shadow. Capitalized on her love for her son....

But he'd wrung the promise from her. She'd stayed until after the first of the year.

The severing had been more painful than any of them had anticipated. He and Nikolaus had driven Rain Shadow, Slade and Two Feathers in the springboard, their lodge and belongings piled in the box, Jack tied behind. In Butler, they'd waited awkwardly for the train, the boys sitting sullenly side by side against the station on a wooden bench, Two Feathers poised on the platform's edge like a wooden Indian, arms crossed, craggy face unreadable.

The eleven-fifty's whistle had pierced Anton's composure, and the train steamed into the station two minutes ahead of schedule. Two Feathers gave Anton a resigned nod and boarded the train. At the last minute Slade and Nikolaus exchanged wooden horses and a bow and arrows, then Slade dashed up the stairs, appearing at a window with a glum wave. Nikolaus burst into tears and clung to Rain Shadow's trouser leg until Anton peeled him off. Anton's eyes met hers, Nikolaus' cries and the shrieking whistle preventing any last words.

She'd kissed him then, pulling his head down, pressing herself against his body and closing her eyes tightly. That kiss disturbed Anton's soul, leaving him wanting to hold her, wanting to keep her with him by whatever means necessary, stamping her taste on his lips as the train chugged slowly away from the platform...away from the station... away from Butler, Pennsylvania... and away from him.

Nothing in his life had been in alignment since.

"She called me 'darling,' Pa," Nikolaus said, dragging Anton from his reverie. "Rain Shadow hugged me and made me not be so scared. She loves me, I think."

Anton released his son and took his hand. He didn't know if anything in his life would ever would be on track again.

Rain Shadow carried a tray through the line and helped herself to a slice of roast, potatoes and gravy. Over the hubbub of hundreds of forks and knives, the buzz of voices in different languages and accents and wooden benches scraping the floor, she glanced around for Slade. Beside her, Two Feathers balanced a slice of pie on his tray, and together they made their way through the throng in the dining tent to a table.

Slade joined them as they ate.

"I wondered where you were." She took the napkin from his tray and laid it in his lap.

"I heard the bell, but I couldn't find you."

"That's okay." She gave him a smile. He hadn't been his usual energetic self lately, and she'd been relieved to see him join the other boys in their games that afternoon. "Did you have fun?"

He shrugged. "It was okay." He took a bite of his meat and chewed thoughtfully. "I wonder if Nikky got my letter yet."

"I don't know," she said. "The mail takes awhile to get that far east."

"Think we can go visit Nikky after Philadelphia? It ain't—isn't—too far, is it?"

She met Two Feathers' eyes across the table. "No, it's not far."

"I told the other kids about Christmas. It was somethin', wasn't it?"

Rain Shadow didn't miss the way he'd been leaving the gs off his words the way the Neubauers did. "It was something, all right."

A memory she'd fought off like a bad cold hit her full force. Christmas with its established customs, laced with sentiment and gay family celebration, had been a grim pleasure. All of Rain Shadow's former Christmases had been spent like any other day: practice, dinner in the dining tents with some six hundred other members of the show and an evening in front of a fire with Two Feathers. Any slim imaginings of the way others spent the holiday came from books, newspapers and pictures.

She remembered a photograph she'd seen once—a family at Christmas dinner, an enormous turkey gracing the table. She had studied that picture, hungrily inspecting each family member's face, identifying their relationships to one another and imagining their lives. She'd examined their clothing, the dishes, the lace tablecloth, even the clock on the wall, and she'd wondered if they always ate dinner at one-seventeen. That image had lodged in her mind, real family behavior as elusive as a butterfly.

Someday, she'd decided. Someday when she found her family, they would sit down to dinner together, and she would belong. She would experience what others took for granted.

She would never take a family for granted.

Rain Shadow could still smell the tree Anton had cut and carried into the cabin for them to decorate. She could still taste the popcorn they'd eaten faster than they could string it. She could still see the delight on her son's face when Anton had held him up to place his paper star on top of the tree, and—a divine disturbance swelled in her heart at the memories of the man she'd grown to love—she could still feel his strong, healthy body as he'd stood behind her and whispered secrets about the gifts he had waiting in the hay loft for Nikolaus and Slade.

Never would a Christmas Eve be as wrought with dear anguish as that one had been. Everything she'd ever wanted, ever dreamed of, danced ahead of her reach, taunted her with the realization of just how happy she would never be.

None of it had been real.

She had tucked Slade into bed, knowing they didn't belong there. She'd sat near the fire with Anton, coping with the fact that he was her husband but that nothing concrete bound him to her. She'd gone to bed in anticipation of another disturbing day to follow and listened to the cabin's night sounds, hoping Anton would come to her bed, praying he wouldn't.

He hadn't.

Day after strenuous day, she had avoided situations and subjects that would make her feelings for him obvious. She loved him. He wanted a proper wife. They'd come to a stalemate. He still had a chance for happiness. As soon as she was gone, he could get on with his life.

Why couldn't she get on with hers? Rain Shadow slid her hand in her pants pocket and closed her fingers around the gift Anton had given her that Christmas Eve. She pulled out the silver-dollar-size pocket watch and ran one finger over the delicately engraved flowers on the gold cover. An unusual gift for a woman, she'd said without thinking. "You're an unusual woman," he'd replied.

She regarded her son with frustration. How could she put Anton Neubauer behind her when Slade spoke of the Neubauers constantly, begged her to return and had even adopted their clipped speech? Stuffing the watch in her pocket, she made up her mind to get their lives back to normal. Slade playing with the other boys today was a good sign. They needed time and distraction. "Want to practice with the hatchets tomorrow?"

His black eyes lit with enthusiasm. The trick was one he'd wanted to learn for some time. "Yes-sir-ee!" His gleeful expression clouded over. "What if I hit Grampa?"

She smiled tolerantly. "You won't throw at Grampa until you're very, very good. Grampa didn't take his place on that target until I'd been throwing for a couple of years."

"Aw, heck." Slade laid down his fork and finished his milk. "Good," he continued, his reaction changing from disappointment to relief in the flash of a second. "I was worried about hitting him. Think I'll be as good as you, Ma?"

"You can be whatever you want to be," she replied, imagining him as a lawyer, a teacher or the head of a big industry. *That's it, Rain Shadow. Focus on your goal. Get back on track.* The contest was less than a month away, and her success depended on giving it her undivided attention.

Her shooting was better than ever. She practiced hours on end every day. Yesterday she'd seen the posters and handbills advertising the contest: Championship Contest between Annie Oakley, Peerless Wing and Rifle Shot, and Princess Blue Cloud, Superb Horsewoman and Crack Shot. Buffalo Bill's Wild West Show. Opens April 14, 1895, Delacourt Park, Philadelphia, Pennsylvania.

It was only a matter of time until her dream came true.

The dream changed. The nightmare evolved into a sensuous panorama of shapes, scents, sounds, textures and temperatures that titillated and tortured. From the edges of sleep Anton moaned at the sensation of cool, silky hair grazing his hypersensitive heated flesh. Velvet-soft skin gliding along his hard muscle and bone was painfully vivid.

Warm, damp lips and tongue caressing his stubble-rough cheeks and furred chest stole his breath and suffused his body with rock-hard heat.

The sensory onslaught haunted him.

Rain Shadow. Cool satin skin and ardent responses.

His own blazing heat and nameless, crushing fear. Apprehension seized his heart and squeezed the breath from his chest. The gentler her touch, the more suffocating the heat. The more passionate her mouth, the more crushing the dread. He was afraid his blazing desire would rage out of control and burn down the defenses he'd so carefully built and protected.

Anton came fully awake and stared into the darkness. Kicking away the coverlet, he allowed the air to cool his perspiring skin. He groped for matches on his nightstand and lit the lantern. The water in the pitcher on the washstand was cold, and he poured some into the bowl and splashed his face and chest.

In the lantern's apricot glow, his harrowing reflection in the mirror distressed him. He hadn't had a decent night's sleep in weeks, and exhaustion was taking its toll. What had he done to himself? He delved long fingers through his damp hair, gripping until his scalp hurt. It wasn't supposed to be this way. He should have been working in his shop, playing *mosche balle* with his brothers, courting Helena McLaury.

Pain lapped at the edges of his mind, rippled through his heart and crested in the parched, barren wasteland of his soul. He gripped the edge of the washstand and let the hurt roll over him in a mounting wave. Black and turbulent, it raged through him, dashing every last defense and leaving his heart raw and vulnerable.

He raised brimming eyes to the mirror and knew why he'd protected his emotions from exposure for so many years.

Love hurt, dammit! He had been in love with Peine, had been enamored of her beauty, education and city ways. He'd tried in the only manner he knew how to make their marriage work, to make her love him, but the effort had been useless.

Sometimes he understood that it wasn't because he was unlovable that Peine had been repulsed by him and obsessed with Jakob.

But it had hurt. More than he'd been willing to admit to himself or anyone else. And the experience had left him unwilling to open himself up to anyone ever again. He'd learned to live without a woman's love. He'd learned not to need companionship. The thought of needing a woman terrified him. Where anyone other than Nikolaus had been concerned, he'd carefully and methodically constructed a barrier around his feelings; it was a shell neither Sissy Clanton nor Helen McLaury could have penetrated, a shell Rain Shadow had dissolved in only a few short weeks.

Rain Shadow. He winced. Thinking her name was like ripping open a partially healed wound.

A tap on the door startled him. The door opened, and Anton ran a hand across his face.

"You all right?" Johann padded into the room in rumpled drawers.

Anton nodded at his father. "Couldn't sleep."

"Seems to be going around." He sat at the foot of Anton's coverless bed. "We need our rest. Spring plantin's hard work."

Agreeing, Anton lowered himself to the bed's edge and eyed the pink scar in Johann's hairline. "You feeling okay?"

"Seems you're the one hurtin'."

Anton felt a muscle in his arm jump. "Seems I am."

"Want to talk about it?"

He shrugged as if he didn't know what to say or where to start. "I think you know."

Johann nodded. Several minutes passed in companionable silence. "Do you love her?"

The familiar acute cramp seized his heart. "Yes."

"What are you going to do about it?"

Anton cut his gaze to the twisted coverlet on the floor. What *was* he going to do about it? Spend the rest of his life feeling like this? Ache for her until the day he died? Court Helena McLaury and, heaven forbid, maybe even marry her because he didn't love her and she couldn't hurt him? Now that was a warped thought.

A dutiful, demure, prim little wife sounded pretty good in theory. But what did sewing and putting up strawberry jam have to do with being a good mother to Nikolaus? Rain Shadow ranked right up there with Lydia and Annette for mothering. Besides, Nikolaus loved her.

Besides . . . he loved her.

Sure, he'd have one hell of a time ever getting her to see anything his way, and it would take one hell of a man to handle a woman like that, and what did any of those wifely qualities matter if the wife wasn't Rain Shadow? After all, she was already his wife!

Anton shot his glance to his father. "I'll go get her." From the nightstand, he picked up the letter he'd received the week before and glanced at the Boston postmark. Abruptly, he yanked open the small drawer and grasped the passenger list he'd taken from Ruiz' belongings. "But there's something I have to do first."

Chapter Seventeen

The train ride raked up memories Anton had buried years ago. Memories of meeting a young, fresh-faced Peine in Pittsburgh for the first time. Memories of marrying her and sharing a sleeper car on their wedding night. Halfheartedly, he watched the countryside chug past the windows. He would never be able to erase Peine. Fragments of the hurt and disillusionment would always remain. But he didn't have to let her haunt him. He didn't have to allow the experience to taint the rest of his life.

That's exactly what he'd done. He'd hardened his heart and hurt others in the process. It wasn't too late. It couldn't be.

Since two days ago when Anton had told him of the trip, Nikolaus had been fairly bursting with excitement over seeing Slade and Rain Shadow again. He slept most of the way, his head cradled in his father's lap.

The station in Philadelphia bustled with activity. Securing their belongings and hailing a ride monopolized Anton's thoughts until they reached a hotel and he dropped his leather satchel and saddlebags on the bed. He glanced around the room, stared out the window at the street below and took Nikolaus downstairs to ask directions.

They had a day to wait until the show opened. Anton hired a horse and, Nikolaus tucked before him, rode to the fairgrounds. A sentry met them as they neared the park.

"Show's not till tomorrow, mister."

"Came a day early. Thought I'd take a look around."

The cowboy tipped his hat back on his head and squinted at Anton. "Don't I know you?"

Anton offered his hand, experiencing a flash of recognition. "Name's Neubauer."

The cowboy grinned and pumped his hand. "Sure! You helped me bury my Belle up in Butler County. Best damned cutting horse I ever had." He released Anton's hand and gestured over his shoulder. "Look around all you care to, Neubauer."

"Thanks." Anton prodded the horse away with his heels.

"Your tickets are on me. Tell them your name at the main entrance tomorrow, and you'll have good seats."

"Thanks again." Anton skirted corrals and livestock tents, the enormity of the encampment taking him by surprise. The entire entourage—gigantic colorful tents, stagecoaches, covered wagons, buggies, excursion cars, housing tents and an Indian village complete with tepees and camp fires lay blocked out and sectioned off military style.

"There they are, Pa! Over there!"

From their vantage point, Anton easily spotted her lodge by its identifying markings. Was she in there? He studied the hide structure he'd once considered an eyesore, and an unexplainable peace enfolded him. She was close. Close enough to see and touch as soon as the time was right. He nudged the horse on.

"Ain't we going down there?" Nikolaus twisted his neck and threw him a puzzled frown.

"I told you I'll do this my way. In my own time when I'm ready."

Nikolaus sighed as if disgusted and turned to ogle the sights.

Tiered planks for seating had been constructed in a colossal oval shape, the entire space for spectators protected by canvas tenting. Workers hammered guardrails into place. Lowering Nikolaus, Anton slid to the ground and looped the reins around a brace beneath the stands.

Nikolaus raced into the enormous arena. An abandoned bull's-eye target on a tripod caught his interest. "I wish I'd brung my bow and arrows!"

"Brought." Anton climbed the planks, his boots echoing across the arena. Halfway up, he sat and studied the place where he'd see her tomorrow. The spot where thousands would watch her ride, shoot and eventually take on Annie Oakley.

What was she doing right now? How was she feeling? Was she nervous? Confident? Lonely? Did she think about him? Miss him? Or had she already dismissed him from her thoughts?

Across the way, two men strung a ponderous banner between tent poles. Annie Oakley's face appeared from the folds, a likeness of Rain Shadow following. She wore fringed ivory buckskin leggings and beaded tunic, two long black braids gracing her breasts, and her violet eyes gazed across the vacant arena.

Anton stared at her image and hoped what he had to offer was enough.

Two Feathers watched Rain Shadow's morning practice. While she cleaned her guns, he traveled to their lodge. From his belongings, he gathered tobacco, sweet grass, a tamper and his sacred pipe wrapped in red flannel. He walked some distance to find a private spot, never an easy task any more.

He sat, cleaned his pipe and rubbed the ash over his hands and arms.

Rain Shadow was better than Little Sure Shot. Of that he had no doubt. But many factors would influence the outcome of the contest today. With one thumb closing the bowl, he drew on the pipe, lit the long strand of sweet grass, laid it on one knee and passed the pipe and tobacco through the smoke.

His daughter would probably win. If her family sought her out as she hoped, what would become of his small family? Two Feathers waved the sweet grass around himself, appealing to the spirits. If her family didn't seek her, what would that do to her?

He cradled the pipe in his left arm, the stem pointing west. *"Tunkasila wiyohpeyata, wacecicive. Onsimala ye. Omakiya ye.* Grandfather where the sun goes down, I am praying to you. Pity me. Help me." Two Feathers dropped the first pinch of tobacco into the pipe bowl. He repeated the ceremony in each direction, then upward to Tunkasila Wakan Tanka, the Great Spirit, and finally down toward Unci Maka, the Earth.

Words became harder and harder to find in his second round of heartfelt prayer. "Grandfather, Great Spirit, You are all powerful and above all things. All things come from You. Let Your spotted eagle look down from the blue sky, which is above all storm clouds. Hear my prayer. I know You can do all things. Help my Rain Shadow in her needs."

A spotted eagle soared above, unseen by the Indian, who had touched one knee to the ground in supplication of Grandmother Earth.

The grounds had been transformed into a milling, pulsating crush of bodies. Holding Nikolaus' hand securely, Anton strolled along rows of wooden stands with red awnings. The throngs tried their luck at games. Wheels spun, shots were fired and balls knocked down cans and blocks while children squealed and dodged adults. Rollicking laughter exploded all around them.

Inside the arena, the band tuned up, and Anton shouldered their way to the ticket wagon. Center-front seats awaited them just as the cowboy had promised. Buffalo Bill's Wild West Show began with an impressive parade, Will Cody leading the cowboys, Indians, *vaqueros,* marching band, coaches, wagons and animals.

Anton and Nikolaus watched a stagecoach attacked by Indians. Nikolaus cheered stunt riders, jugglers and a buffalo stampede. Anton watched South American *gauchos,* Black Elk and the Deadwood Stage. The famed Johnnie Baker exploded blue glass balls in the air with single shots, but none of it compared to the thrill of glimpsing her.

While his attention focused on one spectacular act, the next was set up and the last removed. Unprepared, Anton spotted Rain Shadow emerging from a tent behind her father. He stared at her, the center of attention, while he blended anonymously into the crowd. It pleased him to see her this first time without her seeing him. This was her world, and it took time to absorb.

Two Feathers, dressed in chief's feathered headdress, bartered with the shirtless Hank Tall Bear. The brawny-chested Indian paraded a dozen dazzling white horses past the stoic father. Two Feathers examined them and gestured.

Tall Bear motioned, and his fellow braves dropped bundles of colorful blankets, hats and clothing at Two Feathers' feet. "Chief" Two Feathers poked a box with his toe. Tall Bear knelt and opened the box, holding beads and claw necklaces aloft. Two Feathers pointed to the ring on a brave's finger, and Tall Bear spoke softly to the brave. Apparently, the young man didn't want to part with the piece of jewelry, and the crowd tittered. At last Tall Bear convinced him, and Anton laughed with those around him when the brave made a pretense of being unable to get the ring from his finger. Tall Bear finally bit the ring off, the brave howling, and Two Feathers slipped the ring on his own hand, urging his daughter forward.

Rain Shadow stared prettily at the toes of her moccasins.

A flurry of activity changed the scene, tom-toms and gourd rattles creating a pulsing beat. The white horses galloped away, replaced by a crowd of celebrating Indians.

"There's Slade, Pa!" Nikolaus pointed to a group of Indian children taking part in the mock festivity.

Rain Shadow emerged from the tent once again, this time in full ceremonial garb: a pristine white fringed dress, her braids laced with feathers and beads. A strip of white banded her forehead. The crowd oohed and ahed, the women uttering a collective sigh.

Anton caught his breath. She made a beautiful Indian princess. But then she made a beautiful manure shoveler, too. He grinned.

Hank Tall Bear awaited his bride, his muscular body dressed in a loin cloth, leggings, knee-high boots and a quill vest. The medicine man presided over the ceremony, shook his gourd rattle and led the dancing. Tall Bear and Rain Shadow danced a primitive dance all their own, and the well-wishers formed a circle around the couple.

Watching, a knot of apprehension formed in Anton's chest. Would what he'd come to say make any difference to her? He had to talk to her before the contest. She would probably go back to her tent to change. Anton stood and towed Nikolaus through the crowded stands.

"Pa, where are we going?"

"I have to talk to Rain Shadow."

"Now? The show's still on, and I don't want to miss nothin'."

Away from the crowd and performances, a young voice carried to them. "Nikky! Hey, Nikky! Anton!"

Anton spotted the slender figure running toward them. Nikolaus yanked his hand from his father's and ran to meet Slade. The two boys stopped in front of each other, grins splitting their faces.

"What are you doing here?" Slade asked, and tipped his head back to study Anton.

"We came to see you," Nikky answered. "Pa wants to talk to your ma now, and I'm gonna miss the show."

"You can watch over here with me. Can he, Anton?"

Pleased to see Slade, Anton squeezed his shoulder. To Nikolaus he said, "You stay put until I come back for you, y'hear?"

"Yes, sir." Nikolaus grinned and followed Slade to a dozen bales of hay fashioned into makeshift seating. Several children sat, sprawled or tussled on the bundles.

Anton hurried on. Outside the arena, a line of mounted cavalry soldiers waited their turn. Immediately discovering no safe place to step, Anton realized why Rain Shadow hadn't blinked an eye at shoveling dung.

Nearer the Indian encampment, he wiped his boots on the grass and strode purposefully to her tent. He called out and, at the silence, stepped in.

The interior was just as he remembered, except that the drawers of her trunks were open, clothing, headbands and jewelry spilling in haphazard piles onto the ground. Anton studied the collection and realized she'd played more parts than he'd recognized.

A rider approached. Mouth dry, palms damp, Anton contemplated the tent opening. Anticipation pounded through his veins.

The flap flew back, and she entered the lodge, already untying the leather strips behind her neck. In a split second, she knelt, withdrew the knife from her white knee-high moccasin and leapt sideways.

Anton raised his palms in the air.

It took her longer to recover from the sight of him than it had to crouch and draw her knife. "Anton?"

Lord, the sight of her took his breath away. He doffed his hat. "Rain Shadow."

"What are you doing here?" She stood, looked at the knife in her palm and slid it into her moccasin.

"Watching the show."

She raised a black brow, her amethyst eyes questioning. The white headband she wore made her skin and hair even darker in comparison. Two blue-tipped white feathers dangled near one ear. Face flushed from her run to the tent, she was the most beautiful creature he'd ever laid eyes on.

"I came to see you."

"Is Nikky here?"

"Nikky's watching the show with Slade."

"Anton, what is it?" She stepped closer to him. "Is everything all right? Your father—"

"Pa's just fine. This is about us."

A wary look crossed her features, and she turned aside. "I have to change."

Anton manacled her slender wrist with his enormous hand. She stood in silence, facing away from him. "This is something I have to say now. Before the contest. So you'll know the outcome makes no difference to me."

Her lashes raised in a troubled sweep.

"Rain Shadow, if you don't win, I'd like you to come home with me." Beneath his fingers, her pulse quickened.

"Why?"

"So we can be your family."

She twisted her wrist loose. "Don't insult me by pitying me, Anton. I don't need your pity. I don't want it."

His stomach plummeted. She jerked the headband off, tugged the ties from her braids and ran her fingers through the plaits. Beads plunked and rolled like marbles, and feathers fluttered to the floor.

"Look." He placed his hands on her shoulders. "If you lose, you can still have a family with mine. They're all crazy about you. Especially Nikolaus, you must know that."

She pulled away, grabbed her hairbrush and stroked it through her hair, brushing until the ebony length shone. "So you don't think I'm going to win? You think I'll make a fool of myself and be devastated? Thanks for your confidence." She braided her hair in one long plait, pulling it over her shoulder to tie the end with a leather strip. "You can go now. You've done your good deed. You've made the ultimate sacrifice. Your conscience is clear."

He stared at her, her anger a perplexity. She untied the dress and slipped it forward. He'd come all this way to assure her, and he'd only succeeded in making her mad?

Deliberately, she dropped the dress to the floor and, dressed only in her thong and moccasins, stepped out of the doeskin puddle and turned to her trunk.

Anton stared at the ridges of her spine, fighting to control the desire that pierced his composure at the sight of her honey-hued skin.

She unfolded a dress.

"I said it all wrong," he said softly.

She tossed the braid over her shoulder.

"Rain Shadow." He stepped behind her and, without thinking, spanned her bare waist with his hands, turning her to face him. "I meant to say it differently." Beneath his calloused palms, her skin was as velvet-soft as ever. His hands still made her seem like a fragile, delicate creature, though he was well aware of her strength. "I'm a fool. I need you."

She wadded the dress in her fists and met his gaze evenly. "I'm not Peine. I can never be like her."

He raised his brows in surprise. "I would never have given you a second glance if you were."

"But you loved her. She was everything I'm not."

"Yes." He saw hurt flicker in her eyes. "I loved her. I loved her, but she was obsessed with Jakob. From the minute I brought her home, I was never good enough for her. My lovemaking put her off, my body disgusted her, my scar made her sick. She belittled and made fun of my ear—" He stopped and his voice altered. "She made fun of everything."

"She was the fool, then," she declared.

He'd told her this much, he may as well tell it all. "She tried to kill Lydia."

Rain Shadow's lips formed an astonished *O*.

"She doused the tackle room with kerosene, lured Lydia into it, telling her Jakob was hurt, and set fire to the hay. We chopped a hole in the side of the barn to get in. Jakob got Lydia out, but a rafter fell between Peine and the opening. The fire was out of control. I tried to save her."

"The dream," she whispered.

He nodded. "She was seven months pregnant."

Tears welled in Rain Shadow's storm-sad eyes. "Oh, Anton, I'm so sorry."

"I don't want you to be sorry. Don't you see? You're nothing like her. You're...perfect."

"I'm not."

"You are. I never had a woman want me like you did. You're open. You're honest. Unaffected and unspoiled and..."

Her shimmering violet gaze dropped to his chest.

"And you're beautiful," he whispered. "I want you more than I've ever wanted anything. I lived a lot of years with hurt and anger eating me up inside. I never wanted to care for a woman again. That's why Sissy was safe."

"She can bake and keep house and quilt."

"She can't hold a candle to you."

Rain Shadow raised her gaze to his mouth. "What are you saying, Anton?"

One thumb caressed her spine, sending a delicious shiver up her back. "I'm saying I love you."

Her heart slowed to a dangerous level. Loved her? *Her?* A woman who didn't even know her real name? He could trace his ancestry all the way back to Germany! He loved an orphan with only an illegitimate son and an old Indian for family? He had his own son, father, brothers, nieces, nephews and sisters-in-law. Had he come all this way on a mercy quest . . . or because he loved her? *Loved her?* "Is that what you came to say?"

"Yes."

Hoofbeats pounded up to the lodge. "Princess Blue Cloud?"

"I'm changing," she called.

"'Bout another five minutes. Will's looking for ya!" a young male voice called.

"Tell him I'll be there."

"Yes, miss." The youth rode off.

Blinking away tears, Rain Shadow untangled herself from Anton's embrace and slipped her dress over her head. She picked up her Stevens rifle and her revolvers. "I've worked most of my life for this day. I'm not going to give it all up now."

"I wouldn't want you to," he replied. "Just remember, whatever happens, I love you."

His solemn blue gaze forced her to turn away. She picked up one of her ammunition bags. "I told you I loved you once, and it didn't change anything," she said barely above a whisper.

"Here, let me carry those for you." He brushed past her and took the bags.

She sized up his lack of response. Didn't he believe her? The first time he'd ignored her admission of love she'd been hurt, thinking he had no feelings for her. This time confused her.

Rain Shadow watched him fold the flap aside and carry her bags out. He'd told her he loved her, yet ignored the same words from her. Without understanding, she followed.

As the cowboy band played a lively march, Annie Oakley walked proudly onto the field amid whoops and hollers from the crowd. They loved her, as always. Today's performance was not her usual routine. Her title had been challenged, and she meant to defend it.

She wore one of her leather skirts and a snug-fitting short jacket that emphasized her tiny waist and hourglass figure. Shiny black boots and a flat-crowned hat completed the ensemble. Rain Shadow noticed Annie wore her wedding ring, an unusual occurrence when photographs were to be taken.

A row of cameras formed a bizarre windbreak in the arena, cameramen's legs and feet showing beneath the black drapes. Rain Shadow tried to ignore them and gauged the direction of the subtle breeze. Will announced Princess Blue Cloud. From her perch atop Jack, she balanced herself on her moccasined feet and rode into the arena, arms outspread.

The crowd cheered.

Nimbly, she leapt from Jack's back and took her place, the pony obediently trotting to the sidelines.

Annie Oakley strolled to face Rain Shadow. "The big day's finally here," she said, and turned to study the crowd from beneath the brim of her hat where one of her many medals winked in the sunlight.

Rain Shadow met her gaze when she turned back. "Good luck, Annie."

Annie's brows rose in surprise.

The band fell silent.

Finally, Annie offered Rain Shadow her gloved hand. "Good luck, Princess."

Rain Shadow shook Annie's hand, searching her eyes for a glimmer of uncertainty, but Little Sure Shot was calm and confident.

Will played to the audience with his exaggerated gestures and smiles. He listed Annie's accomplishments, and she warmed up, firing at blue glass balls her husband, Frank Butler, threw into the air.

Will crowed Rain Shadow's abilities, and Hank Tall Bear tossed balls into the air for her practice shots.

"And now the moment we've all been waiting for!" Will shouted into his megaphone.

A hush fell over the crowd.

"Each sharpshooter will be allowed the same number of shots for a total of fifty! In the unlikely event of a tie, the contest will be rescheduled."

Rain Shadow met Annie's eyes. Highly unlikely. But a boon for ticket sales. They smiled at one another, friends, though each had an enormous stake in the outcome of the next several minutes.

"The first event is the target shoot!" Will announced. He signaled to the lad who would hold up a red paper square after each shot was fired. Taking his job seriously, the carrot-haired young man stuck the first square in place on the center of the bull's-eye.

Annie went first. A skilled sharpshooter, she squeezed off ten perfect shots, reloading her single shot rifle after each hit.

Rain Shadow took several deep breaths. Her uncanny ability to zero in on a target and block out all distractions served her well. She'd taught herself that even at practice each shot counted. Concentrate. Breathe evenly. Squeeze the trigger.

Ten perfect shots.

The spectators exhaled in relief and cheered. The contestants changed guns.

Frank threw clay disks into the air for Annie. Ten times she swung the barrel and fired her revolver. Her accuracy enthralled everyone.

Rain Shadow took a deep breath. Tall Bear awaited her signal, knowing after weeks of practice that Rain Shadow preferred hers in more rapid succession. She nodded.

Tall Bear, a jaunty feather standing up from his headband, passed the disks from his left hand to his right, firing one after the other into the sky. Rain Shadow shattered them all.

Ten glass balls came next, none other than Will tossing them into the air.

Annie missed the first one.

A groan rippled through the crowd.

Rain Shadow's heart leapt in her breast. She stared hard at the ground and focused her thoughts. Glass shattered, shards falling to the hard-packed ground. Twice. Three times. Rain Shadow raised her gaze and watched. Nine. Annie had twenty-nine points. Now was her chance to get ahead.

The crowd quieted and waited for the challenger to match Little Sure Shot's skill. Heart thundering, Rain Shadow stepped forward. Will gave her an encouraging nod, and she returned it, signaling her readiness. The first blue orb sailed into the sky.

Quicker than a scared rabbit, Rain Shadow aimed and fired. One shattered. Two. Perspiration dampened her brow. Three. Four. Shots volleyed across the arena as she exercised her skill. Five. Six. Somewhere in the recesses of her mind, she knew she was over halfway there. Seven. Eight. The contest was so close, it could go either way at any time. Nine.

One more and she'd be ahead of Annie Oakley. One more and she'd hold the title. One more—a queasy feeling tumbled in her belly—and she'd find her family. Rain Shadow held her breath. Her finger trembled ever so slightly on the trigger. The bullet resounded. The blue ball hung suspended for a fraction of a second, then fell to earth, landing with a puff of dust.

The crowd murmured before Rain Shadow registered that she'd missed and tied the score. Angry with herself, she lowered her hand, the revolver hanging against her thigh. How could she have missed? She never let nerves get the best of her!

Rain Shadow stifled a curse and calmed herself. All right. They were tied again. Sooner or later Annie would miss.

Twenty shots left.

A row of small red flags on long slender sticks became the next challenge. Five each. "The rule is that the ladies have to snap the stick so that the flag touches the ground," Will instructed.

Annie took aim and snapped the first stick better than two thirds of the way down. The red flag fluttered before it hit the dirt. One after the other, the sticks tumbled like trees felled by lightning. Five shots. Five red flags in haphazard array on the dirt field. Annie met Rain Shadow's gaze, raised her gun and blew delicately on the barrel.

Picking up her Winchester repeater, Rain Shadow smiled, blanked out the crowd's exuberance and concentrated on her first target. The trick was to snap the stick low enough for the flag to hit the ground when it fell. She took a deep breath, released it, aimed and squeezed the trigger. The shot echoed. The bullet caught the stick barely under halfway, the top falling to the right, and the flag hit the ground.

The crowd cheered.

Rain Shadow took aim, squeezed the trigger. The second bullet hit in the same exact spot as the last, the flag careening to the right. The red fabric hit the ground.

She fired three more shots, each bullet felling the flag on the right side of the stick. The downed flags lay in perfect alignment. The crowd went wild.

Rain Shadow met her opponent's pensive gaze and recognized Annie's first glimmer of apprehension.

Annie had a past to defend.

Rain Shadow had a future to build.

Annie would get over it. She'd still have a position with Will for as long as the show lasted. With the addition of the *gauchos* last season, Will had hoped to boost profits. But even with tens of thousands attending and a new manager, the show operated in the red. The future was uncertain for all of them.

Fifteen shots left.

Both women reloaded their guns.

Will announced their next challenge. "Ladies and gentlemen, the next feat these skilled sharpshooters perform will astound you! Their targets are not plates or balls or stationary squares of paper! No! Their next targets are these!" He tossed a handful into the air. "Walnuts!"

Rain Shadow almost smiled. She'd shot enough walnuts out of the sky to feed all the squirrels in Pennsylvania. One of Nikolaus' favorite pastimes had been tossing walnuts for her. She'd learned speed and accuracy in spite of a six-year-old's aim.

"First I'll toss one. Then two. Then three. Then, ladies and gentlemen—four!"

The spectators roared.

Annie took her position. Will tossed the first nut, and she picked it off easily. He tossed the two, and she hit them. Three. Annie reloaded. Four rapid shots and she'd hit all ten.

Rain Shadow traded the rifle for her revolver and took her place. One. *Piece of cake.* Two. Both burst in the air. Three. Rain Shadow reloaded. *Thanks, Nikky.* Four—all close together. The tie was unbroken.

Five shots left.

The next four were paper targets affixed to a platform on a horse's back. The target had to be hit as the horse ran past a scenic backdrop. Annie's shots were exact, as anticipated.

Rain Shadow matched her perfect score.

One remaining shot.

Will stood garnering the audience's attention. All eyes focused on him. He lit a cigar and puffed smoke into the cloudless blue sky. From inside his jacket, he withdrew another cigar and lit it.

Frank Butler and Hank Tall Bear approached him. Will handed them each a cigar. "Miss Annie Oakley and Princess Blue Cloud will attempt to shoot the end off a cigar held in the teeth of a man at fifty paces!" Will shouted.

Rain Shadow watched as Frank and Tall Bear separated several feet. Will called out the paces as they took long-legged strides away from the women.

Rain Shadow glanced at Annie. She was watching her husband and Tall Bear, her rifle cradled in her arms like a baby. Rain Shadow caught Will's gaze as he shouted out, "Fifty!"

They would have to reschedule the contest after all! If Annie was going to miss at any of these last events, it would have been the walnuts.

"Quiet, please!" Will shouted.

Frank Butler puffed on the cigar and turned to face the crowd, the cigar jutting from his mouth. Annie swung her rifle up and took aim. The arena had grown silent. Rain Shadow felt the sun on her shoulders and the light breeze tickling the hair at her nape. The moment hung suspended like a dream.

Annie fired. Frank flinched as the cigar flew from his lips. The crowd burst into applause.

Rain Shadow glanced from Annie to Will. She gave the stands of cheering onlookers the once-over. Somewhere in that ocean of faces, Anton watched her at this very moment. Wondered if she'd make this shot. Hopeless man. He'd traveled all this way to offer her a home with him if she lost. There was no way she could lose now.

If he'd told her he'd loved her months ago, would she have continued with the contest? Probably. They both knew she wasn't the woman he was looking for.

But he'd come for her. He loved her.

Rain Shadow realized the crowd had quieted. All eyes focused on her. She drew a cleansing breath and faced Tall Bear. He smiled and turned toward the crowd, the cigar held between his teeth.

Rain Shadow raised her rifle.

Chapter Eighteen

Above Tall Bear, an eagle soared in the radiant spring sky. Rain Shadow waited for the distraction to fly out of range before she raised the barrel. A horse neighed. A baby cried, reminding her of Anton's dreams. Feverish from his wound, he'd cried out for the baby. She remembered the anguish in his voice, and now she knew why.

She couldn't imagine the hurt and suffering he'd experienced. All he'd wanted was his family and a wife to love him.

She was his wife, and *she* loved him.

In a startling moment of clarity, Rain Shadow realized they'd both wanted the same things all along: roots, stability, two parents for their children. Her heart pounded.

Anton had said he needed her, *loved* her, wanted to become her family. What more did she want? What more could he offer?

Rain Shadow took a calming breath, released it and aimed.

Steady.

Slow.

Squeeze the trigger nice and easy.

Tall Bear's jaunty feather snapped and hung over his eye. He jerked his head toward her in surprise.

It took a few startled seconds for the crowd to realize what had happened. A mixture of remorse and joy rippled in their voices.

Will Cody shouted into the megaphone, "Ladies and gentlemen, the reigning champion sharpshooter of the world, Miss Annie Oakley!"

Annie raised her rifle above her head. Frank ran to hug her. From the stands, hats flew into the air. The cowboy band broke into a victory song. The noise was deafening.

Someone touched Rain Shadow's elbow, and she turned to look up into Tall Bear's unsmiling face.

"Why did you do that?" he shouted. "You had what you wanted."

She shook her head. "I don't think so, Hank." She touched his arm and he bent to press his cheek to hers. "Thanks."

He handed her the unlit cigar and disappeared into the crowd.

The arena became a crush of well-wishers. Rain Shadow caught Annie's attention and saluted her. Absently tucking the cigar into one of her empty ammunition bags, she ran to the back gate and found Two Feathers with Jack.

His dark eyes assessed her knowingly. "Well done, daughter."

She threw her bags over Jack's back and slid her rifle through a loop. "What are you thinking?"

"I want only your happiness."

She studied his sly expression. "If I didn't know better, I'd think you had something to do with this."

He merely returned her gaze. His attention flickered beyond her. She glanced over her shoulder.

Anton stood watching them, his hat brim shading his features.

"I must help with the horses." Two Feathers moved away.

Jack walked behind Rain Shadow as she started toward the encampment. Anton fell into step beside her.

"You okay?" he asked.

"I'm fine."

He hooked one arm around her neck and drew her loosely against him. Oh, his smell. A little bay rum, a lot male. She wanted to turn to him and be absorbed by that smell.

"I'm sorry you lost."

"Are you?" She walked without looking at him.

"Of course I am. Rain Shadow, I didn't want you to lose," he said in a husky voice. "I just wanted you to know it didn't matter to me one way or the other. I still want you to come back with me."

She said nothing.

"Will you?"

She stopped, turned and met the anguished look in his beloved eyes. He'd suffered so much rejection in his first marriage, it was no wonder he'd been terrified to ask her outright. She saw the genuine fear in his eyes. Their relationship had shot holes in his armor, and yet he placed himself in the position for her to pierce his newly mended heart. What courage he possessed!

She slipped out of his easy grasp and opened one of the leather bags. "Do something for me, Anton."

He watched her.

She slid her Winchester out and loaded it. From one bag, she withdrew the cigar. "Got a match?"

He looked at her as if she'd lost her mind. "No."

"It doesn't matter." She thrust the cigar toward him.

"What are you doing?"

"Humor me. Put the cigar in your mouth and walk to that little stump out there." She pointed.

Anton's eyes followed her hand. He stared at her, and recognition touched the blue depths. "You want me to walk out there and hold this cigar in my teeth so you can shoot at it?''

''That's the idea.''

''Why?''

''Don't you trust me?''

He stared at her, a sandy brow raised.

''I haven't killed anyone yet.'' She couldn't suppress a smile.

He drew himself up and stuck the cigar between his teeth. Without moving his lips, he said around it, ''I trust you to take care o' my son if I'm maimed.''

She wanted to laugh, but watched his tall form as he walked away. He stopped in the spot she'd indicated and turned to face her, removing the cigar. ''This is farther than that last shot, isn't it?''

''Precisely.'' She raised the rifle.

''Woman, don't you think—''

''Turn to the side, Anton. Take off your hat.'' She squinted down the barrel. ''And stand still!''

Resigned, he removed his hat and turned. Sticking the cigar in his teeth, he poised, motionlessly.

Rain Shadow drew a breath and released it. She aimed. Slowly, she squeezed the trigger.

The shot echoed. Anton took the cigar from his mouth and stared at the frayed end. ''You did it,'' he said quietly. Then louder, ''You did it!''

Rain Shadow slid the rifle into its loop and met him halfway.

His gaze probed her face, and she watched him struggle with dismayed recognition. ''You lost on purpose?''

She tilted her head in a half nod.

''Why?''

''Why do you think?''

"I don't know. You wanted to win so badly. You practiced so long and hard, and you believed winning would bring your family to you. I don't understand."

"Maybe I was looking the wrong way at the right time. I thought you wanted someone like Annette or Lydia or Sissy."

He offered her a wry shrug. "So did I."

"I knew I wasn't like them."

"That doesn't matter to me anymore."

"Anton, I never sat at a table with a family until I ate with yours. I never saw a meal served on fancy platters with a lace tablecloth under it. I wanted to die that day Annette asked me to set the table."

"I helped you, didn't I?"

She looked at him curiously. "You knew?"

"I suspected."

"I've never had a bath in a tub. We either bathed in streams or heated water in the lodge."

"Want to try it?" He smiled with his eyes.

"Anton, I've never been to church or school. Everything that you take for granted is awkward for me."

"It doesn't matter."

Her heart skipped an uneasy beat. "Doesn't it?"

"No." He set his hat atop the bags on Jack's back and took her shoulders in his easy grasp. "You want to learn all those things, don't you? You want Slade to be comfortable with our ways, to go to school and probably even college. I want those things for him, too. But mostly, I want you."

He wanted her.

"Rain Shadow, I'm crazy for sticking my neck out like this again, but I love you." Quick-shifting apprehension flitted across his expression. "I'm afraid you won't love me back," he whispered.

His honesty reached her heart and twisted it painfully. "Anton, I love you. I told you that."

Behind his eyes exultation melted into confusion and then...embarrassment? "You told me?"

She nodded.

"When?"

"After we made love...the second time that night."

He skimmed his palms up and down her bare arms. She wanted to close her eyes and revel in his touch. He slid his hands to catch and hold hers. Studying the front of her dress, he asked, "Did you say it softly?"

"I think so."

Color tinged his cheekbones.

She waited, watching his gaze drift slowly across her breasts, then back to her face.

"I can't hear with my left ear. I didn't hear you."

Rain Shadow digested that bit of information. "How come I didn't know? Why didn't you tell me?"

He shrugged. "I didn't want you to know."

She took his face in her hands. "Why not?"

"I didn't want you to be put off."

Suddenly, the words he'd spoken that afternoon became perfectly clear. "Peine belittled you because you couldn't hear, didn't she?"

His eyes answered for him.

"Oh, Anton." Unbidden tears threatened to spill over. Beneath her palms his cheeks were smooth from his morning shave. She ran her fingertips across his face, his sun-kissed brows. "She hated your scar." Rain Shadow touched the spot through his shirt. "I love it because it's part of you."

His eyes darkened.

"Your body disgusted her." Brazenly, she pressed herself against him and dropped her head back. "I love every stubborn inch of you. Every time you touch me my heart pounds and my breasts feel heavy. I could touch you forever and not tire of you."

His golden eyelashes fluttered shut, and he inhaled a deep breath.

She slid her fingers through the thick hair at his neck and pulled his head down so that her lips touched his good ear. "I love you."

His hand trembled on her spine. "I want to trust you."

"You already do. You let me shoot at you."

He straightened enough to look at her. "That Tall Bear fellow trusts you enough to let you shoot at him, too."

"Ah, but he knew I wouldn't blow his nose off; you weren't certain."

He smiled. A smile as warm as the afternoon sun.

"Kiss me, Anton."

"Does this mean you'll come home with me?"

"Yes."

He kissed his wife until her toes curled.

"Ma! Anton!"

"Rain Shadow! Pa!"

Childish voices interrupted. Anton raised his head. Beneath her hand, his heart thundered. "I have a hotel room," he suggested with a rasp of need.

"I have a very understanding father."

They smiled into one another's eyes.

Epilogue

"You know, watching the wedding ceremony in the show made me think," Anton said from his comfortable position on the bed. "I don't have a herd of white stallions."

Rain Shadow trailed her fingers through the suds. Replete from their lovemaking, she lay soaking in the enormous tub Anton had ordered carried to his room and filled with steaming water. He watched her, his shoulders propped against the pillows, chest and feet still bare. "If you'd stolen a herd of stallions," she drawled, "you'd be in jail, not making love to me all evening."

"I mean I don't have anything to offer your father except a home." He stacked his hands behind his head.

"The show is the way life was years ago, Anton, not the way we live today. A home is exactly what my father needs. Me and Slade, too. We've missed the farm. I can't wait to go back."

"Jakob and Lydia had a girl this time."

She smiled and tilted her head in a pretty, feminine gesture. "They must be happy."

"Mmm," he said distractedly. He watched her minutes longer, thinking of all he had to tell her. "Isn't the water getting cold?"

"I'm used to cold water."

"You'll shrivel up."

"It feels too good to get out."

He sat up. "I have something to tell you that will make you feel even better."

"What is it?"

"Get out, and I'll tell you."

Reluctantly, she stood.

Even now, the sight of her body sent a shaft of desire through him. He met her with a towel. With gentle hands, he dried her body, wrapped her in a dry towel and led her to the bed. Tendrils of damp ebony hair spiraled at her neck and temples. He touched his fingertip to a droplet of water he'd missed on her collarbone. She relaxed against the pillows.

Sitting beside her, he leaned forward and kissed her. He'd almost been foolish enough to lose her. He'd never take that chance again. "I love you, Rain Shadow."

She placed her hand on his arm, watched her fingers slide across his skin. "Is that what you wanted to tell me?"

"No." His gaze skittered to his satchel beside the bed. Bending, he retrieved a bundle of papers and letters. "I went through Ruiz' things before I took his body to town. I found a passenger list for a wagon train that set west in 1875 and a few letters from a man named Avarato in Boston."

Flying upright, she sat on her knees and stared at him. "A wagon train?"

He smiled at her excitement, pleased he could give her this. "Uh-huh. Seems this Avarato fellow had a daughter who married a man the family didn't approve of and headed west with him."

"Who was she, Anton? Why did Miguel have these papers?" She grabbed the stack from his hands and rifled through them, skimming return addresses on the envelopes until she came to the yellowed list. "Why are all these names circled?" She pointed to the names on the parchment. "And these checked off?" She grabbed his arm. "Anton?"

"Let me tell you. The letter hinted at the fact that Ruiz knew where this man's daughter might be. It seems Avarato was paying Ruiz to track her down—or her locket, anyway—"

"Locket!" Her hand flew to her bare chest.

He'd been surprised that she hadn't been wearing it that afternoon when he'd removed her clothing, and then he'd recalled she hadn't had it on earlier in the day when she'd undressed in front of him. The day after Ruiz' death, Anton had handed the locket to her. She'd stared at it for a moment, and then tucked it into her pants pocket. "Where is it?" he asked.

She let her hand drop to her bare knee. "In a trunk. Somehow I couldn't wear it after he had it." She shook her head. "Anton, is my locket the one this man wanted?" A look of astonishment flattened her features. "Is Avarato my family?"

"I'm convinced it's the same locket he gave his daughter years ago, but no, she wasn't your mother. I have a feeling Ruiz wanted you to pretend she was to bleed Avarato."

"How can you be sure?" she asked, disappointment tinging her voice.

"Avarato had done most of the work in going over this passenger list. He hired private investigators years ago, and followed up periodically. His daughter had no children."

"But it's the right wagon train?"

"It is. How else would you have gotten her locket? Two Feathers found you wearing it, right?"

She nodded fervently.

"We can only guess that Juanita Avarato, her name was Wilkins by then, gave it to you. Or maybe you just picked it up wandering around after the attack."

Rain Shadow's heart pounded so hard she knew Anton could see it. She ran her fingers reverently over the aged paper. "That means my parents are on this list!"

Anton nodded. He slid a few envelopes from the stack. "Over the years Avarato or his men looked into all of the names. Ruiz checked out the sources and obviously agreed with their findings. Avarato's daughter died."

"But after all these years how would we ever find these people?" The task sounded impossible.

"Avarato contacted the families years ago. He kept names and letters and telegrams. When I wrote, he was sympathetic to your cause and gladly gave me all the names and addresses of survivors. All I had to do was write each one. Several came back without being delivered. Most came back with replies saying they knew of no dark-haired little girl on that wagon train."

Rain Shadow let her eyelids flutter closed. She swallowed and opened them again. So close! How could she have come so close? It had been too many years! They'd never find the families of the passengers now!

"But this one," Anton said, drawing a heavy parchment envelope from the pile, "came from a woman whose daughter and son-in-law had a dark-haired, violet-eyed three-and-a-half-year-old girl."

Rain Shadow had never fainted in her life, but she feared this might be the first time. Her head grew so light, her vision grayed. Anton's face blurred; the room faded from view. She dropped the papers, gripped Anton's forearms and forced herself to focus on his features.

"Are you sure?" she whispered, excitement sharpened to an unbearable peak.

He secured her waist and smiled into her eyes. "I'm sure. She described your parents. You must have your father's hair and eyes and your mother's small size. Your grandmother said you were a beautiful but headstrong child. Can there be any doubt?''

"Oh, Anton!" she cried, every nerve ending atingle. "Oh, my—" Passionate tears filled her eyes. Releasing one arm, she grabbed the envelope and blinked trying to see the handwriting. "What's her name?"

With his thumb, Anton wiped tears from her cheekbone. "Her name's Melisande Snow. She's French. Snow's her married name."

With trembling fingers, Rain Shadow slid the heavy sheet of paper from the envelope and unfolded it. Impatiently, she wiped her hand across her eyes and focused on the letter, her eyes devouring the words. "Amorette and Thomas Westcott."

"Your parents," he said, emotion clogging his voice.

She pored over the remainder of the letter and took great care in folding it and replacing it in the envelope. Her finger touched the postmark. "She lives in London."

"And she wants to come to America to visit you just as soon as you say it's all right."

It was all too much! Taking a breath, she unfolded her legs from beneath her, settled back and forced her limbs to relax. "I have a grandmother," she said staring at the ceiling in awe.

"Yes. You do, Alexandria."

She shot a glance at him. "Alexandria Westcott." She tried the name out on her lips. A long-forgotten memory flitted across her consciousness, an intangible blur of her mother's face and voice. "Lexie Westcott," she whispered. "They called me Lexie."

Anton leaned over her, his eyes a vivid blue. "Lexie Neubauer, you mean."

She smiled and wrapped her arms around his shoulders. "Oh, Anton, if I'm dreaming, I don't want to wake up."

He kissed her, running his thumb across her shoulder and under the towel she still wore. "If I'm awake," he said against her mouth. "I don't ever want to sleep."

A delicious shiver ran down her side. He slid his palm beneath the towel and cupped her breast. "Thank you," she whispered into his good ear.

"Thank you," he replied.

He covered her mouth with his, pressing her into the soft mattress, and she welcomed her husband's ardent caress, knowing she'd always crave touching him the way she did now. She needed him exactly the way he was, wanted him enough to bridge their cultures and loved him more than enough to last for time and eternity.

"I love you," she sighed as he tossed the towel on the floor.

He smiled. "I want to hear you say that every day for as long as I live."

"You will."

* * * * *

Harlequin®
Historical

Looking for more of a good thing?

Why not try a bigger book from Harlequin Historicals?

SUSPICION by Judith McWilliams, April 1994—A story of intrigue and deceit set during the Regency era.

ROYAL HARLOT by Lucy Gordon, May 1994—The adventuresome romance of a prince and the woman spy assigned to protect him.

UNICORN BRIDE by Claire Delacroix, June 1994—The first of a trilogy set in thirteenth-century France.

MARIAH'S PRIZE by Miranda Jarrett, July 1994—Another tale of the seafaring Sparhawks of Rhode Island.

Longer stories by some of your favorite authors.
Watch for them this spring, wherever
Harlequin Historicals are sold.

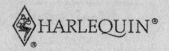
HARLEQUIN®

MARRIAGE *BY Design*

Harlequin proudly presents four stories about *convenient* but not *conventional* reasons for marriage:

- ◆ To save your godchildren from a "wicked stepmother"

- ◆ To help out your eccentric aunt — and her sexy business partner

- ◆ To bring an old man happiness by making him a grandfather

- ◆ To escape from a ghostly existence and become a real woman

Marriage By Design — four brand-new stories by four of Harlequin's most popular authors:

**CATHY GILLEN THACKER
JASMINE CRESSWELL
GLENDA SANDERS
MARGARET CHITTENDEN**

Don't miss this exciting collection of stories about marriages of convenience. Available in April, wherever Harlequin books are sold.

HARLEQUIN®

Don't miss these Harlequin favorites by some of our most distinguished authors!
And now, you can receive a discount by ordering two or more titles!

HT#25409	THE NIGHT IN SHINING ARMOR by JoAnn Ross	$2.99 ☐
HT#25471	LOVESTORM by JoAnn Ross	$2.99 ☐
HP#11463	THE WEDDING by Emma Darcy	$2.89 ☐
HP#11592	THE LAST GRAND PASSION by Emma Darcy	$2.99 ☐
HR#03188	DOUBLY DELICIOUS by Emma Goldrick	$2.89 ☐
HR#03248	SAFE IN MY HEART by Leigh Michaels	$2.89 ☐
HS#70464	CHILDREN OF THE HEART by Sally Garrett	$3.25 ☐
HS#70524	STRING OF MIRACLES by Sally Garrett	$3.39 ☐
HS#70500	THE SILENCE OF MIDNIGHT by Karen Young	$3.39 ☐
HI#22178	SCHOOL FOR SPIES by Vickie York	$2.79 ☐
HI#22212	DANGEROUS VINTAGE by Laura Pender	$2.89 ☐
HI#22219	TORCH JOB by Patricia Rosemoor	$2.89 ☐
HAR#16459	MACKENZIE'S BABY by Anne McAllister	$3.39 ☐
HAR#16466	A COWBOY FOR CHRISTMAS by Anne McAllister	$3.39 ☐
HAR#16462	THE PIRATE AND HIS LADY by Margaret St. George	$3.39 ☐
HAR#16477	THE LAST REAL MAN by Rebecca Flanders	$3.39 ☐
HH#28704	A CORNER OF HEAVEN by Theresa Michaels	$3.99 ☐
HH#28707	LIGHT ON THE MOUNTAIN by Maura Seger	$3.99 ☐

Harlequin Promotional Titles

#83247	YESTERDAY COMES TOMORROW by Rebecca Flanders	$4.99 ☐
#83257	MY VALENTINE 1993	$4.99 ☐
	(short-story collection featuring Anne Stuart, Judith Arnold, Anne McAllister, Linda Randall Wisdom)	

(limited quantities available on certain titles)

	AMOUNT	$
DEDUCT:	10% DISCOUNT FOR 2+ BOOKS	$
ADD:	POSTAGE & HANDLING	$
	($1.00 for one book, 50¢ for each additional)	
	APPLICABLE TAXES*	$ _____
	TOTAL PAYABLE	$ _____
	(check or money order—please do not send cash)	

To order, complete this form and send it, along with a check or money order for the total above, payable to Harlequin Books, to: **In the U.S.:** 3010 Walden Avenue, P.O. Box 9047, Buffalo, NY 14269-9047; **In Canada:** P.O. Box 613, Fort Erie, Ontario, L2A 5X3.

Name: _____

Address: _____ City: _____

State/Prov.: _____ Zip/Postal Code: _____

*New York residents remit applicable sales taxes.
 Canadian residents remit applicable GST and provincial taxes.

HBACK-JM

INDULGE A LITTLE 6947 SWEEPSTAKES
NO PURCHASE NECESSARY

HERE'S HOW THE SWEEPSTAKES WORKS:
The Harlequin Reader Service shipments for January, February and March 1994 will contain, respectively, coupons for entry into three prize drawings: a trip for two to San Francisco, an Alaskan cruise for two and a trip for two to Hawaii. To be eligible for any drawing using an Entry Coupon, simply complete and mail according to directions.

There is no obligation to continue as a Reader Service subscriber to enter and be eligible for any prize drawing. You may also enter any drawing by hand printing your name and address on a 3" x 5" card and the destination of the prize you wish that entry to be considered for (i.e., San Francisco trip, Alaskan cruise or Hawaiian trip). Send your 3" x 5" entries to: Indulge a Little 6947 Sweepstakes, c/o Prize Destination you wish that entry to be considered for, P.O. Box 1315, Buffalo, NY 14269-1315, U.S.A. or Indulge a Little 6947 Sweepstakes, P.O. Box 610, Fort Erie, Ontario L2A 5X3, Canada.

To be eligible for the San Francisco trip, entries must be received by 4/30/94; for the Alaskan cruise, 5/31/94; and the Hawaiian trip, 6/30/94. No responsibility is assumed for lost, late or misdirected mail. Sweepstakes open to residents of the U.S. (except Puerto Rico) and Canada, 18 years of age or older. All applicable laws and regulations apply. Sweepstakes void wherever prohibited.

For a copy of the Official Rules, send a self-addressed, stamped envelope (WA residents need not affix return postage) to: Indulge a Little 6947 Rules, P.O. Box 4631, Blair, NE 68009, U.S.A.

INDR93

INDULGE A LITTLE 6947 SWEEPSTAKES
NO PURCHASE NECESSARY

HERE'S HOW THE SWEEPSTAKES WORKS:
The Harlequin Reader Service shipments for January, February and March 1994 will contain, respectively, coupons for entry into three prize drawings: a trip for two to San Francisco, an Alaskan cruise for two and a trip for two to Hawaii. To be eligible for any drawing using an Entry Coupon, simply complete and mail according to directions.

There is no obligation to continue as a Reader Service subscriber to enter and be eligible for any prize drawing. You may also enter any drawing by hand printing your name and address on a 3" x 5" card and the destination of the prize you wish that entry to be considered for (i.e., San Francisco trip, Alaskan cruise or Hawaiian trip). Send your 3" x 5" entries to: Indulge a Little 6947 Sweepstakes, c/o Prize Destination you wish that entry to be considered for, P.O. Box 1315, Buffalo, NY 14269-1315, U.S.A. or Indulge a Little 6947 Sweepstakes, P.O. Box 610, Fort Erie, Ontario L2A 5X3, Canada.

To be eligible for the San Francisco trip, entries must be received by 4/30/94; for the Alaskan cruise, 5/31/94; and the Hawaiian trip, 6/30/94. No responsibility is assumed for lost, late or misdirected mail. Sweepstakes open to residents of the U.S. (except Puerto Rico) and Canada, 18 years of age or older. All applicable laws and regulations apply. Sweepstakes void wherever prohibited.

For a copy of the Official Rules, send a self-addressed, stamped envelope (WA residents need not affix return postage) to: Indulge a Little 6947 Rules, P.O. Box 4631, Blair, NE 68009, U.S.A.

INDR93

INDULGE A LITTLE
SWEEPSTAKES

OFFICIAL ENTRY COUPON

This entry must be received by: APRIL 30, 1994
This month's winner will be notified by: MAY 15, 1994
Trip must be taken between: JUNE 30, 1994-JUNE 30, 1995

YES, I want to win the San Francisco vacation for two. I understand that the prize includes round-trip airfare, first-class hotel, rental car and pocket money as revealed on the "wallet" scratch-off card.

Name_____

Address _____ Apt. _____

City_____

State/Prov._____ Zip/Postal Code_____

Daytime phone number_____
                              (Area Code)

Account #_____

Return entries with invoice in envelope provided. Each book in this shipment has two entry coupons—and the more coupons you enter, the better your chances of winning!

© 1993 HARLEQUIN ENTERPRISES LTD.   MONTH1

INDULGE A LITTLE
SWEEPSTAKES

OFFICIAL ENTRY COUPON

This entry must be received by: APRIL 30, 1994
This month's winner will be notified by: MAY 15, 1994
Trip must be taken between: JUNE 30, 1994-JUNE 30, 1995

YES, I want to win the San Francisco vacation for two. I understand that the prize includes round-trip airfare, first-class hotel, rental car and pocket money as revealed on the "wallet" scratch-off card.

Name_____

Address _____ Apt. _____

City_____

State/Prov._____ Zip/Postal Code_____

Daytime phone number_____
                              (Area Code)

Account #_____

Return entries with invoice in envelope provided. Each book in this shipment has two entry coupons—and the more coupons you enter, the better your chances of winning!

© 1993 HARLEQUIN ENTERPRISES LTD.   MONTH1